How To Survive Camping

The Man With No Shadow

Bonnie Quinn

PREFACE

"How to Survive Camping" was initially written as a series of posts in a the r/nosleep subreddit of Reddit.com. The premise of the subreddit is that all posts tell "true" stories and that commenters must play along and treat every story as if it is real. I wrote the first post and it was well-received enough that I was inspired to keep going. The story only grew from there.

I began to get requests to publish a "How to Survive Camping" book. I asked people which they would prefer: an as-is collection or a rewrite. I received enough feedback in favor of an as-is collection – so they could easily re-read and recommend it to others – and once I reached a good stopping point I began editing the posts into this book.

I've made minor changes to remove parts that were there to conform to the subreddit's rules. For example, the intro to each story was mostly a placeholder for links to prior parts or the first post for newcomers. Most of the intros have been removed, with a few exceptions to address instances where the comment section was relevant to the plot. Otherwise, I've kept them true to the original.

If you're new to the series, I hope you enjoy the journey.

If you're a returning fan... it shouldn't need to be said, but don't follow the lights.

How to Survive Your Camping Experience

1. Have a sturdy, waterproof container that holds a spare change of clothes and a blanket. This will ensure you have something warm and dry if your tent floods.
2. Place solar lights near your tent stakes. This will keep people from tripping over them or the ropes at night.
3. If the ground is soft from heavy rain, reinforce tent stakes either by weighing them down or by using longer stakes. They can get pulled out of the ground by a strong wind, otherwise.
4. When planning your camp, allocate three extra feet per tent. This leaves rooms for ropes and stakes.
5. If you're camping on an incline, dig a 1" wide and 3" deep trench that will direct water around your tents and common area. This will minimize flooding.
6. To maintain adequate water pressure, don't split a water hose more than three times. Always ask permission from the campers with the spigot on their land before attaching a hose.
7. Cheap tents and pop-ups from Walmart are not designed for weather. One strong breeze is enough to collapse or flip them. If you insist on using a pop-up, weigh it down and stake it so it doesn't turn into a hazard when it goes flying off.
8. Plan for a tent or dayshade collapse. Store valuables in strong containers that won't break if something hits them. Leave your tent closed when you leave, storms can show up unexpectedly.
9. Pack some heavy blankets. It can get cold at night.
10. Map out your campsite in advance. During peak camping season the amount of land allotted to a group is limited. Ask for the square footage of your group's tents and make sure they will fit.

How to Survive Your Camping Experience

1. If you hear something trying to enter your tent at night, sit up and say in a clear, calm voice that you are not receiving visitors, but it is welcome to visit in the morning. If a stranger appears the next day asking for entrance to your camp, invite them in and give them food and drink. This will give you good luck for the rest of your stay.

2. Fairy rings are generally benign. If there are the remains of a small animal inside the ring, however, inform camp management immediately.

3. Don't follow the lights. I can't believe I even have to say this one. *Don't follow the lights.*

4. If you see a group of people dancing in a circle around a fire, you may join them. If they welcome you in, dance with them until the music ends. Do not look at the musicians. If they do not welcome you, but instead stop and stare, back away slowly and then leave. If they follow you, you can try to run, but it is likely already too late. Pray that death comes swiftly.

5. If you think you're lost, stop and look at your surrounding. If the everything appears a little gray, like the color has seeped from the world, then you're no longer in the campsite. Seek out the highest hill and beg whatever you find there to return you to the camp. Pray it is in a benevolent mood.

6. Do not sleep unless you are in your tent or in a hammock that you have setup with your own hands. No matter how drowsy you suddenly feel, do not lie down and sleep. You will wake in an unfamiliar place and even if you are found again, you won't be left particularly whole.

7. If you wake and something is already in your tent, lie very still and say nothing. Do this until it leaves, no matter what it says to you. It can mimic the voices of those you know. Do not be deceived.

8. If you find yourself surrounded by a group of people whose faces you cannot see, not matter how hard you look, give them whatever they request. They will ask for an insignificant part of your body, such as a piece of your earlobe or a single digit from a finger. Try not to scream when they cut it off, or they will help themselves to more. Do not refuse or try to escape. They will take far more from you if they must obtain it by force.

9. The lady in chains is not in distress. Do not try to help her. It is a trap and she will kill you.

10. Keep track of what time the charge on the solar lights typically runs out. If the solars go out before then, do not leave your tent until sunup. Do not open the tent, not even to look. Stay in your tent, try to sleep, and wait for daybreak.

11. Deer do not grow to be the size of a horse. If you see a large deer, do not stare at it and especially do not make eye contact with the person riding on its back. Consider bowing until it passes. This is a sign of respect and it may bless you with its favor.

12. If you're approached by a stranger offering you a drink from a cup made out of a human skull, accept. It will taste foul and you will not be able to eat without vomiting for the next 24 hours, but this is better than what they will do to you if you refuse.

13. If you find evidence that an animal has tried to get into your food overnight, contact camp management. Don't move anything, so that we can inspect the area. It is likely a racoon, but it's better to be cautious.

14. If you are wandering the campsite with friends and you discover that one has gone missing, contact camp staff immediately. Under no circumstances should you try to find them yourselves, not even if you discover that they're only a short distance away. That might not actually be your friend.

15. The woman with an extra set of eyes will help you. You can trust her. If she invites you to her house for tea, accept. I think she's a bit lonely.

16. Don't eat food you find sitting out around the campsite. It's not yours and worse, it might be an offering and you will offend whatever it is intended for.

17. Be wary of a friendly man that may approach you in shaded areas. Try to convince him to move into the sunlight. If he casts a shadow, you can assume it's another camper and proceed accordingly. Otherwise, end the conversation immediately. He is trying to earn your trust.

18. You can buy ice from the children that approach your camp ONLY if they have a wagon. Those are the children of other campers trying to make some extra spending money. They only upcharge by a few dollars, so consider tipping. If a group of children approach without a wagon, do not buy from them. Act like they don't exist. They will eventually leave.

19. While it can get cold at night, you should not see frost forming inside your tent. If you are woken by the cold and see frost, call the camp emergency number. Stay calm and stay in your tent. We will come get you.

20. Drink enough water[1]. Insufficient hydration has resulted in far more cases of people needing medical intervention than anything else at this camp.

---

[1] Vodka mixed with Gatorade is not an acceptable substitute.

CONTENTS

HOW TO SURVIVE CAMPING

Posted Aug 03 2019 19:02:47 GMT-0400

I run a private campground. My family has owned it for generations now. It's about 300 acres, most of that shaded by forest and the rest is an open field. We host events, like dog clubs, music festivals, etc. We've also got open camping weekends throughout the year and in the height of summer we're open full-time for general camping. A lot of people take advantage of that. It's a cheap and pleasant vacation. Hammocks get erected in the trees. Grills get unloaded from the backs of trucks. There's some pretty elaborate setups from the people that come back year after year.

The return campers are smart. They know what they're doing. Everyone knows their job when they roll in. They unload as a group. Tents start to go up. Community areas and kitchens go in the same place year after year, where they've found the land suits their setup best. Tent locations might change, but every camper knows where their tent is going in their allotted land. It's a far cry from the disheveled masses that show up and simply expect everything to work out with no prior planning. By noon on setup day the experienced campers are sitting under their dayshades, sipping beer, while the newbies are relocating tents because they didn't leave enough room for walkways.

I've tried to help. I put together a guide that everyone receives in the mail once I have their registration info and payment. Sure, the postage is a bit of an expense, but I feel having a hardcopy makes them more likely to read it. Not having to fill out as much paperwork with the police is worth the money. I've titled the brochure "How to Survive Your Camping Experience." I wish people would take that name more seriously.

The first page is full of practical advice. Stuff like:
1. Have a sturdy, waterproof container that holds a spare change of clothes and a blanket. This will ensure you have something warm and dry if your tent floods.
2. Place solar lights near your tent stakes. This will keep people from tripping over them or the ropes at night.
3. If the ground is soft from heavy rain, reinforce tent stakes either by weighing them down or by using longer stakes. They can get pulled out of the ground by a strong wind, otherwise.
4. When planning your camp, allocate three extra feet per tent. This leaves rooms for ropes and stakes.

The second page is advice more specific to the area. This campsite has been in the family for generations, after all, and a parcel of land obtains a sort of significance when it's been passed down from heir to heir. It is an old place in the world, perhaps not an ancient place, but old enough to have attracted the attention of those things that prefer old places to make their homes. (we will have to sell the campsite before it becomes an ancient place, as it will be unusable at that point, but there are still many generations to go before that happens)

This is the part that the new campers don't take seriously. They think it's a prank, some little joke of the reclusive camp manager who perhaps doesn't spend much time around other people. The experienced campers try to tell them otherwise, but they don't always listen. I feel my rules aren't onerous. Here's a sampling:

1. If you hear something trying to enter your tent at night, sit up and say in a clear, calm voice that you are not receiving visitors, but it is welcome to visit in the morning. If a stranger appears the next day asking for entrance to your camp, invite them in and give them food and drink. This will give you good luck for the rest of your stay.

2. Fairy rings are generally benign. If there are the remains of a small animal inside the ring, however, inform camp management immediately.

3. Don't follow the lights. I can't believe I even have to say this one. *Don't follow the lights.*

I confess it's a haphazard list, but there's a lot of vicious things out there and they all function in slightly different ways. I do some things as part of camp management in an effort to minimize the danger to my campers. We set out traps for the creatures stupid enough to fall into them, so that they can be dispatched by my uncle and his two sons. We're closed during Pentecost, on midsummer day, and other significant times of the year. But we can't do everything. We can't save people from themselves.

Every morning I circle the camp on a four-wheeler. My staff does the same, a couple times a day. We look for any new developments on the land (a tree that needs pulled down, for example) and campers know they can hail any of us if they need something. I leave directly after I finish my breakfast and a cup of coffee. My house is on the campsite, so it's especially easy for me to take the morning shift.

There's never many people awake yet, so it was especially noticeable when I saw a man approaching me ahead, walking down the middle of the road. He looked unremarkable (they always do) but he walked slowly and deliberately, his head bowed so that it was difficult to see his face, and he carried before him in both hands a human skull. I pulled the four-wheeler over and waited, my stomach twisting with fear.

Rule #12: If you're approached by a man offering you a drink from a cup made out of a human skull, accept. It will taste foul and you will not be able to eat without vomiting for the next 24 hours, but this is better than what he will do to you if you refuse.

I have drunk from the cup before. It is how I learned of his existence and subsequently added him to the rules. He stopped me on the road and at the time, I thought he was a camper needing assistance, until he handed me the skull cup and bade me drink. I did, as I had already learned that when a being of power asks something of you, it is better to comply.

It may not be enough to save you. Sometimes they invite you to partake in your own demise, but the odds of compliance are better.

He lifted the cup to my lips and I drank. One swallow. Another. He kept the cup there; his thin fingers brushed my hair back when it slipped past my ear, and I drank it in entirety. The water inside tasted bitter and salty with a vegetal undertone. My stomach twisted and I swallowed hard, struggling to keep it down.

"Thank you for the drink," I said when I was done, trying to sound sincere.

He knew I lied, for he smiled briefly in wry humor, his dark eyes flashing with cold amusement.

"It was wise to not refuse," he replied.

He told me what he would have done, had I not drunk, and my insides crawled with horror as he spoke and I wanted him to *stop* but to interrupt would have been a dire insult. His words were etched into my memories and for days after I wept whenever I thought of the fate I had so narrowly avoided. I still feel cold and small when I think of the things he told me.

That evening, I threw up my dinner. I threw up the crackers I ate. I even threw up water. Finally, I stopped eating and drinking altogether and waited a full day to try again. I was weak and miserable, but I survived.

Now, seeing the man approaching on the road, I mentally cursed my misfortune. This was our busy time of year. I couldn't afford to be sick for a day.

He stopped just before he reached me. Raised a hand and beckoned for me to come closer. He didn't raise his head until I stood just across from him and when he did, he flashed that thin, dry smile at seeing the expression of dread on my face.

"Are you not thirsty?" he asked mockingly.

"Not particularly, but if you wish to offer me a drink I will not be so rude as to refuse."

My heart hammered in my chest. Let him release me, I silently pleaded. He put a hand over the top of the skull, covering up the carved opening and the water inside.

"Be at ease, I did not come to offer you a drink. I came to give you a warning. Some of your charges have conducted business with the children."

I stood there, staring blankly at him in incomprehension. He sighed, almost imperceptibly, and even though his expression did not change I felt the weight of his disapproval when he spoke next. These ancient beings do not enjoy having to explain themselves.

"The children with no wagon," he said, speaking slowly, as if that would help me understand. "Someone bought ice from them."

"Oh," I said dumbly. "Oh god."

"He won't save them." The man walked past me, his shoulder brushing against mine as he did. "No one will."

Rule #18: You can buy ice from the children that approach your camp ONLY if they have a wagon. Those are the children of other campers trying to make some extra spending money. They only upcharge by a few dollars, so consider tipping. If a group of children approach without a wagon, do not buy from them. Act like they don't exist. They will eventually leave.

It wasn't until he was almost out of sight that I realized I didn't have any idea which campsite had purchased the ice and there were a *lot* of people here right now. I did the dumb thing. I jumped on the four-wheeler, turned it around, and went after him. I pulled up along the side of the road, a respectful distance away, and called out to him.

"Hey, what campsite was it?"

He paused almost imperceptibly.

"Are you thirsty after all?" he asked and even though his words were mild, I understood it for the threat it was.

"Nope, I'm good, sorry for bothering you."

I drove away before he changed his mind on granting me mercy. This was a terrible dilemma for me. I hadn't had *anyone* buy from the children without wagons before. Most people find their silent stares creepy and the normal children are pretty aggressive with their ice routes anyway, so that no one needs ice by the time those other children show up. I had no idea what to expect. I had no idea how to undo what had been done.

There was, however, someone I could ask.

I went to my most senior camp. They're a group of friends that have been camping here for over two decades. The members have changed, to the point that the founders have all been replaced, but they've kept the traditions and are willing to work with me. As a result, I've given them the best campsite. It's up on a hill, nestled in a clear spot among the trees so that their camp has shade most of the day and there's spots to hang hammocks. A gas line runs up the hill, so I have to keep part of it free of trees, which funnels the breeze straight into their camp. It's noticeably cooler there than the rest of the site.

It's also the most dangerous.

I heard their shouting before I arrived. I slowed, cutting the noise of the engine down enough that I could make out words. I needn't have bothered. It was nothing but cursing. I couldn't tell if it was an inter-camp dispute (doubtful, they kept the drama to a minimum) or if they were angry at another group (plausible, they had a couple feuds going on with the younger camps) or if it was something else. Bracing myself, I hopped off the vehicle and walked in past the line of tents that marked their boundary.

There were five people in the common area, clustered around the beer kegs. They had a cooler that was outfitted with four taps and they ran lines up through a steel plate that was packed with ice, providing access with chilled beer from the tap at any time. The kegs were all homebrew. Right now, they had all four taps open and dark liquid was spilling out onto the ground. There was an odd smell in the air that turned my stomach.

Like a butcher's shop, I thought, finally placing the smell.

"Is that... blood?" I ventured, walking closer.

"YES." The woman that did the brewing kicked one of the kegs. "All of them are blood."

I told them I've come to talk to the thing in the dark. I had a question, I said, and I could also ask about the kegs while I was at it.

"Sure." She jerked her head at the back of their camp, where the trees crowded in close enough so that their shadows overlapped and the forest floor was noticeably darker under the lattice of their branches. "We haven't seen the solars go out all week though, so maybe it's not home."

Rule #10: Keep track of what time the charge on the solar lights typically runs out. If the solars go out before then, do not leave your tent until sunup. Do not open the tent, not even to look. Stay in your tent, try to sleep, and wait for daybreak.

I crept into the forest, wincing at the branches that cracked under my feet. Some of the creatures in the campsite were less malevolent than others. So long as they were respected, they wouldn't kill you or even seriously harm you. I'd spoken to the creature in the dark only once before, when I thought to put the senior camp near its lair. I asked if their proximity would disturb it. It replied that they would not, but nor would it hesitate to take any of them were they out in the open when it passed by.

I don't know what happens to the people it takes. Their bodies are never found. The entire camp dreams of dying, however, of slow and torturous death in whatever manner they fear most. I dream of the little girl and the beast and when I wake I know that I'm going to be talking to the police yet again.

The creature's lair is nothing more than a mound of broken branches, easily mistaken for a pile of stacked debris. There are some signs, however. The air grows colder as you approach. Sound falls away, encasing you in silence so that the only thing you hear is your own heartbeat. Mine was growing steadily faster as I drew nearer and it felt like the darkness in-between the piled branches was reaching out, gathering up all the light, and dragging it to its doom. Flowers littered the forest floor - the white, parasitic ones with bowed heads, feeding on the tree roots running below the barren soil.

"Excuse me," I whispered, my voice cracking. I coughed and tried again. "Sorry to bother you, but I have a question."

A long silence. I waited, wondering if this was in vain and perhaps the creature wasn't there. Then it spoke and its words were rough like stones rolling against each other and I winced in pain, for it felt like my head was between those stones and my skull would crack under their weight. It asked me what I wished to know.

I told it about the children. That someone had bought ice from them. And also about the kegs, as an afterthought.

"The children are displeased by their lack of prey," it finally replied and I pressed my fingers against the bones near my ear, as if that could help relieve the pressure. "They rejoice at finally being given an opportunity."

"To do what?"

The pile of branches shifted. The *earth* shifted and I stumbled, realizing in sudden terror that that small lump of debris was not nearly enough to contain the creature inside and it was far larger and perhaps far more terrible than I'd imagined. Its *shrug* had nearly thrown me to the ground.

"The kegs are just the start," it sighed. "More will suffer. *All* will suffer. And then the dying will begin."

My entire campsite was at risk. I felt cold inside. I could evacuate, I thought. I could claim there was something - a gas line rupture? Disease outbreak? There were some options available that would explain why I was throwing everyone out. But then what about my livelihood? Would people return? I'm a little ashamed that greed factored into my choices, but this campsite has been in my family for three generations and I wasn't going to ruin it all now.

"Eliminate the one that started it." The ground bucked, violently, and I was thrown to my hands and knees. "Everything else will unravel."

I stumbled to my feet, thanking it profusely. I gibbered my apologies for disturbing it and my gratitude for its advice. Then I fled, fighting the urge to look back the entire time.

Eliminate the one that started it. Those words rattled around in my head as I went from campsite to campsite, asking if they'd bought ice from the children today. I received quizzical looks from the newer campers, but the older ones answered solemnly, understanding the gravity of my question. They'd read the rules. Finally, I found the camp that bought the ice and they identified the person that had made the purchase. He was elsewhere at the moment, but I could stop by later, they suggested. I said it was fine. I wasn't ready to talk to him. I wasn't ready to take the creature in the dark's advice.

I thought... how bad could it be? It was only just beginning. Perhaps I could find some other way to resolve the situation. I spent the evening digging through my books of camp management and folklore, trying to find some sort of ritual or appeasement I could try. Yet the creature had said that the children were tired of not having prey - prey I'd denied them with my rules - and that this would only get worse and worse until people started dying. That everyone was in danger.

Night fell and I reluctantly abandoned my efforts until the morning. My worry made it impossible to sleep through the little girl weeping outside my window and begging to be let in. (she's not in the rules. She only harasses members of my bloodline) I was almost relieved when the beast came and dragged her off while she screamed in mortal terror, signaling that dawn was near.

I threw on some clothing and jumped on my four-wheeler. I even skipped making coffee. I needed to see what had happened overnight.

The man with the skull cup stood on the road, staring off into the trees and calmly sipping the water inside like he was taking his morning tea. I pulled up close by and killed the engine so we could talk.

"Skipped your coffee, did you?" he asked. "Want a drink?"

"I am quite satisfied, but I will gladly accept if you wish to share," I replied with gritted teeth.

That thin smile again. Now he was just messing with me.

I looked in the direction he was staring. A slew of people - twelve in all - dangled in mid-air. For one brief, horrifying moment I could only think of the time I'd found someone that hadn't heeded my rules, their gutted body dangling uncomfortably close to my house, like it was a warning. How the police had let me do most of the work getting it down while they waited on the ground with their damned paperwork.

I don't make my staff clean up the remains. That's asking too much.

These were alive. I almost wept with relief. They'd been pulled from their tents and stripped naked, then taken into the woods. Their bodies were covered with bruises and scratches from being violently dragged across the ground. Then they'd been hoisted up into the trees and left hanging by their ankles from the boughs.

"Next time it'll be their flayed skins hoisted in the branches," the man said. "You should end this quickly."

"I'm surprised by your concern."

"I need people to share a drink with," he murmured. "I can't do that if everyone dies."

I had to get my brother and both my uncles to help get the terrified campers down. They didn't fight much while we were doing this, just hung there limply, crying or whimpering softly. It made the job a lot easier. Dead weight is predictable and we could pull them towards the ladder, get a good hold on them, and then cut the ropes and pass them down to the ground.

Eliminate the one that started with it. As the abducted campers were taken off to the local hospital for treatment, I delegated the police paperwork to my brother and jumped on my four-wheeler. I returned to the camp that had bought the ice and called the man responsible aside for a conversation. I asked him if he'd bought ice from some creepy children with no wagon and when he said he had, I asked why he'd broken one of the rules of how to survive camping. It was rule #18. Hadn't he read it?

"Oh," he said bleakly. "That one. Well, there *are* a lot of rules."

I took a breath. Held it a moment. Reminded myself that the majority of people are good-intentioned and don't do things simply to be contrary or cause trouble. That it is my responsibility as both camp manager and a decent human being to be understanding and help people, because we have a common goal. I want them to have a safe and fun camping experience so they come back and they want to have a safe and fun camping experience so they *can* come back. This man didn't ignore my rule simply out of spite. It was an accident. An unfortunate accident.

I asked him why he'd glossed over that rule. My tone was polite and friendly without a hint of condemnation or judgement. That's the important bit - people respond in kind. So long as I didn't accuse, he wouldn't become defensive and we could have a productive conversation.

I've done a lot of reading on conflict resolution and behavioral change.

He hadn't taken them seriously, he admitted. He'd certainly *read* them. Intently, in fact, because he thought it was a joke but it was a clever joke and he enjoyed it. But real? Nah . He pointed to his tent, showing how it had three feet of clearance between the other tents (rule #4) and that they'd brought a longer hose so they didn't have to split the closer one more than three times (rule #6). The will was there. My system was flawed.

It didn't change what I had to do. I thanked him for talking to me and walked away. Then I went into the woods and gathered some things. It took a while to find them all, but I'm familiar with my campsite and I know where these things are likely to be found. Then I returned to my house with the mushrooms in hand.

They're called "destroying angel." Amanita virosa.

I crushed it and took the resulting juice (careful not to touch it with my bare hands) back to his camp. I poured it into his reusable water bottle, swirled it around to coat the sides, and then left it to dry.

They wrote the initial symptoms off as mere food poisoning. By the time his campmates took him to the ER, he was suffering from liver and kidney failure. They did their best, but I had put a *generous* dose in that bottle and his body simply could not keep up, not even with medical intervention. He was dead within thirty-six hours.

The police dropped by, of course. I talked with them for a bit, we commiserated on how difficult it can be to protect people from themselves, and that was the end of it. They understand what it's like in the forest.

I feel I am to blame. I know rules are ineffective, but they were *easy* and that's what I relied on. I wrote off the deaths as isolated incidents instead of warning signs that I wasn't doing enough to determine if my rule list and other measures were accomplishing their intended purpose.

You know what *does* help people change their behaviors? Storytelling. It's one of the most effective techniques, far more effective than a list of rules, which according to research is the least effective method (and the most prone to "antisocial behavior" which is basically people deliberately sabotaging the system out of spite). Instead of telling someone "do this", you tell the person a story that demonstrates the behavior you want. Preferably true, as that carries more weight. And the more personal it is, the more the individual will relate and subsequently accept what you are trying to tell them to do.

I'm a camp manager. I don't have a list of rules because I'm trying to ruin your fun. I have a list because I'm trying to help you from coming back to camp and finding your tent collapsed and full of rainwater and having no dry clothes or nowhere to sleep. I'm trying to keep you from spending half a day setting up tents because you didn't plan where everything would go in advance. And I'm trying to keep you from doing small, simple things that could result in a horrific and most assuredly agonizing demise.

RULE #4 – THE DANCERS

Posted Aug 09 2019 15:55:18 GMT-0400

Every morning I take a four-wheeler out and circle the grounds, before most people are awake. There are some benefits to being an early riser. Solitude. Seeing the sun rise. Finding the human torso lying in the middle of the road before anyone else.

Yes. The torso. Just the torso.

This was back before smartphones. I was twenty-one. I'd been in my last year of college, finishing up a business degree with a minor in horticulture. The campground was staffed in part by my extended family, but its ownership passed only to direct descendants. My life was planned out from birth and so my degree choice was deliberate. I believe my parents would have supported whatever I chose to major in, so long as I took ownership of the campground, but I've loved this place my whole life and wanted to prepare myself to be the best steward I could.

It was the start of the spring semester when my mother forgot to close a window. My father woke in the middle of the night to find the little girl sitting in the mangled ruins of mother's abdomen. Enraged, he seized the girl by her hair and dragged her out the back door and into the yard. She shrieked, she pleaded, but he couldn't be swayed. He threw her to the beast and after it was finished with her, it turned on him. The police found his hand. That was all they found.

I know this is what happened because I dreamed of it. It was a true dream. If you've ever had a true dream, you know they feel different, and you know you can trust them.

I never finished college. I regret that, some days. I don't need a degree to do my job, but I think it would have been nice to have. There's an empty spot on my office wall. My parents had cleared it before they died so they could hang my diploma there, in preparation for when I took over management. I can't bring myself to put anything else up in its place.

I was well-prepared to take ownership of the camp despite my age. I'd been training for it my whole life, after all, and I had my entire extended family to help me. So when I found part of a body in the road, I knew what to do.

My flip phone's coverage was limited and I couldn't make calls while under the canopy of the trees. Instead, I carried a digital camera and took photos from all the important angles that the police would be interested in. Then I took out the large black trash bags from the back of the four-wheeler and edged the body in. I tied it shut, put another bag around it, and tied it again. Then I hoisted it onto the back of the vehicle and strapped it down. The blood was fresh enough that I could wash it off into the dirt with the couple gallons of water I carried for this specific purpose.

Now, I understand that some of you may be astonished that I would clean up the scene of a violent death without first contacting the police. However, my family has an understanding with the police. The campground is important around here. It brings a lot of people in and during the peak of summer we double the county's population. They spend a lot of money on local businesses. A *lot* of money.

The police don't mind if we take certain liberties to ensure the normal operation of the campsite isn't disrupted. It would be upsetting to campers if they came across a dismembered body or an active police scene.

I called the police as soon as I was back at the house and then I started calling family members. I'd only found the torso, after all. That meant there were two legs, two arms, and a head yet to be found, and I had no idea how many pieces those parts were in. While my extended family scoured the woods for the remaining bits, I could deal with the police. Officer Thomas responded. He'd been helping with our campsite difficulties since before I was born. He's close to retirement now. We sat in my office and he looked through the photos I'd taken on my computer, then requested to see the body out in the backyard.

I pulled it off the four-wheeler and cut the plastic open. Mercifully, the body was still fresh that it hadn't started to smell of decay; just the sour, meaty smell of early death. Officer Thomas inspected the severed sockets, picking at the edges of flesh and muscle delicately with his fingers, before sitting back on his haunches and stripping off his stained latex gloves.

"This is different than the other cases," he finally said.

I blinked, taken aback and suddenly feeling woefully inadequate to the challenges of my family's campsite. I'd *known* that this could happen someday, that I'd be the one to deal with something new moving in, but it was a distant sort of knowledge, the sort that you decide to handle some other day and live in blissful ignorance until that time comes. Like writing a will. We all know we should, but that's a problem we regulate for the future and try to ignore its specter in our present lives.

Thomas explained that the limbs were severed methodically. When we were dealing with a wild animal - whether natural or otherwise - the bodies would be haphazardly torn apart. There'd be additional injuries of teeth or claw marks. The torso was otherwise untouched. There wasn't even bruising. This indicated that the victim hadn't even been restrained - at least, not by a method that left marks.

The police might not be able to tell us what we were dealing with, but they could help narrow the possibilities.

Thomas had brought the police van, so we put the body into a bag and tossed it in the back for transport to the morgue. He asked that we bring the other parts by, once we found them, and they'd start trying to identify the victim. I would also check in with the other campers to find out if someone was missing and perhaps any information about what they'd done or where they'd gone. Then Thomas would come back with some paperwork about a wild animal attack and that'd be it.

We'd lose some campers, of course, once the rumors started to spread. That was unavoidable. Business would be slow for the next year, but it would bounce back once people began to forget that urgent sense of danger and slipped back into complacency.

We hadn't formally acknowledged that this was an old land yet. The rules wouldn't come until later, when we had too many creatures that were intelligent or powerful enough to elude our attempts at removal.

We found all the body parts by midday. They'd been left deliberately, placed so that someone actively searching for them could find them, but the casual passer-by was unlikely to notice. My cousin found the head. She called for me on the walkie-talkie, asking that I come look, and she sounded deeply shaken.

My cousin is two years older than me. I was quickly finding that having the camp manager title conveyed the perception that I was better equipped to handle *anything*, no matter how horrific.

The head was placed on a stake in the center of a narrow clearing. The ground was spongy, as it sat in a depression that collected water every time it rained. Four more stakes were stabbed into the earth in a circle around it. I pulled out my compass and checked their orientation. They sat askew from the cardinal directions. I frowned. This was a deliberate perversion.

"Look," my cousin whispered, pointing at the head on the stake. "He's still alive."

I edged closer, peering at the head. My skin crawled and I felt goosebumps break out on my arms as I crossed the perimeter of the circle. A middle-aged man, perhaps in his forties. His jaw was missing, leaving behind the upper row of teeth, and his eyes were wide with silent suffering.

He blinked.

I swore and stumbled backwards. Rounded on my cousin and told her to leave, to go take a break and recover her composure and then start going around and asking camps if all their members were accounted for. I'd take care of it from here.

Perhaps watching my parents die, a silent observer in a dream that felt like reality, had prepared me to withstand this sort of horror. I confess that it angers me, to see someone die in a manner that no one should have to endure, but I've long since accepted that this is life. My world no longer has room for the blissful illusion that humanity has no predators.

I told the man on the stake that it would be okay, that I could put an end to this and he'd finally, mercifully, die. A couple tears ran down his cheeks and I saw relief in his eyes. Then I went to the stakes and pulled them free from the ground. After I wrenched the last from the earth I stood and watched the man's face. His eyes remained open, long past when he should have blinked, and I was satisfied that whatever ritual bound him here had been disrupted. The air felt different as well. Lighter. It no longer pressed in on me.

I left the remaining detective work of identifying the victim to the police and the rest of my staff. I locked myself in my office. It was still odd, thinking of it as mine. The marks of my parents were strewn everywhere and I moved slowly in replacing their presence with my own. The books on folklore and camp management were worn, the bindings broken, the pages crumpled and smudged. I wondered how many times my father or mother had leafed through these, searching for answers.

Folklore is not a tidy thing. Monsters and creatures of power don't fall neatly into categories. It is not so different from the natural world in this regard. We can look at a bird and know it is a bird, but what kind of bird is it? Bird of prey or waterbird or woodpecker or pigeon or any of the many many other types?

Similarly, am I dealing with a spirit or a demon or a fairy or a god or something that falls into that gray area in-between? And even if I *could* narrow it down, there were still variations within a category. If we're dealing with an incubus, is it one in the classical sense or is it the kind that attaches only to one person for life or is it the kind with chicken legs from the knee down?

Yes, chicken-footed incubi are a thing. No, we haven't had to deal with them yet at this campsite.

I decided to try a couple things. The use of ritual made me suspect fairies, but the perversion of it also made me think spirits. I gathered up some deterrents from the shed: iron stakes, hawthorn branches, stones with holes in them, that sort of thing. Then, I went about the campsite and left them in strategic areas, mostly at crossroads and along the edge of the designated camping areas.

I erred. We were used to dealing with brute creatures that could be driven off, captured, or killed. I don't regret my attempt. It is my responsibility to keep my campers safe. However, I am far more cautious now when I try to drive off something that is intelligent. They recognize these attempts for what they are and take offense at such aggression.

That night, I was woken by the sound of someone's voice outside my bedroom window. I'd at *least* cleared out the master bedroom and made it my own, for my childhood bedroom had been turned into a study after I left for college. I didn't catch the words, for I came to awareness at the end of the conversation. Someone was talking to the little girl that cries outside my window.

That made me sit up straight in my bed. Who - or what - would talk to the little girl?

Her weeping stopped. There was the soft sound of her feet running in the grass - away from the house. Someone - or something - had sent the girl away. My heart began to hammer in my chest and I quietly slipped out of bed, thinking of the shotgun I keep in the bedroom, wondering if it'd do anything at all.

Then my house shook as something slammed against my front door *and* my back door in unison. A pause. Another impact that rattled the doors in their frames. A third, final impact and the crack and crash of both doors being torn off their hinges.

I stumbled out of bed, blind with fear, thinking of how my father had died, how he'd clawed with his bare hands at the beast's face as if he could fight it off even as its teeth severed his body into two. My hands closed over the shotgun's stock as footsteps echoed down the hallway. I stood, turned - and there was a hand against the shotgun's barrel, pushing it up and away, and then another palm against my cheek.

"That's enough," a female voice said. She sounded amused. I couldn't see her face in the darkness of my bedroom. "How about you go for a walk with us?"

I don't remember much after that. I left the house and I think I told them I couldn't, not without the beast coming for me and she'd laughed and said they'd sent it away. I'm not sure how many others were with us. Only the woman spoke to me. We walked out into the forest and I'm not certain of the route we took, for it comes and goes as if I were slipping in and out of sleep.

When my awareness returned I found myself standing beside a lit campfire, in among a ring of people around it. The ground around me was packed earth. The woman moved from person to person, a ceramic pitcher in her arms. She slipped a cupped hand inside and came up with a handful of water, which she dribbled on the brow of the person before her. Something felt wrong about this ritual. Unsettling. I tried to move or speak, but I found my body was slow to respond to my desires.

Finally, she stopped in front of me.

"Why don't you join us?" she murmured, pouring the water on my brow. It ran down my face and neck and into the neckline of my nightgown. It felt gritty and I tasted salt when a drop touched the edge of my lip.

They began to dance and I was compelled to join them. Step. Turn. Stretch our hands to the night sky, spines arched. Twist and bend. Touch the ground. Then up, a hop, and then the music quickened. (and I saw, as we spun, that the music came from a hunched group at the edge of the light.

A violin. A hand drum. Something that reminded me of a flute)

We danced. My legs began to ache. My breathing grew labored. Bright pain stabbed through my feet and ankles and I thought, madly, that I felt *liquid* against my bare feet with every step. Still, the dancers continued, their movements growing more aggressive, more frenzied, and I wept and pleaded in broken, panicked fragments for them to release me.

They did not.

I collapsed before the music stopped. My chest heaved in spastic gasps, wracking my entire body with convulsions as it instinctively tried to bring in more oxygen to my battered body. My feet burned, pain shooting up my legs with every beat of my heart. I lay there, writhing in the dirt, whimpering and openly weeping.

The dancers clustered around my prone form. One of them crouched and I felt fingers in my hair, close to the roots, and she lifted my head from the ground so that I was forced to look up at her. The firelight was to her back and I could only see her chin and lips in the flickering light.

"The little girl and the beast have laid claim to your life," she said and she smiled, her white teeth shining in the darkness. "None of us will contest their right. However, there is still *so much* we can do to you before you succumb."

She leaned in close and I felt her breath against my ear. Her body smelled of earth and plants.

"Don't try to drive us off again," she whispered.

She released me and as a group, the dancers and the musicians turned and walked away. I'm not sure how long I lay there shuddering on the ground. It was one of my senior campers that found me. I heard his footsteps approaching at a run and then he hit the ground next to me, turning me over onto my back. A flashlight shone in my face and I squeezed my eyes shut tight.

"Oh thank god," he breathed. "You're alive."

He didn't recognize me. That's not uncommon, I don't socialize with the campers much. I was able to tell him to not call 911, that I was the camp manager and I just wanted to go back to my house and rest. I could take care of myself from there or call my aunt to come help.

He deposited me on the sofa in my living room and remained at my house until my aunt arrived. At one point, he asked me what had happened. The dancers, I said weakly. The dancers found me. His attention focused on that and he asked a few questions - specific questions.

"Weird," he finally said, convinced we'd encountered the same people. "I danced with them a few nights ago. I don't think I've ever felt so happy in my life."

Even in my exhausted state his words triggered a memory of something I'd read. Dancing is used as a *cure* for supernatural afflictions. The sick individual is sat down in the middle of a circle and the dancers move in a circle around them, thereby banishing their illness. Yet something felt *wrong* about their ritual, from the off-center placement of the stakes to the mockery of anointment. Were they a group of dancers that had been cursed? Were they demons enacting their own, abhorrent, version of the same ritual?

Without being certain, I didn't dare try to drive them off again. However, I at least wanted to understand the difference and why one person had survived and another had not. I could convey it to my campers, somehow. I had not yet written my rules, but I had a vague idea that perhaps I could inform them so that they would know of the hazards. We already spray-painted the poison ivy patches fluorescent pink. Telling people to stay away from the dancers wouldn't be too dissimilar in theory.

When the wounds on my feet were healed enough that I could walk, I went out into the forest after the sun had set. I wasn't concerned about the beast. It stayed close to the little girl and the little girl never went into the forest.

I drove about on my four-wheeler, searching for campfires. There were many, but the later it got the fewer remained to check. Finally, sometime after midnight, I found the dancers.

They moved in a slow, sinuous circle. Their movements were languid, the music slow, their shadows stretching out into the darkness beyond the orange glow of the campfire. I killed the engine and walked down through the thin line of trees to the clearing. The music stopped as I approached. The dancers turned to stare at me and while I couldn't see their faces, I felt their hostility. The woman stepped out to meet me. She was short, I noticed, not even my height. She stood out from among the other dancers - tall and lean - and I wondered if there was a reason for that or if it was mere coincidence.

"You should go," she said evenly. "You aren't welcome."

"I figured as much," I replied. "I'm not ready to leave yet, though."

Her hand snapped up. She grabbed me by the neck, raising her arm up, her fingers digging into my tendons.

"What *are* you trying to do here?" she hissed.

I stood on tiptoes, trying to ease the pressure on my throat.

"Finding out what prompts you to kill people."

Her eyes went wide. She stared at me in disbelief for a moment and then let go of my neck. I stumbled backwards, coughing. She laughed, a high delicate sound like the chime of a bell.

"You take advantage of your immunity from death," she said in amusement. "I like your boldness. I will tell you. Knowing what displeases us won't be enough to keep people from resisting the temptation of joining in our dance."

They had to be welcomed, she said. Permitted to join. She would not elaborate on what sort of person they would welcome and who they would reject. There wasn't any sort of criteria, she said with a shrug. They just knew who they liked. As for the other offense that would merit someone's death...

She directed me to look at the musicians.

I did.

They raised their heads and looked back at me.

My next memory is of being on my knees, my fingernails stained with blood, the skin around my eyes and down my cheeks burning from where I'd clawed it raw. The dancers were gone and mercifully, they'd taken the musicians as well.

I don't leave the safety of my campers entirely up to themselves. I do what I can. Sometimes I take risks and sometimes I suffer for them. This is my responsibility as the camp manager. We do the hard and dangerous work to make sure you have a pleasant and safe camping experience.

The least you can do is follow the directions that I suffered to obtain.

Rule #4: If you see a group of people dancing in a circle around a fire, you may join them. If they welcome you in, dance with them until the music ends. Do not look at the musicians. If they do not welcome you, but instead stop and stare, back away slowly and then leave. If they follow you, you can try to run, but it is likely already too late. Pray that death comes swiftly.

WHEN IT RAINS

Posted Aug 17 2019 00:12:32 GMT-0400

There aren't any rules about the rain. I cannot possibly make a ruleset to encompass all potential threats. Our world is a dangerous place. The books in my office are filled with sticky notes marking the pages for everything from invasive beetles to the causes and cures for werewolves. I could not hope to condense this much information into a simple list of rules, especially since I already struggle with getting people to read the ones that already exist. Instead, I target the most immediate threats. The ones that I know exist on the campsite and that campers are more likely to encounter than others.

Since the majority of my campers stay under their shelters when it rains, I don't have to worry as much about them encountering one of the things that come out during storms. The campers stay in one place and drink and the unnatural creatures of the woods tend to avoid large groups. They prefer to prey on lone individuals wandering through the trees.

Most of these creatures leave when the rain stops. There are a handful, however, that do not and have to be dealt with by camp staff.

It rained last week. A few days ago, one of my camp staff showed up at the office with a rather shaken camper in tow. Our campsite was mostly deserted at this point, as our big open camping event had ended and we were prepping for our next wave of campers. Just a handful of people, families and couples wanting to get away for a few days, nothing organized like our events. My employee told me that he'd been clearing out some of the underbrush that posed a fire hazard when he'd heard some shrieking. He'd gone to investigate and found this young man on the ground, pinned by a woman.

A naked young woman with green hair.

They're called rusalki (singular rusalka). I've also heard them referred to as water spirits or mermaids (but with legs instead of a tail). They originated in Russia. They don't need the ocean to appear, any body of water will do - even something as small as a puddle left behind after a rainstorm.

She was in the process of tickling him to death.

If you laughed just now, stop and think about it for a moment. Imagine what it's like being tickled to the point you feel you can hardly breathe and your stomach and chest aches with exhaustion. Now imagine that doesn't *stop*, it keeps going and the pain just gets worse and worse until your lungs seize up and you pray that darkness sweeps you away just so it'll *stop*.

Imagine how long it would take to die in such a way.

If you're not ticklish, the rusalka merely finds a convenient puddle of muddy water and shoves your face in it until you drown.

Unless it's one of the northern variants. Those smother their victims with their breasts.

If you're thinking - that's a great way to die! - I should add that their breasts are iron and I suspect it's less smothering and more "crushing their victim's face and skull into a pulpy mass of flesh" but hey, I only know what the books told me. I haven't actually seen a northern variant kill someone.

All of our four-wheelers are outfitted with useful supplies both mundane and occult. This particular staff member had paid attention during orientation and the bi-yearly refresher meetings and knew to grab the branch of hawthorne before charging at the rusalka. She snapped her head up, her beauty vanishing as her face contorted into a grimace; her lips peeled back and her gums protruding, her eyes nearly swallowed up in the puffy folds of flesh. My employee averted his gaze, "flailed a bit with the branch" (his words, not mine), and she fled. Then he'd helped the camper up onto the back of the four-wheeler and brought him to my office.

I called the police so that they could talk to the victim and take his report and tell him they'd press charges once they found his attacker. It makes my campers feel safe. The police just throw the reports in a special file back at the office and never touch it again. Dealing with the rusalka would be my job.

To do that, I would need some help from my staff.

I have a new employee. I'll call her Turtle, since that was part of the username she contacted me under. She's an internet hire. I don't typically do internet hires. I recruit locally, as my campground's support of the community is one of the reasons the police are willing to work with me whenever an accident occurs. However, there is a lot of value to be found in bringing in outside ideas, so when Turtle made a good suggestion and said she was between jobs... I brought her on.

I was also short-handed at the time, even before Jessie was put in the hospital.

I've been doing something new. Ever since the man with the skull cup spoke with me about the children selling ice, I've been making a point to greet him when I'm out on my four-wheeler.

Interesting fact about the man with the cup: it isn't always a man. Some people are approached by a woman. They look like a different person to everyone that encounters them and I haven't been able to find a pattern to their gender or appearance. However, I only see him as a man.

I'm also encountering him more often. I wonder if this is because I'm actively looking for him, as before now I was dreading his presence.

It's a calculated risk. I want to learn more about him and what he knows about this campground, but he isn't willing to forgo giving me a drink every time we meet. One time I wasn't thinking things through and took a drink from my water bottle to get the bitter, salty taste out of my mouth and wound up puking beside the road while he watched. It felt like he was disappointed in me.

About two weeks ago we heard someone scream over the radio. We all carry one. I asked everyone to check-in and Jessie was the only one that didn't respond. I told my staff to group up and start searching the campsite in pairs. Then I left my office to go check the land around the thing in the dark. I don't ask that of my staff. I didn't get very far into the woods before I noticed the man with the cup standing by the side of the road. I stopped and asked if he knew where Jessie was.

"Back there," he said, nodding to the trees behind him. "I offered her a drink. She accepted, but she wasn't polite about it. I left her impaled on a tree branch."

So after that I was desperate for extra staff and Turtle seemed like a good fit. And she has been. It's working out so well, in fact, that I thought I'd give her a bit of extra responsibility.

I called Turtle to my office and asked if she could wear something nice to work tomorrow. It's not some weird dress code thing, I hastily explained. The ritual requires a maiden to be dressed up and while we didn't have the right clothing - indeed, I don't even *know* what it should look like because the book didn't describe it - I've found that substitutions can be made. It is the symbolism that matters. Clothing that is reserved for special occasions would signify that *this* is a matter of elevated importance, thereby conveying ritual status to what we were going to try.

Turtle stared blankly at me when I finished. She seemed open to strange things when I hired her, but I think this was a bit beyond what she'd anticipated. Generally, when a boss tells a female employee that they should be ready to throw their clothing at a murderous mermaid in case things go horribly wrong, that's going to merit a sexual harassment lawsuit. However, this is an old land, and things are a little different here.

As with any supernatural creature, there are a myriad of ways to banish a rusalka. There's also a number of different ways to protect yourself against one. We were going to try a fairly simple ritual, in which a young lady is dressed up and sent out into the woods. She is the avatar of the rusalka and her symbolic "banishment" from the village (in this case, the staff lodge) would transfer on to the rusalka and banish her from my campground. If something went wrong, Turtle could buy herself time to escape by throwing her clothing at the rusalka. They're obsessed with clothing. They desire it more than anything and will stop to pick up and put on any article of clothing thrown their way.

I showed her the route to take on a map. She'd start at the employee lodge. All of the staff would be present to see her off. She'd walk through the woods, all the way to the opposite property line. It's about a half mile walk. I'd be waiting there with the four-wheeler to take her back.

"That's it?" she asked, somewhat surprised by how easy it sounded.

"Well, if it goes wrong you might be *running* that half mile," I said. "Just be ready to throw something behind you to slow her down. I don't recommend throwing your shoes. The road turns to dirt at the base of the hill and there's a lot of rocks. You'll want your shoes."

She agreed with my advice and said she'd wear a cardigan over the dress and throw that first.

The next morning Turtle showed up in a sleeveless mint dress with a lace overlay. A neat white cardigan and running shoes completed the outfit. She looked uncomfortable and understandably nervous. I left her with the rest of the staff, reassuring her that this would be fine, that I'd be there waiting for her at the edge of camp. Then I got on my vehicle and headed out.

My staff relayed what was happening via radio. They told me that Turtle had left the lodge and they'd seen her off. That the rusalka had apparently been lying in a ditch near the edge of the field (wallowing in the remaining rainwater, perhaps?) and snapped to attention as Turtle walked by. That the rusalka had then slipped off into the woods after her.

"Well that's not good," I said.

"She's got a cardigan," someone offered hopefully.

There wasn't much I could do except wait. I kept track of the time. I had a rough idea of how long it would take someone to walk this far and then I added another five minutes past that. After that, it became apparent that something had gone horribly wrong and Turtle wasn't making the rendezvous. I started the engine on my four-wheeler and began driving slowly down the dirt road, listening intently for the frantic cries of someone being tickled to death.

Instead, I heard a bird call. Okay, it wasn't a bird call. It was a human voice yelling "kaw kaw!" at me in an attempt to subtly get my attention.

It wasn't really that subtle.

"Turtle?" I asked hesitantly.

"Yes," she hissed back. She was hiding behind a sizable tree. I watched as she poked her head out from behind it. "I don't think it worked. The rusalka wound up chasing me. I did what you said and threw my clothing at her.

"Are you at least wearing-"

"NO. I had to throw ALL my clothing away before she stopped."

So she was not wearing undergarments. With that question answered, I went to fetch something from my four-wheeler. While not ideal, it would at least let me get her back to the employee locker room.

It's not in the rules but I'm thinking of adding it: always carry a spare tarp. They come in handy if the rain does something unexpected, your tent fails in some way, or you need an emergency cover-up for a naked employee.

I dropped her off at the employee lodge and once she was dressed, we reconvened in my office to discuss what went wrong. The rusalka had come at her as soon as she entered the woods, Turtle related. There'd been a gleeful, almost childlike expression on her face, but Turtle wasn't going to take chances that the rusalka wouldn't hurt her. (which is good, I think Turtle is going to work out as an employee) She'd thrown her cardigan and the mermaid had stopped to pick it up and put it on. Turtle had run for a bit, trying to put distance between them, but she was quickly winded and had to slow down into a brisk walk. From behind her she'd heard someone humming, growing closer, and when she turned the rusalka was only a few yards behind. There was a smile on her face and an unnerving intensity to her gaze. Turtle had kept walking, unzipping the back of her dress as she did, and then she stripped that up over her head and tossed it back to the rusalka.

Inside-out, which probably bought her a handful more precious minutes as the mermaid struggled to turn it right-side-out again.

And so it went. Turtle would gain some ground, the rusalka would catch up - humming the entire time - and my newest employee would discard another item of her dwindling wardrobe.

"I should have worn more layers," Turtle sighed. "It was like the worst game of strip poker; where the loser dies at the end."

Finally, the rusalka had seemed content with the clothing she'd put on - or perhaps she got bored or distracted - for the humming ceased and when Turtle turned around that last time she discovered she was alone. Then she found a tree to hide behind and waited until I came looking for her.

I'm still not certain why that banishment failed. Perhaps because it's used to remove a rusalka from around a settlement and my campground includes forest, which is where rusalka are traditionally banished *to*. Regardless, I needed to attempt something else.

"There's another ritual we can try," I said.

I explained what we'd do. Turtle went pale. Her eyes darted sideways, gauging the distance between her and the door. She didn't need to have worried. She's a good employee, after all. I had her handle procuring the supplies we needed: the wood, the gasoline, the drugs from the pharmacy (they know how my campground works and are willing to fulfill "special" orders). She even took on the task of slipping the pills into Jessie's water bottle while they were both in the camp breakroom, which surprised me.

Jessie didn't make it very far before they kicked in. She'd been cleared to return to work but she still had stitches in and wasn't moving very fast. Turtle - bless her - tried to catch Jessie when her knees buckled, but Jessie was flailing a bit and she went down hard. It was an embarrassing scene, her rolling around on the ground, gasping and screaming and her camp uniform getting stained with blood from a broken stitch in her stomach.

We dragged her back into the breakroom and I had a couple more female staff members (I felt it was proper to respect her dignity as much as we could) help me strip her and dress her up again in another one of Turtle's dresses. It didn't fit that well, but it didn't matter. She only needed to be wearing it for as long as it took for her to burn.

There's another ritual to banish a rusalka. An effigy is created to resemble the rusalka, dressed in clothing it covets, and then burned. I was going to use something a bit more *significant* than a crudely bound bundle of twigs.

You see, the man with the skull cup said something else that had me concerned. He called to me, as I was hurrying into the woods to locate Jessie and get her to the hospital.

"Her behavior reflects poorly on you," he said. "If it happens again, I will hold you responsible as well."

I fear the little girl and the beast above all because that is the most likely cause of my eventual demise. However, after what the man told me he would do, if I ever refused to drink... My parents didn't exactly die quickly, but they still died *better* than what the man promised.

We took Jessie to a clearing in the woods where a pile of firewood waited. Jessie cried and fought the whole way, but the drugs made her uncoordinated and weak and it was like the tantrum of an infant. We dumped her on that first layer of wood and then heaped more up and around her so that she was partially buried, emptied a couple cans of gasoline onto it, and then I lit a twisted knot of newspaper and tossed it on.

Jessie went up like a candle. Her screams didn't last long, but they were piercing - the shrill, agonized terror of someone not wanting to die like that. She writhed, jerking convulsively, before falling still and her form was obscured by the thick black smoke from the burning gasoline. Most of my staff have seen something terrible before, so they were merely unnerved. Turtle seemed the most bothered, staring firmly at the ground until one of the other staff members gently took her arm and suggested they go back to the breakroom and dispose of Jessie's old uniform. I've slipped an excerpt from the employee handbook into her locker, just in case she forgot about our healthcare plan. She's entitled to a free monthly counseling session with a local therapist who knows about the campsite and will accept stories of demons and monsters at face-value. It's the least I could do, really.

I don't think Turtle will have to help me with something so unpleasant for a while, though. I wasn't listening to Jessie scream. I was waiting for something else - the sound of a second scream, coming from somewhere off in the woods. An echo of Jessie, that same helpless, desperate cry. I'm not sure if anyone else heard it. It died away shortly before Jessie succumbed.

The rusalka isn't dead. She's merely banished. Regardless, it'll be a while before we have to deal with her kind again.

I run a private campground. It's a little different from others, where the people aren't intrinsically tied to the land and there is no significance in the trees and the earth. Perhaps you think I'm cruel in how I literally fired an employee that refused to respect the creatures of the forest, but being disrespectful of ancient beings is a serious transgression and should not be taken lightly.

I saw the man with the skull cup today. He smiled at me and this time, it was neither mocking nor condescending. I think he approved and his approval means safety for me, for my employees, and my campers.

And that's what I'm here to do. Keep all of you safe by any means available.

RULE #3 – THE LIGHTS

Posted Sep 03 2019 22:37:52 GMT-0400

I admit my campground is a dangerous place. My staff takes care of what threats we're capable of handling, but I do ask for a modicum of common sense from my campers - such as not blundering off into the woods after oversized fireflies.

This should be obvious. Anyone who has ever paid attention to anything should have heard the folklore by now. Will-o-wisps. Marsh lights. Fairy fire. Whatever you call them, you should know that they lead travelers astray, sometimes to their deaths.

And yet that's rule #3 on my list. Don't follow the lights.

Why they didn't have Gollum do an eyeroll after pulling Frodo out of the swamp when the dumbass followed the lights, I'll never know. Real missed opportunity, there.

There aren't a lot of terrain hazards in my campground. No lakes to drown in (though there is one in a neighboring area but that's not old land and the lights don't go further than the property line) and no cliffs to blunder off of. A few steep hills that could result in a broken ankle, I suppose, but that's about it. It's not like the middle ages, either, where getting lost in the woods could leave you walking for days before you get out. As long as you walk in a relatively straight line you'll find *something* manmade to lead you back to civilization. I've had many campers call the camp emergency line asking for a ride back to camp after they wound up on the side of a nearby county road. Before cellphones, they had to hitchhike, and we lost a couple people that way. That's a story for another day.

The real hazard of the lights and the reason they merit a mention on my list is because they leave people vulnerable to the other *denizens* of my campground.

This is only partially about the lights. It's more about how I met the thing in the dark.

It was the summer we renovated the barn. It's the biggest structure on our property, with a high ceiling and intermittent support poles to hold up the vast, open space. Initially my father had hoped to make it into a show ring for horses but after the whole cannibalism incident he decided perhaps that wasn't a good idea. It became a meeting space instead for our various events to use as an indoor area when it rained and they couldn't use the field. The acoustics were terrible, however, and our events weren't utilizing its space to the fullest. My mother and father often argued about doing something

25

different with it, but my father's heart was set on that horse ring.

I waited quite a few years before I finally let go of my father's dream. It was part of grieving, I think. I remember standing in front of the barn and being unreasonably *angry* that they'd never done anything with this space and now I was stuck with a useless barn that could go to much better use. And as I stood there, fuming, hating my father for his stupid, unreasonable dreams, I think I realized I was more angry at the fact that he'd gone out into the darkness and let the beast kill him.

Because that's what he did. He went out there to die and he left me without both of my parents.

I couldn't undo that. I wasn't certain if I'd ever stop being angry. However, the camp *was* mine now and I couldn't hold onto things exactly as they were forever. It wouldn't bring them back.

The next day I started calling in contractors to make estimates. We'd clean up the vehicle garage and use that as the indoor meeting space. It was a little smaller than the barn but would suit the events' needs just fine. The acoustics were still terrible, but at least sound wouldn't have to travel *as* far. We could construct a much smaller garage for the vehicles. We were only using a fraction of that space.

The barn would be a camp store and a restaurant, I decided. That was what my mother wanted. Not a fancy restaurant. Things like hotdogs and grilled cheese sandwiches. I was losing so much revenue to the food trucks during our large events.

I thought at that time that I was getting a handle on running the campground. I was going to make some renovations, start some new cash streams, and perhaps this was all going to work out. I knew what I was doing. I could do just fine for myself, even with this being an old land.

I got complacent. I didn't notice that the mound of leaves and broken branches was growing bigger out in the woods. It'd been there for almost a decade and perhaps it grew, but it was so slow that I didn't realize. I thought it was just an oddity in how the forest debris accumulated and it wasn't in the way, so I left it alone.

That year it grew two feet. And then two feet the next year. And two more feet before it finally stopped. I should have realized that something was changing and in an old land, that meant something dangerous was happening.

It was two in the morning when I was woken up by the radio I keep on my nightstand. This was while cellphones were still quite new and not everyone had one. Those that did couldn't get reception down in the woods. My staff patrolled the campgrounds, once an hour, 24/7, and campers knew they could flag them down for help. That is exactly what had happened. Someone was missing, my staff member said. They'd seen something in the woods and wandered off to go see what it was and their campmates didn't think much of it until someone got up to pee in the night and realized their tent flap was open and they hadn't come back.

"Did they follow the lights?" I sighed, fumbling for the switch.

"Probably?"

"I'll help look. If we don't find them in an hour I can call in more staff."

Which would mean overtime pay. It couldn't be helped. I dressed quickly and the little girl outside the window heard me moving around and her crying stopped. She hiccupped twice.

The only time I cannot leave the house is when the beast is present and unless something unusual happens (such as the night my parents died) it only appears in the hour before dawn. The little girl is certainly a threat, but she is bound by certain rules. She can only enter through "formal" entrypoints and can only harm my family if we leave by those same formal entrypoints.

Garages don't count. They especially don't count if I'm already on a four-wheeler and I floor the gas as soon as the garage door is up.

I glanced back at the house once I was past the edge of the driveway. The little girl stood at the fence, her hands on the pickets, watching me leave.

I met my staff member at the last spot the missing camper was seen. It's a woman, he said, which is why their campmates were so concerned. Their fear was understandable, but they were worried about the wrong things. There were non-human predators in this campground and they zealously protected their territory from *lessor* predators. Of course, they wouldn't pass up an easy meal, either. I wasn't worried. Most of the creatures at this point of time required some sort of... trigger, such as the dancers or the man with the skull cup. The ones that actively hunted we could typically locate and dispose of before anyone was hurt.

I remember this summer not only because we remodeled the barn, but also because the nature of the campground started to change. It was inevitable, I suppose. The only way to stop it would be to sell it to someone outside the family and then the creatures would slink away and the forest would be... diminished. The trees would appear sparser. The imperfections would stand out more. The outside world would press in harder and we would lose that sense of serene isolation that my campers come here for.

I left my vehicle behind on the road and went on foot, carrying an electric lantern. I am not afraid of the forest at night. My parents took me out after sundown so that I would learn its ways and grow up to respect the woods. The night quickly swallowed me up so that I walked in a bubble of light cast by my lantern. Trees appeared out of the darkness like looming sentinels, quickly vanishing behind me as I pressed on. I wasn't walking in any particular direction. I was looking for the lights.

It took perhaps half an hour before I saw them. They hovered just ahead, neon green orbs about the size of a soccer ball. Motionless in mid-air, perhaps mere yards away. I knew this to be a trick. I could never reach them. They would remain forever out of my grasp, seemingly not moving, but steadily leading me further and further into the woods.

And then I'd eventually come out near the highway, I don't know, like I said, there's not a lot of terrain hazards in the campground.

I angled slightly to the right of them instead. There's a trick to it. Search near where the lights are first seen, but avoid following them. If the missing camper had tripped over a branch and sprained her ankle, she'd hear me. Otherwise I'd have to assume she'd just kept walking and would have to hitchhike her way back to camp on her own.

That could be a danger of its own. The odds were greatly in her favor, at least. The locals around here are nice.

I called her name as I walked. Her campmates had given it to my staff. It didn't take long before someone answered, frantically crying that yes, here, she was here. Her voice was hoarse. I wondered how long she'd been here on her own, screaming for help. The forest swallowed up sound unless people were actively listening. Another quirk of an old land.

She was buried in the ground to her waist. I paused, staring down at her in surprise. The earth around her was packed down and her frantic clawing at the dirt had only produced thin scratch marks. Her fingers were bleeding and her face was covered in tears and snot. I crouched in front of her and pulled a handkerchief from my pocket and gave it to her.

"I'll have to call for my staff to dig you out," I said. "It'll be okay. You followed the lights, didn't you?"

She nodded glumly.

"Are they… actually…" she whimpered.

"Yes," I confirmed. "They're will-o-wisps. This whole burying thing is new, though. I guess they got tired of merely leading people to the property line."

Perhaps I shouldn't have told her that, for her breathing sped up, on the verge of hysteria. I opened my mouth to reassure her that everything would be fine, that will-o-wisps were generally harmless -

- and the lantern went out.

All light went out.

I froze. I could feel my heart speeding up as a sudden cold shiver of dread ran down the back of my neck. This was *definitely* new, and as such… I didn't know what to do.

There's a few options when confronted with a supernatural creature you can't identify. Running is generally a poor choice. Predators are *designed* to outpace their prey, after all. Hiding is similarly useless. Confronting the creature directly sometimes works out, so long as you are respectful and they're the sort that are willing to talk or bargain - such as the man with the skull cup. For everything else… groveling is the way to go.

I dropped to my knees and grabbed the woman's hands. I told her to lower her head and close her eyes and *keep* them closed, no matter what she heard or felt. Become nothing. Become like the dust on the ground. Beneath notice. And perhaps whatever presence was approaching would pass us by.

It was like a weight on my back. Like the very air was growing thick and it slumped to the ground, dragging me with it. I struggled to breath and I heard the woman in front of me gasping, shaking violently with terror.

There was a faint touch against the back of my head. Something immense, I realized, but so very in control that it could touch me as light as a fly. I struggled to remain still, burying my own trembling deep inside me where it twisted around my chest and stomach. And since we had not escaped its notice... I went to the next stage of groveling.

Begging.

Look, sometimes you just have to throw your pride out the window and do whatever it takes to survive.

"I'm sorry," I gibbered. "I was just trying to help her. Please. I beg you - pass us by."

I felt pressure against my back, like a lead blanket weighing me down and pressing my body into the ground. I cowered in the dirt, holding on tight to the wrists of the half-buried camper, whimpering in the back of my throat.

I think she opened her eyes. I think that's what happened. She began screaming, over and over and over - a high, raw scream of mindless terror, pausing only to fill her lungs and then it started over again. A rumble, like stones rolling downhill, and the earth around me shifted - loosened, and I felt my body slide backwards. My throat constricted with fear, I thought for an instant the earth was going to swallow me up like it had swallowed her - but I did not dare to open my eyes.

My body was pelted with debris. Small sticks and stones, the very earth around me torn up and thrown into the air, spun around in a whirlwind that howled in my ears like a beast and stole away the woman's screams. I covered my face with my arms as pain slashed across my exposed skin and I felt hot blood trickling down the back of my hands. My body was curled tight into a ball as the ground bucked and rippled beneath me. I heard the agonized groan of the trees as they shifted in the frenzied wind. I kept my eyes firmly shut.

Then it ended. The wind vanished, the weight lifted, and everything was silent. I remained exactly where I was, arms over my face, eyes shut tight, until I heard a cricket resume chirping from somewhere nearby. Only then did I open my eyes.

My lantern lay nearby, casting light again, covered in a thin layer of dirt. The ground around me had been stripped clear of leaves and debris, leaving behind a five foot diameter circle, the dirt swept into grooves that spun outwards in a spiral. There was no sign of the woman or the hole she'd been trapped in.

I returned to the road. I radioed the rest of my staff that were working that night and told them that we were missing a camper and I didn't think we'd be finding her alive. They were to keep an eye out for her body but they were not to leave the roads. Not until morning. And if their lights abruptly stopped working... drop to the ground and *keep your eyes shut.*

The police were there the next morning to talk to the affected campsite and take down a missing person's report. I filled out the paperwork mechanically, exhausted from an evening spent in the library, digging through volume upon volume in search of an explanation for what had happened. I found nothing and my nerves were worn thin by the many cups of coffee and the steady wailing of the little girl just outside the window.

It's no use yelling at her to shut up. She only cries louder.

It took a few more encounters and subsequent disappearances before I put together the pattern. The lights vanishing. The sensation of something immense passing by. The whirlwind that takes away anyone that looks at the creature. The dreams everyone has of dying in the way they fear most. Finally, I realized that the pile of debris in the woods was growing rapidly and I went to investigate and found that I *recognized* the feel of the presence that dwelt inside.

It spoke to me. I do not remember what it said. I only knew what I had to write in the rules when I returned to my office.

I also added rule #3. I put it high up on the list because it's one of the more common hazards that people will encounter. (there isn't actually a system to how I organize the rules. It's however I feel about it at the time when adding a new one)

Anyway. I'll make this last bit short because my elder brother Matthew - who just returned from finishing a graduate program in Europe - stuck his head in and said that Turtle is sprinting across the field with what might be an empty bag of lemondrops, chased by a horde of our local carnivorous rabbits (that also greatly enjoy lemondrops). I think it'll be okay, but Bryan wants to release his dogs and I'm not sure the situation merits that kind of massacre yet. I should go make sure no one does anything dumb.

Anyway, I'm a campground manager. I'm trying to keep you safe. Please, for the love of my sanity, rub a couple brain cells together when you're out in the woods and *don't follow the lights.*

WHY WE DON'T KEEP HORSES

Posted Oct 05 2019 13:34:14 GMT-0400

I've been somewhat lax in updating since my last post. It is close to the end of the camping season and there's a lot to do. The weather is pleasant and people want to get their weekend trips in while they can. We're also having to prepare for Halloween. While we won't have campers on site, I still need to protect my staff and family, as well as ensure that the inhabitants of my campsite are contained.

The latter is the important one. The rules of how the world functions shift on Halloween. People disguise themselves as monsters. Monsters disguise themselves as humans. And all the boundaries grow weak as all the world becomes an old land.

The whole town takes precautions for Halloween. My campsite has to take the most. However, I've found a little bit of breathing room here to sit down and type this out because my elder brother Tom - who finally returned home after his craft brewery in Kentucky went under - has agreed to take upon himself some of the preparations. He's been urging me to let him handle them and I've resisted, as he's been away for so long and this is important enough that I feel I should handle it myself. After all, I've been managing this site for a decade now and he's been off galivanting on a boat as a crewman for some deep sea research expedition. Which I suppose is dangerous, but it's a *different* sort of danger. However, he's finally prevailed and I feel I can trust him with some of the easier rituals.

I've still put some other projects aside to write this, but they aren't urgent, and I felt a little guilty with everyone clamoring for another post.

I alluded to a couple events that have happened on this campsite in my last installment. The hitchhiking incidents and the cannibalism. Unsurprisingly, I've gotten the most requests to find out about the cannibalism. It's not a pleasant story, perhaps more unpleasant than the rest simply because it involves animals. I'm loathe to describe things in such a way that they necessitate warnings to my audience... but perhaps I can scrub my soul of the screams of the foals by doing so.

I think that's warning enough.

My most vivid memories of my father are while he was resplendent with joy at the thought of keeping horses. The mundane memories all blend together, him sitting at the dinner table, him sitting in his study leafing through his books, him helping carry lumber to some part of the campsite... I could not tell you any of these moments individually because they are unremarkable points in the fabric of my life. The months leading up to the horses, however, are like gold thread woven into the tapestry, catching the light and reflecting it back at me. They shine because he shone.

I remember him coming outside to where I was playing in the yard. He said it was all settled, the money was paid and the construction of the barn would begin. And I, only dimly aware of these proceedings, stood there dumbly until he picked me up and set me astraddle on the swing, saying that by this time next year I'd have a horse of my own and be riding it around the campsite.

He bought me a saddle for Christmas, while the barn sat finished but empty until the spring. It was for both of us, my younger brother and I, but I knew in my heart that it was for me. Already my brother had failed to display much interest in the campground and even at that young age we knew who would be taking it over in the future.

Then, while the snow melted, the horses arrived. My father didn't want to just own horses, he also wanted to breed them. He had four mares and a stallion - no special bloodline, but fine, adequate horses. I remember mother saying dourly that he was being too ambitious, that none of us had much experience with horses, but my father dismissed her concerns. We had someone on staff - Louisa - whose family did raise horses for a while, until they sold all but one. That last lies buried on their property, its head under the oak tree and the four halves of its torso at each corner of the field. Another story for another time, I suppose. Anyway, Louisa knew what to do and had been given a pay raise in preparation for her additional responsibilities.

She lies buried in the cemetery. No need to do to her body what was done with her parents'.

That first year all four mares gave birth. I claimed the biggest - a chestnut - as my own. I named it Chestnut (I wasn't an imaginative child). My brother at first refused to call any of them his own. He interacted with the horses grudgingly, perhaps resenting the attention our father was giving them.

He was more like our mother. I took after our father and I wonder if my brother sometimes wishes he had a closer relationship with dad. He's never spoken about it.

Around mid-summer I noticed that he was spending time with the small dappled gray foal. He'd lean on the fence and stare at it for hours while it stood there staring back at him. I was young enough that I didn't think much of it, other than to assume my brother was weird, and honestly growing up like that we were *both* a little weird.

I think that's why my brother got married and I didn't. He left the campground behind when he went to college. I did not.

Near the end of the spring my mom woke me up, saying that my father needed my help. He was in the horse pasture. I dressed and went to where he was, just outside the fenceline, his clothing stained with mud with a pile of dirt nearby.

I think I knew. When I hopped the fence and followed my father through the tall grass to a round spot of trampled grass, the earth stomped flat and soaked with blood, I think I knew. The foals were dead. All but the little gray one that watched me as I helped drag their bodies to the waiting grave. I remember that I didn't cry.

Autumn and winter passed. Spring came and the four mares once again gave birth to four foals. By then, the small dappled foal was no longer small, but a full-grown horse that towered over all the others. He'd suckled on the mares all through the previous summer - all four, not just his own mother - and he'd grown quickly because of it. He was beautiful, but wild, and only my brother could ride him. I hated him for it, watching him use the saddle that had been given to both of us but was really meant for *me*.

I remember that this was the spring that my brother grew distant. Like he wasn't there, staring off into the distance and day-dreaming, and I remember our parents getting cross with him repeatedly for it. I remember our father snapping at him, telling him to pull his head out of his ass, and I was shocked to hear the frustration in his voice. I didn't make the connection until I was older that he was worried about the horses, afraid that whatever killed the foals last year would return, and it bled into every other aspect of his life.

My father loved this land but after we got rid of the horses I think he resented it.

One night in the early summer I woke to the little girl calling for me. She went quiet when I sat up in bed. My bedroom was on the second floor but that didn't stop her shadow from being visible through the sheer curtains over my window.

"What do you want?" I yawned.

"Your brother left the house," she said.

I'd had conversations with the little girl before. She stopped talking to me after my first period; the mark of adulthood, I suppose. She doesn't talk to adults. She only weeps.

And no, I never got her to say anything about herself.

"We're not supposed to leave the house at night," I whispered.

"He's going to be in tr-ou-ble," she sang. "You should go after him."

"And the beast?"

"Not here yet. Be sure to leave through the garage."

I shoved the covers back and put on my shoes. The little girl hummed the entire time and as I descended the stairs her humming stopped and turned into weeping, from just outside my parent's bedroom.

I wasn't certain where to go as I left the yard via the driveway. It was the screaming of the foals that led me to the pasture.

The barn doors were open. Father had taken to checking them every night, compulsively, and ensuring they were locked tight. The foals were out in the field. The big dappled gray stallion was loose as well. My brother clung to its back. I watched from the fence as the stallion ran down one of the foals and kicked it, knocking its legs out from under it, and then it half-reared and came down and I heard the crunch of bone from where I stood. The foal began to scream. I felt like I was frozen in place by the sound, helpless to watch as my brother slipped off the stallion's back and knelt over the wounded foal and slit its throat.

And the dapple gray horse bent his head and began to eat. It ripped the skin off in long strips, tossing its head back as it swallowed, and then buried its nose again in the foal's steaming body. It ate and ate, stripping muscle off of bone, tearing open the organs and devouring those, leaving not a scrap of meat behind.

This was how the foals died the previous year. This is what killed my Chestnut. My brother and his big gray horse.

I ran back to the house. It was close to dawn so I went to my room and covered my ears with my hands and counted the minutes until the beast arrived. The little girl's screams reminded me of the foals in the field.

The next morning I helped my father bury the bones of the foals. I remember how angry he was and how my brother was no help at all, off in the other corner of the pasture with his dapple gray stallion. The horse seemed even bigger now, fully as large as a clydesdale. My father snapped at him over lunch and I thought that perhaps today wasn't a good day to tell them what had happened. Perhaps tomorrow when dad wasn't as upset.

This is what almost got me killed.

That night I woke to the sound of scratching against my window. The little girl again, hissing so that I would wake. I tried to ignore her. I wasn't in the mood to talk. She, however, was insistent and finally, I opened my eyes, annoyed by the interruption to my sleep. My brother stood over me. In the darkness, I could barely see his outline, but he felt… vacant. One of his arms was raised and in his hand was a kitchen knife.

I threw the stuffed bear I slept with at him on instinct. Then, while he batted that away, I seized the lamp off the nightside table and smashed it into the side of the face. From outside my window, the little girl screamed in fear and I think that was what woke my parents up. They came running upstairs, flung on the light, and found me sitting on my bed with my brother groaning at my feet and bruises already swelling around his eye socket.

He sometimes reminds me of the black eye I gave him. My retort is that he was *going to kill me.*

Our parents took us downstairs and mom made hot chocolate while my brother held ice against his face. He said that the dapple gray horse had told him to kill me. Now that the stallion was big and strong it was time for my brother to take what he deserved.

Inheritance is not strictly to the eldest. There is plenty of precedent in stories for the youngest child to inherit. However, before that could happen, something had to disqualify the eldest as a worthy successor. I had to be removed.

My brother was bewildered. He didn't even *want* the campground, he said. He wanted to go off and be an astronaut or maybe something with math. Our parents sent him to his room after that and they argued about what to do with the stallion. They finally settled on selling it. Mom started searching for a buyer immediately and quickly found one. The dapple gray stallion was a beautiful horse, after all. In the meantime my brother wasn't allowed out of his room except to use the bathroom and for meals. At night they locked the door and they had me sleep at the foot of their bed. At the time I thought this was a fair punishment. He'd killed my Chestnut, after all, and deserved this. I didn't think about how it was all precautions to ensure he didn't try to kill me again.

I told you earlier that Louisa was helping us with the horses and that she's now buried in the cemetery. When the buyer arrived, my father sent her to bring the dapple gray stallion to the waiting horse trailer. I was lingering nearby, wanting to see with my own eyes that the horse was gone.

I remember watching as Louisa approached the dapple gray stallion. How she tried to slip a harness over his head and how he let her and I thought that wasn't right, that he was being too compliant. And then how he snapped his head up and to the side and the reins wrapped around her wrists and I remember that look of perfect surprise before he turned, pulling her forwards, knocking her off-balance so that she fell face-first into the ground.

I remember him rearing and how he remained there a half second, poised in the air, his breath steaming in the early morning chill, and the arc of his hooves as he brought them down onto Louisa's skull.

I remember how he began to eat her body.

And I remember my dad's face, set into a severe line. It couldn't be sold now, he said. Nothing left to be done but put it down. None of us said anything to him, we merely looked on in solemn witness as he took the shotgun down and loaded it, tucked it under his arm, and left in the direction of the barn. My mother held my brother as he cried silently.

We heard the shotgun go off and when dad returned he said that it was done. It wasn't until late that night, after my brother was asleep, that I heard my parents talking downstairs. I'd been sleeping only lightly and woke at the sound of voices. I crept down the hallway to listen.

The dapple gray stallion was still alive. It'd broken down the stall door and the shotgun blast had been my dad trying to kill it before it reached the doors to the barn. He'd missed, it'd escaped, and vanished into the woods. He didn't want my brother to find out. Better if he continued to believe the horse was dead.

We didn't see the dapple gray stallion after that, not until the fall. I was walking past the barn when I became aware of a commotion from inside. The barn door was cracked and I peered inside the dim interior.

One of the mares flew through the air, past my line of sight, and slammed into the wall of the barn. It struggled to stand, crying out in terror, as the gray stallion advanced on it. He put one hoof on the mare's shoulder and opened his mouth - his teeth were sharp - and he clamped down on the mare's neck. That desperate, agonized shrieking was finally silenced when the stallion jerked his head back and ripped the mare's throat out.

I stood there, transfixed, watching as the horse ate. He turned to look at me, calm, as if daring me to do something about this. Chunks of meat fell from his lips as he chewed. Then he swallowed, turned his head back to the mare, and ripped more meat from her corpse.

This is when I ran to find my father. When he returned to the barn with his shotgun it was far too late. All that was left of the four mares and the one stallion were bones. I helped him bury them out beside the foals.

My brother doesn't like horses anymore. Neither do I. You see, the dapple gray stallion is still around. I tell my staff to keep an eye out for hoofprints or horse dung. We let Bryan's dogs loose if we find signs. I'm sure it's alarming to the campers to see a pack of enormous hounds running around, but it's better than the alternative.

We've found that the horse will feast on human flesh as readily as the bodies of its own kind.

I'm a campground manager. This land has a long history and its share of tragedies. Sometimes they echo, down through the years. Remember: we don't keep horses on our campground. If you see a chestnut foal walking through the pasture, know that it won't hurt you, but it isn't *really* there. Its bones lie buried under the mound on the east side of the field.

And if you see an immense gray stallion, be wary of approaching. It isn't on my land anymore, but it is somewhere out there. Perhaps it will merely crack your skull and feast on your body. Or perhaps it will accept you as its master and whisper to you dreams of power and position until you are driven to kill the innocent to slake its hunger and you are master no more, but slave to the dapple gray horse's bidding.

MY BROTHER IS NOT MY BROTHER

Posted Oct 09 2019 23:12:15 GMT-0400

I received quite a few inquiries about my elder brother. Wasn't I the eldest? And how come his story was different every time myself or Turtle answered a question about him? Did he work in the oilfields? At an amusement park? Was he away on a ship for a deep sea research expedition? And why did his name keep changing?

Let me make this absolutely clear. I do not have an older brother. I'm the eldest and I have only one brother and his name is Tyler.

Now then. Let me explain what happened, starting with the staff meeting. I try to not hold many emergency staff meetings. Reserving them for actual crises ensures that everyone attends. For lesser matters I utilize the whiteboard in the staff breakroom. I did the trendy thing and bought whiteboard paint and painted an entire wall. It's popular for leaving notes like "I brought in cupcakes, they have pink frosting, don't eat the ones with green frosting I don't know what left them" or "the woman with extra eyes says she's out of chamomile", or "can anyone cover my shift this Friday???" Sometimes there's pictures or a game of hangman. I reserve the upper right corner for my announcements and that's how I convey non-urgent information to my staff. That way, when I call an impromptu staff meeting, they know it's something important.

The employee hall is another barn-like structure with a corrugated steel roof and thin metal walls. Enormous fans keep the air circulating so that it stays tolerable in the summer. There's a breakroom with a fridge, sink, stove, and countertop space. A couple general purpose rooms, including two at the entrance that we open up during our larger events for volunteer usage, and the meeting room.

I've been trying to convince my uncle to take some camp funds and build himself a new house on the property so we can use his current one for our staff building. They'd appreciate A/C and I like its central location. My uncle isn't convinced yet. He doesn't like change.

The cupcakes with the green frosting were on the conference table when I entered. Subtle. Real subtle. I took them outside and left them on the ground. Hopefully the birds would dispose of them for us. My staff trickled in, nervous at there being an emergency meeting and disgruntled at being interrupted in their Halloween preparations. The timing of this was less than ideal. Everyone was already on edge from it being October.

"Everyone knows my elder brother, right?" I said. "He just got back from

37

hiking the Appalachian trail."

The words flowed from my mouth so easily that for a moment I forgot why I was having this meeting. Everything was fine. There was no emergency. Then I glanced down at the framed picture sitting on the table before me and I looked back up to see my staff all staring back at me, smiling happily and nodded. Of course they knew Steven who spent the past year by the ocean finishing his novel. James who got back from California where he's a firefighter. Eric who just completed his master's degree in medieval history at a European university.

I held up the picture.

"See this?" I told them. "Since this is an old land, we take our family history very seriously. This is our family tree. It hangs in my office. Does anyone notice anything strange about the last entry?"

No Steven. James. Eric. No elder brother.

"I only have one brother," I continued. "He's sitting right there and he's younger than me. I'm not sure what this 'older brother' is but he's *not my brother.*"

I told them that I didn't have answers but that I was going to work at finding them. While this was certainly unsettling to hear - that the boss doesn't know what's going on - I believe in being honest with my staff. In the meantime, I wanted them to act like nothing was wrong, but to take extra caution around this interloper. Don't go anywhere with him alone. Work in pairs (and this was the standard procedure for October *anyway* but it especially needed repeating now). And I told them all to get out their cellphones and set a reminder for every fifteen minutes that I only have one brother, a younger one. No one could forget this, I said. And I got out my phone as well and we all sat there in silence for a few minutes while people tapped on their screens.

Then I told Bryan to come with me. We were going to go on a visit.

I took a shopping bag with me. Bryan brought two of his dogs. The rest he instructed to patrol the campsite. Bryan's family is from Ireland. They came over in the potato famine and have retained that Irish heritage fairly strongly in their bloodline. Most of the family has red hair, except for Bryan and his dad. They have black hair.

We took two of the four-wheelers down through the camp road to the eastern edge. I haven't done much development to the eastern side of the camp. It is still thick forest that drops into a depression along the southern side. It floods every year and the groups that camp in this area have developed a multitude of ingenious methods for dealing with the mud. I didn't build this area out because I didn't have to - these campers roll in, unload, and do all the construction themselves. It's frankly impressive.

The lack of human structures also means that it's easy to hide things among the trees. The forest crowds in around things that don't want to be found. I shut my vehicle down and took my grocery bag and told Bryan to wait for me at the road. To come find me if I wasn't back in two hours. Then I started off into the woods, hoping that the person I was looking for was in the mood to receive visitors.

One of my staff members first found the lady with the extra eyes some years ago. He'd had a particularly bad week. His wife had left him. I can't say he didn't deserve it, he's honestly a jerk, but that's still a hard thing to go through. The lady with extra eyes found him and invited him in for tea. He told me, later, that he didn't know whether to refuse or not and which would get him killed, so he accepted because he honestly didn't care if she *did* kill him and figured he'd at least die with a nice cup of tea first.

And the lady hadn't killed him, merely made him some tea and served him some biscuits and let him tell her all about his wife leaving.

There isn't a happy ending to this. She didn't give him any life-changing advice. Just tea. He wasn't able to make amends and the divorce went through and he's been bitter ever since. At least his bitterness makes him a hard - albeit angry - worker.

Today, I was in luck. The lady was receiving visitors. I found her cottage - a single room with stone walls and a thatch roof. Smoke curled up from the chimney. I knocked on the door and it creaked open at my touch. Inside, the woman was busy with a tea kettle hanging over the stove.

"I brought you chamomile," I said, holding up the grocery bag.

"Lovely, lovely. Put it on the shelf."

The floor of her cabin is packed dirt. The interior is merely a round dining table and another rectangular one against the wall for food preparation. I'm not sure where she sleeps. I'm not sure *if* she sleeps.

The lady herself is rather plain, appearing in her early thirties with long brown hair. Her eyes are gray. She has a lot of them. They cover her forehead and her cheeks. I don't know how many there are. Staring at her long enough to count them all would be rude.

She brought the hot water over along with two cups and threw some leaves into each before filling it with water. Then she settled herself in across from me and we waited for the tea to cool enough to drink. I told her about my brother that isn't my brother and she listened. Then, because I think she's lonely and just likes to hear people talk, I told her a bit more - about how I'm sharing these accounts online and she thought that sounded delightful.

She says hello and says you should all come to visit her. I'm sorry if that sounds ominous. It's not.

I wasn't certain what I was hoping for. She was my first recourse because of all the potential allies, she's the safest to talk to. The man with the skull cup would be my second recourse and if that failed... I would implore the thing in the darkness.

"I can't get rid of him for you," she said when I finished, "if that's what you're here hoping for."

It was. It would be rude to say so, however, and I remained silent.

"I can give you some assistance at least, and you will have to deal with this problem yourself."

The tea, she said, was her first gift. It would allow me to retain a clear head while in the presence of my not-brother. This was one of the patterns we'd identified in the staff meeting. Anyone talking to my not-brother or merely in the general vicinity would immediately believe that he was my brother, that he had every right to be here, and give him absolute trust. This effect could last for hours. It took an outsider to point out the problem and even when it was right there in front of me on the screen, I still struggled to realize that my brother *is not my brother.*

I asked her how long the effect would last. She waved her hand dismissively.

"I don't know, you humans are the ones with the cellphones, google how long it takes to metabolize tea."

The second gift, she said, was the gift of sight. She asked me if I had an optometrist I could see on short notice. I replied that I should be able to get an appointment in the next few days and asked why she inquired.

"Because I'm pretty sure you'll need one to get this back out."

And she took up a miniscule splinter from the table, rolled it between her fingers, and stabbed it into the sclera of my eye.

For the record, my optometrist won't see me until next Friday. That splinter is still in there and it is deeply irritating.

I stumbled around her tiny one-room house for a minute or so, clutching at my face and bumping into the tables. I *trusted* the woman with extra eyes and so when she'd stepped up close to me I hadn't thought to react until it was too late. She busied herself with cleaning up the tea cups while telling me that the splinter would grant me the ability to see what really was for the next twenty-four hours and after that it would be nothing more than a splinter that the doctor would need to remove.

"One last thing," she said as I stared up at the ceiling, blinking rapidly as my eye filled with tears. "Keep that eye closed until you're out of the woods. There are things out here that aren't safe for a mortal to see clearly."

Now, I'm sure you're desperately curious as to what I could have seen in the forest with that splinter lodged in my eye. However, I have spent so much time and effort trying to convince other people to follow a set of rules that are designed to keep them from suffering a horrific fate and I wasn't about to do the stupid thing and go ignoring the lady with the extra eye's warning. So depth perception be damned, I kept that eye *shut tight.*

Bryan graciously let me ride on the back of his vehicle after I almost walked into a tree.

My house was different when I walked inside. The light from the windows was brighter. There was a gold sheen across every piece of furniture, like it glowed with light from within. I went to the office and the books on the shelves, the ones my father collected and the ones passed down through the generations, they sparkled like stars. I cried, but not because of the splinter in my eye. I think I understand a little better what it means to be an old land. It isn't all bad. It isn't all dangerous. Some of it is beautiful, radiant with the life of those that came before us.

I closed the one eye before I went into the bedroom, the master bedroom that I now claimed as my own, the one my mother died in. I wasn't certain what I would see… and I was afraid to know. Perhaps it would glow with the warmth of those that came before me…

Or perhaps it wouldn't.

I suppose I'll never know.

I took the shotgun down from its spot and returned to the living room. I got on the radio and called for my elder brother (and this time, a name did not appear unbidden in my mind) to come by the house. I had more Halloween preparations I wanted him to take over, I said.

He was quick to respond. I waited in a chair, the shotgun loaded and resting over my knees. I listened as the front door opened and shut behind him, listened to his footsteps as he rounded the corner.

I wish the lady with extra eyes had warned me. I wish she'd tried to prepare me in some way. As it was, I could only stare for a moment, my voice swallowed up by the cold terror settling in my stomach.

He was empty. His abdomen and chest cavity were open and hollowed out, the skin rolled back and neatly tied on either side of his body like one draws curtains. His sternum was gone, the ribs cracked so that they protruded from either side of his body like fangs. I could see clear through to the smooth muscles at the back of the cavity, to the bulge of his spine. He stared at me a moment and asked what was wrong, why I'd gone so pale all of a sudden.

I stood, raised the gun and pointed it at his chest, and asked him what he was.

He was silent a moment. Then he lunged at me - I fired - and the blast hit him in the center of his mass because that's where I'd *practiced* to hit, that's where my dad taught me, but there was *nothing* left to destroy. It knocked him down but he flipped to his feet, barely even stunned, while I desperately tried to reload. Then he was springing forwards, his hand closed on the gun, and he wrenched it from my hands and threw it across the room.

I found myself on the ground. Dazed, unsure of how this happened, aware of a sharp pain in my knee. Then he was over me, snarling that this campground was rich pickings for him and if he couldn't replace me, then he'd *dispose* of me instead.

I felt his nails against my abdomen and wondered what he'd do with my organs, once they were removed.

That was when Bryan's dogs came in through the window.

My not-brother jerked to his feet as the glass shattered. I caught a glimpse of his face, his lips peeled back in frustrated rage, and then he turned and ran. The dogs pursued, knocking over furniture as they went, bounding over top of my prone body in one jump. The dogs are Irish wolfhounds. Perhaps it was a trick of the light, but their gray coats looked almost black.

According to my staff, the dogs pursued my not-brother off of the campgrounds. He ran impossibly fast for a human, but I suppose that's to be expected of something that isn't actually human. The chase seems to have broken the effect he had on all of us as well, as my staff were able to see clearly what he was as he went running by with a pack of baying hounds close behind.

I really wish one of them had been quick enough to catch it on video. I would have liked to see that thing running for its life.

I'm a campground manager. It's a dangerous job sometimes, but it has its benefits. I have the trust of my staff and those that camp here are under my protection. For that reason, I suspect that my not-brother will be back. Had he been successful in replacing me, he would have had easy access to all those people that come and stay here. He may yet try again.

Because of this, I am adding a new rule to my list.

Rule #20: I only have one brother. He is younger than me and his name is Tyler. If you meet anyone claiming to be my older brother, inform camp management immediately. He is not my brother.

RULE #8 – THE PEOPLE WITH NO FACES

Posted Oct 26 2019 23:17:21 GMT-0400

I hate rule #8. It's a monstrous thing to ask of my campers. Could you just… *go along* with being maimed? And maybe try not to scream in the process? That's really messed up. I can't believe I had the gall to include it with the others, but what choice did I have?

Let me tell you about the people with no faces and perhaps you'll understand something of my helpless rage.

I initially tried to write this while drunk. I learned a few things about myself in the process.

First, I have been neglecting my liquor cabinet. Getting drunk off some pepper vodka that you thought would make for interesting mixed drinks and half a bottle of wine because the only other alcohol left is whiskey that's too expensive for mere inebriation is no way to live.

Secondly, I am an enthusiastic but incoherent drunk.

Thirdly… when I'm drunk, I refer to my mother in the present tense.

I learned about the people with no faces from my mother. She told me a lie, when I asked her why I only have nine toes, and it was a beautiful lie. I gave my missing toe away, she said, when I was little. I came across a fairy in the woods who had no nose. She was crying and when she told me why she was sad, I said she could have my nose if it would make her happy again. And the fairy refused, because it was too great a gift. So I offered the fairy a finger and that could become her nose instead, because I had ten fingers. And again the fairy refused. Then I offered her a toe and the fairy thought and thought about it and finally said that she supposed a toe wouldn't be missed *that* much and she took the smallest of my toes and it became a cute button nose.

But not as cute as my nose, my dad would say, and he'd pinch it to make me giggle.

Then mother would say that the wicked fairies that stole the crying fairy's nose was still out there. She'd say this so solemn and sad that I'd stop laughing and listen as she explained that this was why I couldn't go into the woods by myself yet, that I had to go with someone else. Someday I could go alone, she promised me. Once I knew how to protect myself from the evil fairies. This is how my parents introduced me to the dangers - and wonders - of an old land. They told me stories of heroes and monsters and one day I saw my uncle carrying the remains of something that looked almost human out of the forest and I realized the stories were meant to be warnings. I think that was my first step out of childhood.

It wasn't until I was in highschool, helping my father bury the remains of a camper who was divested of their liver, that I thought to ask my mother for what really happened to my missing toe. I'm not sure why I waited so long. It just didn't occur to me to ask, because it was such a trivial thing, something I'd grown up with and was as natural to me as my hair color.

There's creatures in the forest that don't have faces, he said. They travel in a group and they weren't sure what they are. Demons, perhaps, but there was no way to know for certain, not without encountering one directly and using a specific countermeasure and seeing the result. They seemed to avoid the staff. We never saw them, not unless we were walking through the woods unprotected.

He spoke absently, in short phrases here and there as he stabbed the shovel into the earth. It was the middle of summer and the earth was parched, packed hard and brittle. His face was flushed with exertion and sweat shone on his brow.

He wasn't certain why mom went into the woods without one of the four-wheelers and its associated pack of equipment. Especially not while she was so close to her due date. He stabbed the shovel into the ground and stared at it dully for a moment, old frustration etched into the corner of his eyes. I thought about the fights I'd overheard, when they yelled at each other in hushed voices, their anger simmering low, as if that could keep from waking me or my brother up. I wondered if this was what they fought about.

Maybe she didn't know, herself, he sighed, and scooped up another shovel full of soil. I thought that was directed at himself instead of me. Then he continued his story. Mom had been approached by the people with no faces. They wore raincoats, she said. Thin, dull gray, with the hoods raised and no matter how hard she'd peered at them, the memory of what their faces looked like slipped away as soon as her eyes were directed somewhere else. They carried scalpels, each clutching one tightly in their fist.

They needed something from her, they said. And my mother said she would grant it if it were in her power, because she was surrounded and when confronted with creatures so much more powerful than yourself the best strategy is to simply go along with what they ask and hope for mercy.

They asked for a toe, but not hers. And they called me by my name, the one my mother had picked out but hadn't told anyone yet, not even my father.

I haven't told you my name, have I? It's Kate.

And they took the smallest of my toes and left behind an incision in her stomach, not even an inch long, but my father rushed her to the hospital when she came staggering into the house and the doctor delivered me four days early via emergency c-section.

I think this makes me safe from them. I've seen them out in the forest and they just smile at me and nod and while I cannot see their smiles, I know they're there. They've never asked for anything from me.

Not everyone in my family has been so lucky.

In one of my office desk drawers is a knife. The handle is bone, the blade is bone, the binding is sinew. It was a gift and I keep it because it was a gift and I am obligated but I will never use it.

It was given to me because of how my great-aunt died. I am not certain if it was meant as a mockery or as some obscene token of respect, for despite the circumstances I must reluctantly admit that my great-aunt *chose* her time to die and took her fury with her all the way to the grave.

It started with my second cousin; her grandson. He went into the woods by himself. I remember his father coming out of the woods, carrying him in his arms, his face set and grim. My second cousin was screaming, a blind terror that froze my limbs and I stood there, shocked and senseless, until my father appeared and ordered me back into the house. The bite of his words snapped me back to myself and I turned and ran, but not before I saw how my second cousin's legs moved.

They flopped limply from the knee down. Swaying back and forth with every step my uncle took. Like noodles, I remember thinking. Like noodles. And the next time my mom made spaghetti, weeks later, I only took three bites before I thought of my second cousin's legs and threw up on my plate.

That evening, after the hospital had gotten him sorted out, my mother sat my brother and I down and told us what happened. We were both in highschool now and they didn't tell us lies our campground. Our second cousin had encountered the people with no faces, she said. They'd asked for the tip of one of his fingers and he'd tried to escape instead. Thought he could reach the four-wheeler if he just sprinted. So they'd taken the tibia and fibula from both legs. The doctors amputated the limbs just below the knee.

He does most of our desk work now. Payroll. Financials. Purchasing. He lives in town and rarely has to visit the campgrounds.

After he lost his legs, my great-aunt became a fixture on our campground. I remember thinking it odd that she'd be here, constantly, sitting in the rocking chair on our porch with her knitting in her lap. The campground had belonged to her until it became clear that she wasn't going to marry (I suppose I take after her) and ownership passed to her brother's line (my grandfather). My great aunt didn't have much to do with the campground once she relinquished control, however. She felt it would be crass to hover and instead let it go and let the next generation make of it what they wished.

I remember my father saying that she hadn't even said anything about the horses. Grandpa certainly had and my father was bitter about that. He was bitter about everything to do with the horses, though.

I liked having my great-aunt around. I did my homework out on the front porch, sitting on the floor with my back against the house, and sometimes she'd tell me things about the campground. It'd changed, she said. Sure, back then the trees had that *thick* quality to them - how they seemed to close in around you and tuck you away from the world - but it didn't feel *dangerous* like it sometimes does now. She didn't blame anyone for that, she sighed. It's just something that happens. The forest never did belong to humans. That's why we cut it down and build our houses in its place.

There's many things she told me but this is the one I remember the clearest, for it was the last story she told before she died. She kept one of our radio units nearby and it crackled as one of the staff reported that they'd seen a small group of people moving through the woods in jackets. Great-aunt set her knitting aside and said it was time for her to go.

I thought she meant 'go home' so I didn't say much else other than tell her goodbye. Then, after a small amount of time, I realized that I hadn't heard her car engine start. When I looked, it was still in the driveway.

There'd been a finality to the way she said it was her time to go. The pieces started to fall into place. I grabbed the radio and frantically broadcast that I thought great-aunt had gone into the forest. Then I went after her. I took one of the four-wheelers. I didn't have a plan. I just wanted to find her before she found the people with no faces.

This is something I've had to learn. You can't save people, especially when they don't *want* to be saved.

I caught up with my great-aunt as the last of the people with no faces encircled her. I killed the engine and tumbled off the four-wheeler, running the rest of the way on foot. I hit one of them, grabbing its arm and trying to use my momentum to knock it out of the way, to give me room to get through to my great-aunt. It was like striking a stone. The person didn't even flinch, merely shook their arm and broke my grip as if I weren't even there. I tried again, grabbing at their jacket and then at the hood, trying to yank it back.

They turned at that. Seized my wrist and took a step towards me, forcing me back and away from the circle. I think the fact they'd already taken one of my toes before I was even born was the only reason they didn't harm me, even as I screamed and kicked at the one that held me at arm's length.

Through all this, my great-aunt remained stoic. She never even looked in my direction. Just stood there, gray-hair like silver in the filtered sunlight, back straight, shoulders set. Great-aunt was in her mid-nineties, but there was strength in her, like all her frailty had been tossed aside for this one last task.

One of the people with no faces asked for the tip of her ear. A small thing, they said, quickly taken and easily forgotten. And my great-aunt said yes, of course she would grant their request for such a small, simple thing.

It raised its scalpel, positioning it near the tip of her ear. Her hand moved so fast - shot up and seized its fingers, twisted, and then *she* had the scalpel and the person with no face was stepping backwards. I sensed its surprise.

My great-aunt stabbed it in the face.

It screamed, a high, shrill sound and the birds exploded from the nearby trees with shrieks of their own. I screamed, covering my ears, and the person holding me back released me and turned towards my great-aunt. They converged on her, brandishing their scalpels, and she lunged at another with her stolen weapon. Behind her, the one she'd stabbed first had collapsed to the ground and was convulsing. Then it went still and limp, like the body was flattening into the earth.

My great-aunt fought like a wild beast. I don't know how many of them she stabbed. Their screams were deafening. But she was outnumbered and they overwhelmed her and forced her to the ground and then they began removing her organs.

I heard her scream at me to run. So I ran.

I'm not sure how far I went. I was running blind, not even on the trail, barely able to see through my tears. I don't know who - or what - grabbed me. There was just a hand suddenly on the back of my shirt, jerking me to a halt, and then before I could even rationalize what had happened they had spun me around and was holding me close, burying my face against their shoulder.

They told me that it was okay. That my great-aunt had *chosen* her time and I shouldn't weep. So many don't get to choose.

That's all I can make out. Their words and the press of their fingers against my back. Then I next remember walking out of the forest, across the grass, back towards the house. It is a long walk through that field and my mother came running out to meet me.

I didn't cry at my great-aunt's funeral and I remember wondering if something was wrong with me. I understand now that we all grieve differently and I had already mourned her out in the forest with that stranger that I am now convinced was not human.

Our "relationship" with the people with no faces remained unchanged, despite the attack. I suppose they recognized that this was a personal thing between them and her. Vengeance for what they'd done to her grandson.

I didn't encounter them again until the day I took possession of the campsite. I'd returned from the lawyer's office to finish up the paperwork involved and was exhausted from a day of working through my parent's will. The people with no faces were waiting for me when I pulled up to the house. I stopped the car in the driveway and got out, walking to where they were clustered at the base of the patio steps.

"The hell are you doing here?" I yelled at them, stopping a few steps away. "You aren't *invited*."

I don't know if they followed the rules of property or not. They seemed like the kind that would, however. When a creature has rules to their interactions with humans they generally follow the rules of property as well.

The one in the lead bowed its head and acknowledged that they'd trespassed, but that they came to deliver a gift. Of course I accepted it.

A knife. They told me how it was made. The handle was carved from my second cousin's fibula. The blade was a sharpened rib from my great-aunt and the sinew was from the muscles of her heart.

I'm a campground manager. I wrote these rules to keep you safe, to ensure that the horrors I have seen do not stretch out their hands and claim new victims. I hate that they exist, because it is a reminder of how powerless I really am. That all I can do is warn people and hope they heed me, because even if I were to take that knife from my desk and go out there and confront those monsters head-on it wouldn't be enough to save everyone.

Perhaps someday I will, when I am old, and ready to die. Perhaps I will release all this rage and hate inside me and choose the manner of my death, as my great-aunt did.

Rule #8 - If you find yourself surrounded by a group of people whose faces you cannot see, no matter how hard you look, give them whatever they request. They will ask for an insignificant part of your body, such as a piece of your earlobe or a single digit from a finger. Try not to scream when they cut it off, or they will help themselves to additional pieces. Do not refuse or try to escape. They will take far more from you if they must obtain it by force.

I WENT TRICK-OR-TREATING WITH THE MAN WITH THE SKULL CUP

Posted Nov 01 2019 18:02:06 GMT-0400

Normally October is terribly busy, but preparations for Halloween had wrapped up nicely and I even had some free time this weekend to write about the people with no faces, on account of the rain. Then things started to go wrong on Monday. One of the staff members came to me with an idea to put together a haunted house.

"Think of how much money we'd make," he said, which was certainly tempting.

Then he said the second part of his idea, which was to staff it with our *other* campground inhabitants and if a couple people went missing to sate their hunger, then oh well. And I looked out the office window and saw the children with no wagon staring at the house from the road and wondered where this idea had come from.

He's taking an extended vacation. With pay. Somewhere outside of town, just until his head clears and his thoughts are his own again.

Then on Tuesday I had someone leave a 1-star review on Google for my campground because - get this - the solar showers were cold during their visit earlier in the week.

It's late October and it was *overcast*. Solar. Showers. What did they expect???

This is why part of my rules are dedicated to basic camping knowledge, because the general public is full of dumbasses.

And on Wednesday, the sheriff dropped by to see if we were all finished up with our Halloween preparations. I'm pretty sure he thinks Reddit is slang for the new weird fad that the youth are doing, like planking or tide pods, so I'm going to go ahead and say this here. I don't like him. We don't get along.

I miss the old sheriff.

I heard the new one berating poor Turtle out in the driveway. She was getting the second box of liquor out of the trunk while I put away the first. Look... I don't drink *that* much. A lot of that is going to be Christmas gifts for staff. Yes, Turtle knows, I'm not ruining the surprise by saying this.

Anyway, Turtle was doing her job by trying to find out the reason for his visit instead of just letting him blunder into my house - we've all been a little on edge about that since the not-brother incident - and then next I hear is him about biting her head off because doesn't she know who he is?!

I stuck my head out the front door and told her to go sweep the hay out of the barn (which is code for GTFO) and then invited him in. He sprawled authoritatively in the chair opposite me and rested his hand on his gun, which I suppose was meant to be intimidating but I've survived a direct encounter with the thing in the dark and I just don't get intimidated by humans that easily anymore. I coldly asked him what I could do for him.

"There won't be problems this year, right?" he asked.

Referring to Halloween, of course. I'd already discussed my preparations with the local police force and we had our points of contact established for if containment failed at any time.

"There's always problems," I replied and I wasn't able to keep the bite out of my voice. "I'm surprised you're concerned, seeing as this isn't an election year."

So that was the wrong thing to say and I paid for it with an overblown lecture about his duty to protect the people and how my campsite was a liability and blah blah blah. I tuned it out and fixed a solemn expression on my face, nodding occasionally, and let my mind drift until he seemed to be wrapping it up. Then I reassured him that yes, of course I understood, and we were doing all we could to ensure this year was uneventful.

When he left I double-checked our preparations myself, cursing him under my breath the entire while. I also found Turtle in the barn, sweeping an already clean cement floor in obvious consternation. I guess no one taught her the code phrase. Whoops.

Anyway. Halloween day arrived with me already in a foul mood on account of the aforementioned difficulties. It didn't help that the day started with ill omens. A minute after midnight the little girl woke me by rapping on my window.

"Today is All Hallow's Eve," she whispered. "Will you honor the dead?"

It's been so long since she spoke to me. Sitting here, typing this, I still wonder if I imagined it.

I rose from my bed without a word and went out from my house to the family cemetery. It's tucked in a grove of trees close to the house, sheltering it from sight of the campers, encircled by a wooden fence with "STAFF ONLY" signs. I lit candles and left them on each of the grave mounds and remained there until morning, sitting in front of my parents' shared grave, until the distant screams of the little girl signified that the beast had come and gone.

A headless bird lay on my front porch when I returned to my house. Could be a gift from one of the barn cats. Could have been an omen.

Was probably an omen.

I wish I could say Halloween was uneventful. None of my staff were harmed, despite the dancers deciding that they'd collect half my staff for their Halloween party. I received word via our radios that the dancers were processing through the forest, carrying torches and wearing masks. They were gathering up everyone they passed, dragging them into the procession and forcing a torch into their hands. I felt I should go check on them myself, as the rest of my staff were occupied with a possible break in the fence and the police were trying to decide if the reports of a hitchhiker near the highway were just that or... something *else*.

I didn't make it far. I opened the door to my house and *someone* was there, standing directly on the other side, their form looming out of the darkness at me. I screamed and stumbled backwards, regaining my wits enough to grab the edge of the door in an attempt to slam it shut. The visitor put up a hand and the door stopped short. I backed away, thinking of where my shotgun was stored, and then I saw the cup he clutched in his other hand. The white bone shone in the moonlight.

"Oh," I said. "You."

The man with the skull cup nodded faintly. I let the door swing open again but he did not enter and nor did I invite him in.

"I need to go," I finally said, as the silence between us grew awkward. "I need to check on my staff."

"They're fine," he said. I heard wry amusement. "Hospitality laws are in effect."

"So the dancers *are* fairies," I said.

He shrugged, his gaze sliding away from the doorway.

"Fairies aren't the only things that follow hospitality laws. Even humans practiced them at one point, though that tradition has sadly waned in modern times."

"So they *aren't* fairies?"

He ignored my question.

"It's Halloween. Aren't there traditions to be honored?"

I babbled an apology and went back to the kitchen and fetched the rest of my costume. I'm the same thing for Halloween every year. It doesn't take much work, just some black leggings, a black turtleneck, and a printed cardboard box I bought online.

I'm an enderman.

Look. It's easy and kids love it.

I put the head on and took up a bowl of candy I'd prepared - just in case. I offered it to him, he hovered over it a moment, and then his hand dropped to the side and latched around my wrist instead. He pulled me out onto the porch. I let the candy bowl fall from my hands, protesting in sudden panic that I had work I should be doing. I needed to *leave*. He laughed and inquired as to whether I was confident that my preparations had been enough and whether I could trust my staff to do their jobs.

"I'm never confident," I said. "I live in constant fear that I'm not doing enough."

"See, that's the problem. You never relax. It's Halloween. Let's enjoy it."

He threw his arm around my shoulders, as if we were friends, but his fingers tightened, digging his nails into my muscle until I flinched.

"Let's go trick-or-treating," he said.

His tone indicated this was not a request that could be refused. I at least managed to send a quick text to my brother letting him know what was happening so he could take over making sure nothing terrible occurred in my absence.

At the campsite entrance we paused. The Halloween preparations serve three goals. Containment, protection, and surveillance. We have bundles of all the materials known to ward off supernatural entities hung up around the perimeter. This isn't always enough, but it keeps a lot of stuff trapped inside the campsite on this day when borders no longer matter and they're free to go where they will. This protects the town. Then, since all those malicious entities are trapped here with us, we need to protect ourselves. We've reinforced the securities on the various buildings and staff only leave in pairs with their own personal protections. Finally, we have cameras setup around the campsite and most of my staff are running surveillance. If anything gets out, we notify the police. I can't do this year-round because it's far too labor intensive.

The man with the skull cup eyed the gate as I ran the flashlight over it and then he turned to me, his thin lips curling up into a smile.

"Would you," he asked politely, "open the gate?"

I stared at him a long moment.

"You can shut it behind us."

His words were very soft. *Something* in that bundle of protections we'd tied up and fastened to the bars of the gate was keeping him from exiting the property.

"I'm not obligated to," I replied.

I could stop him right there. Easily. He considered for a moment and then said something and I silently went to the gate, removed the bundle, and swung it open for him to pass through. Then I replaced the bundle and joined him as he walked off down the road that led towards town.

My plan was to make the trip into town on foot and hopefully that would take long enough that he wouldn't have time to cause mischief before midnight. Then someone going into town stopped and offered us a ride because they recognized me and they clearly didn't recognize who was *with* me, and of course the man with the skull cup accepted, smiling that soft, smug grin the whole time we were in their backseat.

There's still people in town that haven't read my rules. I don't hide the fact that they exist. I'm not sure what I'm doing wrong here.

They dropped us off at the edge of town, where houses sat side-by-side for a few blocks. Old houses with wooden shingles and gnarled trees in their yards. This was the only place to trick-or-treat in town. Everywhere else had acres of land sitting between them and the next driveway. Kids ran past us, oblivious to the inhumanity of my companion. Their parents were a little more observant.

Everyone we encountered realized who I was, even with a cardboard box over my head. I've used this costume in the past before, so it's pretty apparent what's going on when a 5'4" enderman shows up on the doorstep with a man carrying a skull cup. Or woman. Or whatever people other than me see him as.

And the man with the skull cup just solemnly intoned, 'trick or treat' as each door opened for us and then stood there, his cup clutched in both hands, until the homeowner handed me the candy, not really sure what else to do. I hadn't brought a bag so I took off my enderman head and used that to store the candy in.

Then we reached a house and after receiving our candy, the man in the skull cup offered the person at the door a drink. I stood a pace behind the man and I frantically pantomimed to the homeowner to take a sip. They did, their eyes wide and fixed on me the whole time. Then the man with the skull cup walked away and I followed him, casting nervous glances backwards to the person that'd just been poisoned.

That wasn't the only person he offered a drink to. I started to sweat, despite the cold air. Drops of perspiration beaded up on the back of my neck and I was flushed with anxiety, watching all this unfold.

After about an hour, I began to notice a trend in which houses he offered a drink.

"Are... are you only poisoning the people giving out shitty candy?" I asked.

"Maybe," he replied with a thin smile.

Now, while this may *sound* amusing, just think back to how I said the people in town haven't all read the rules. I'm sure some of them were hugging their toilets last night. But it wasn't until the last house of the night that I really ran into trouble. It was getting close to ten and most of the kids had gone home. The porch lights were starting to go out. The man with the skull cup was walking quickly now, up to the last house on the edge of town. The streets were dark with shadows, as we'd left streetlights far behind.

"I'm sorry, I *just* ran out of candy," the woman that answered the door said, visibly growing more nervous as she took in who I was and who I was with.

"It is tradition to present all that visit with a gift," the man with the skull cup said cordially and he held out his cup in one hand and a knife in the other.

I understood what he was asking. I know how these things go. Behind him, I pantomimed to the woman cutting her palm open with the knife while mouthing the word "sacrifice" to her. I saw comprehension dawn in her eyes and she nervously took the knife from him and put the point to her palm.

She seemed surprised at how easily it cut through her skin. His knife is *very* sharp. Then I mimicked turning her hand over and she did this and let the blood drip freely into the bowl of his cup. We stood there for a few moments, the woman growing pale, not from the blood loss, but from the sight of it, from the growing pain in her palm as the nerve endings finally realized what was happening.

Then the man thanked her, she snatched her hand back and clutched at her wrist as if she could hold back all sensation, and the man turned to go. I followed. Behind us, I heard the door slam shut and the heavy click of a deadbolt.

"Old blood from what was in the cup before," the man with the skull cup murmured as we walked back to the street. "New blood freely given. I need only one more ingredient to refill my cup."

"Wait, refill? You have to *refill* it?"

He did, he said. I just hadn't noticed, or at least, I hadn't made the connection when I found the bodies. The ones with their throats slit. And his eyes slid sideways towards where I stood beside him, slowly growing cold inside at the realization of what he was saying. The last ingredient.

Blood forcibly taken.

And I made to turn, to run, but he seized my hair and wrenched my head sideways and I felt - briefly - the line of his knife against my neck - then I twisted and pulled and I left behind a clump of my hair but I was free and running down the road, the line across my neck burning as it bled freely into my shirt, but it was *intact*, my artery was intact.

I was heading away from town by necessity. The man stood between me and the safety of the houses. I'd cut across the field, I thought desperately, and circle back towards town.

I'm in shape from all the work I do on the campground, but I'm not a runner. That's a different kind of athleticism. I quickly exhausted my stamina and was reduced to a fast walk, clutching a hand against the stitch in my side. My neck stung where his knife had broken skin but the blood flow was slowing. I angled my direction more towards the beckoning lights of the town. I was quickly running out of field - there were trees ahead; I couldn't tell if it was merely a windbreak or a stretch of forest.

Then I saw, somewhat behind me and to my right, the man with the skull cup. He walked at an even pace, cutting a straight line between me and my destination, so that even if I sprinted I'd run the risk of being intercepted. Even if I *could* sprint. So I changed tactics. I'd head back towards the campground. That was a straight line and if I could reach the gate, I could get my hands on the bundle that guarded it and whatever it was that he feared inside.

Have you heard of persistence hunting? You walk an animal to death. You keep pace with it, so that every time it slows you're right there, threatening it, spurring it to keep moving, keep going, step after weary step until it finally collapses of exhaustion.

I didn't have my cellphone on me because it'd fallen out of my pocket in my struggle to break free of his grip. This is why women need real pockets on our clothing. My pants barely fit my cellphone in the best of circumstances. Worse, it was late enough at night that the road was deserted, and so without any hope of rescue, I had no choice but to keep going.

And each time I looked back, the man with the skull cup was there.

I collapsed long before I reached the campground. My thoughts were hazy at that point, worn thin by exhaustion, and I remember thinking that all this was *futile*, that I was dealing with creatures far more powerful than I and my time was simply *up*. That it'd be easier to give in than to keep going for a minute longer.

And *that* resignation broke as soon as I heard gravel crunch under his feet as he approached. I struggled to stand, my legs burning with pain, and I stumbled blindly forwards, driven only by an instinct to survive, pushed well beyond the limits of my endurance. His hand closed on my hair, right at the roots, and he jerked backwards. I stumbled, fell, and then he was straddling my legs, pinning them in place, and he twisted his wrist to force my head back and expose my throat. His body felt cool against my back. Not cold... just... not as warm as a human should feel.

I clawed at his wrist as he raised the knife. I'm surprised at how clear my thoughts were - that I was going to die - and I wondered if this was how my father felt as he walked out to meet the beast. Like floating. Like the world didn't exist anymore and it was just myself, alone with the beat of my own heart.

The knife point slipped along the line of my throat and there was no pain and I waited for my body to catch up, waited for the hot blood to soak my shirt... and then his wrist shifted again and there was a flash of pain along my jaw.

He dropped the knife and picked up the cup, holding it just below my chin and now I felt the heat of blood trickling along my neck, saw it dripping into the cup and mixing with the blood and water already present inside.

Then he released me and took the cup away. I pressed a shaking hand against the cut on my jaw and watched blood run down my wrist and soak into the sleeve of my shirt.

It was a long time before I could speak.

"I thought you were going to kill me," I whispered.

"Perhaps I was," he murmured. "Would it have been forcibly taken if you'd known you weren't going to die? Wouldn't you have simply acquiesced, knowing that it was easier to submit than to fight the inevitable?"

"But... why me?"

A selfish question, perhaps. But I've grown accustomed to others being the ones that die and I the one that lives.

"It's my gift to you. A reminder of the dangers of your campground. After all, familiarity breeds complacency. Think of how your mother died. I'd prefer you lasted a little while longer yet."

He walked away. I watched him go, dizzy with pain, shaking with exhaustion. When he was no longer within eyeshot I simply lay down there on the shoulder of the road and there I lay until my staff thought to come looking for me and took me back to my home.

I wish I could say that my ordeal was the only consequence of this incident. See, we have a tenuous relationship with the town at times. Not everyone feels the benefits of the campground outweigh the dangers. After the man with the skull cup poisoned a number of locals... they've decided to reopen the issue.

There's a town meeting in a few weeks. My presence is requested.

I'm a campground manager. I spend much of my time preoccupied with the unnatural, with things that have their own rules and customs and I suppose I've ignored *other* threats, the human threats, and our tendency towards blind, rash panic when threatened. I think I forgot myself inside my helpless anger and insulted the wrong person.

I wish Halloween were uneventful. I wish my problems were not of my own making this time.

At least the man with the skull cup is in my debt, in exchange for opening the gate. I can only hope it will be worth it.

A BIT OF LOCAL HISTORY

Posted Nov 21 2019 00:07:01 GMT-0400

We keep the deaths and injuries that happen on our campsite quiet from the outside world largely through the cooperation of the local police. The campground falls within the jurisdiction of one of the few towns that sits nearby and they're the ones that respond whenever something happens. They don't come by to arrest or prosecute anyone. They bring paperwork and assurances for any out-of-town campers that something will be done. Then I bury the bodies and they make up some story and we continue on as if nothing unnatural has happened.

Perhaps this is wrong of us. What else can we do, however? Our legal system makes no allowances for things that are not human and so forces us into a lie.

Our relationship with local law enforcement was formalized shortly after my grandfather took possession of the campground. I've mentioned the "scandal" that drove my great-aunt out of ownership before. It's a little more complicated than simply a child out of wedlock. We're not certain at what point our land transitioned to being old land, as it happened gradually. There have always been strange things in this world and our town was not without its troubles. It wasn't until someone sat down and looked at all the reported incidents and saw the concentration on our land that everyone put it together.

The locals began to say that we should break up our land and sell it. We weren't putting it to good use, after all, except to collect monsters. Back then, it wasn't *really* a campground, not like it is now. They opened up some land to campers, but it wasn't the sole usage of the land. Rather, we owned the land just to own it. My family was among the first settlers of this area and had significant holdings.

One of the reasons we dedicated ourselves fully to running a campground was because it altered the local perception of the family. We weren't entitled, elitist landholders anymore. We had an honest living.

But at the time of my great-aunt, we had that against us still. Then she showed up with a baby. She tried to keep it quiet but word got out and rumors started churning through town. Having a child out of wedlock was one, of course, but there was another, more dangerous, rumor that began to spread. They said the child was a changeling. And Bryan's ancestors were among the most vocal proponents of that rumor, on account of their heritage.

Great-aunt decided to turn her enemies into her allies. She went to them, with the child, and let them inspect the baby. And she told them the real story and the identity of the father.

Great-aunt took that secret to the grave. So did Bryan's grandparents.

I don't think there was anything *unnatural* about the father. Bryan's grandparents would not have been swayed to great-aunt's side otherwise. I think it was local politics. Someone influential. Possibly an affair. My great-aunt must have liked him quite a bit to not drag him down with her.

The campground was transferred to my grandfather to make the town happy. It settled most of the grumbling. Great-aunt could step out of the public eye to raise her confirmed not-a-changeling baby in peace. The transition to my grandfather let people believe that now that the land had changed hands, the monsters wouldn't keep showing up.

They were naive. My family, less so, but we had bought ourselves some time to recover from the scandal.

Then something started robbing the graveyard.

My uncle liked to tell this story. He was twelve years old at the time. My father was fourteen. Dad doesn't like to talk about this because I think he pitied the things he killed. He had a soft heart. Even though it was necessary, he didn't like to kill things simply because they were acting on their nature. He didn't like killing *anything*. In this, at least, I take after my mother.

The first handful of graves were quickly discovered by the groundskeeper and he buried them again, telling their relatives nothing. Not about the holes, the disturbed headstones, and certainly nothing about the shattered coffins and the missing bodies. He understood that these things happened and it was best to not upset people unnecessarily.

The first grave theft that was discovered by the town was when one of the local families made their routine Sunday trip to the cemetery to leave flowers on a relative's grave. He'd died unexpectedly, possibly from a heart attack. The story that went around is that on the day of the theft, the mom thought that something was strange because there was loose dirt strewn all around the cemetery as they were approaching the gravesite. She believed at first that maybe the groundskeeper was doing some maintenance but told the children to stay back. She had a bad feeling, she said.

The grave had been partially dug up. A hole that exposed half the coffin, dug in a slope like a dog digs, kicking the loose soil all across the ground around the grave. The coffin itself was shattered, the wood splintered and snapped apart, exposing the dark hollow of the coffin inside.

Then one of the children shrieked, coming across a human skull, and the mother ran to them and told them they were leaving. The skull was fake, she said. It was just someone's idea of a bad prank. She knew. She could tell it was a fake skull.

In her heart, she knew the truth, but this little lie at least distracted the children until they were old enough to handle the reality that something had dug up their father's grave and devoured all of it but the skull and a few ribs that had fallen into the grass when it cracked the sternum free.

Perhaps it would have ended there, if the oldest of the boys hadn't climbed out the window when he and his brother heard their father's voice calling to them from outside. The boy, too, was devoured.

The mother blamed our campsite. We aren't *that* far from the cemetery, as it was placed on the outskirts of town and we're not *much* further than that. She also needed someone to blame, I suspect, and we were still at that time an easy target. A town meeting was held. The issue of whether our land should be split up and sold was opened once more. Grandfather went to the meeting - the entire family went to the meeting. They stood in the back, silent and watching, and perhaps this was deliberate. To remind the town of just how long my family has been around and how many of us there actually are. To remind them of how hard our eyes are, the grim set of our silent stares, the strength of our will.

Grandfather told the town that our family would take care of this creature, regardless of whether it came from our land or not. We weren't the only ones whose land harbored strange things, he said. We *were*, however, the ones that had the resolve to *deal* with the things it attracted. And let them come to our land, he continued. We - none of them - could keep the things *out*. They all knew someone that suffered dead livestock, strange claw marks on doors, apparitions and visions without explanation. We would do this, and more, if they at least had the courtesy to treat us with respect.

Then he walked out without even giving them a chance to respond. The meeting continued but without the family there it felt hollow, lacking in purpose, and if any decision was reached no one remembers what it was.

Grandmother set to the work of turning our land into a proper campground and opening it up fully to the public. The more campers we brought in, they reasoned, the more money they'd spend on the local economy. Certain goods wouldn't be available on site. Food, for instance. The general store's supplies were kept deliberately lean and maps of local shopping was printed for the main office. In time, we *would* expand, but not before being certain that our campers would still dump a significant amount into business outside our property. But at that time, these were all plans for the future.

Grandfather dealt with the more immediate problem of the monster stalking the graveyard.

It was a simple plan for a simple creature. He and his sons stood watch in the graveyard each night until the monster returned for another body. My uncle was scared. He'd never hunted anything more dangerous than rabbits and could only think about how the boy that had been eaten was only a few years younger than him. Fear tightened around his neck like a noose and the shadows took on life, hunkered under the thin moonlight like malevolent beings, waiting for him to turn his back. His knuckles were white as he gripped his rifle like a lifeline. It was an effort to keep his gaze poised on the side of the graveyard he'd been assigned to watch. Grandpa and my father were at his back, watching the darkness beyond the edge of the faint bubble of light their lantern permitted, and he ran this through his head as a mantra to fan the flames of his dwindling courage.

His father and brother were there. He'd be safe.

On the third night my uncle fired on something that was moving around the edge of the graveyard. The gunshot echoed through the night, followed by the rustle of grass as something fled. Grandpa scolded him for firing. It was too small, he said. He probably fired at a groundhog. Don't shoot until you're certain of what you're shooting at. Didn't he remember that, from when he went hunting for rabbits?

And my uncle, embarrassed, swore he wouldn't make that mistake again.

It almost got my grandpa killed. But no one held that against my uncle and my uncle, for his part, knew it wasn't entirely his fault. He was only twelve, being asked to do something that the grown men of the town wouldn't do.

He saw it, in the corner of his vision. A subtle streak of movement, like water flowing along the ground. Pale, dead flesh. A trick of the light. The latter is what he told himself it was, as he forced his fingers to relax their grip on the rifle. They ached from hours of strain in the cold night air.

It came up just at the edge of his vision, sliding between the tombstones, in a blind spot where none could see it clearly. It moved like a dog, belly to the ground, the yellowed flesh draped loosely on its bones. My uncle, so determined to not shoot at shadows again, kept his gaze fixed on the darkness at the edge of the graveyard, searching for something *real,* and missed the faint impression of movement at the edge of his eyesight.

Missed it, until it was almost upon him.

Grandpa didn't leave his sons entirely on their own. He watched over them as well as his own third of the graveyard and he saw the ghoul before it could lunge at my uncle. He stepped between them, raising his shotgun, but the creature was in mid-leap and it hit him squarely in the chest. My uncle screamed and threw himself backwards. My grandpa hit the ground hard, the air knocked out of him in a rush, and the creature landed on his chest. It clawed at his shoulders and his neck until my grandpa got the barrel of the shotgun interposed between them. The ghoul threw its full weight against the gun, stretching out broken fingernails towards my grandpa's eyes.

My dad was the one that knocked it off him. He'd been standing by in agony, unable to find an opening with which to shoot the creature, not without risking hitting my grandpa. He didn't trust his aim, not with the two twisting and thrashing on the ground. The ghoul bobbed like a bird, kicking and clawing, trying to land its teeth in something vital enough to put an end to my grandpa's resistance. Then, in a flash of inspiration, he ran around to the side of the combatants and stuck the rifle down and angled the barrel back up into the ribcage of the monster. It froze for a second, but it was too late, and my father pulled the trigger.

The bullet ripped through its chest and exited up and out. The force of the gunshot threw it off my grandpa and it landed just a few feet away, directly at my uncle's feet. My uncle stood frozen, clutching his rifle to his chest. It seemed pathetic, rolling on the torn grass in front of him, its skin rippling as it convulsed in pain from its injuries. Its cries were like that of a cat, whimpering and mewling.

It raised its head and stared up at my uncle. Its lips were peeled back from a row of perfect white teeth, its eyes were bright, and its face was familiar. He'd met this man before, in the grocery store when my grandma took him on her errands. While he was still alive, before he died of a heart attack and was buried and before the ghoul dug him up and ate what scraps of flesh remained on his bones.

My uncle couldn't move. He couldn't think, he couldn't breathe. The human face staring up at him with mindless hate in its eyes robbed him of all reason.

Then grandpa got to his feet and limped over. He shot its legs and then caved it skull in with the stock of the gun. He didn't stop until its head was a mess of battered tissue, a gelatinous heap the consistency of cold oatmeal.

My uncle said that he didn't hesitate after that. These things were monsters, he realized, regardless of whose face they wore. He taught his children the same and they were the ones that went hunting when we had something on our campsite that *could* be hunted.

After the ghoul was dispatched my grandpa went back to the town hall and told them the problem was dealt with. If we had the cooperation of the town, he said, and especially the police then we could continue to deal with these things. We could keep our old land as old land and all those *things* out there would flock to it and with nowhere else to go, they'd be trapped. Contained. And everyone else would be safe.

This is the arrangement we have with the town. I wonder how many of our campground inhabitants are here by choice, how many are here because they have nowhere else they can survive, and how many we've compelled to stay.

I need to find out if anything falls in the last category. It's not something I've ever considered before, but I feel it will soon be very important to know this.

Every now and then the town starts to forget the dangers and question if our role is necessary. My parents were called to the town hall three times in their tenure as owners of the campground. They were polite and diplomatic, but also firm. The campground would remain in our hands. It would remain old land. Didn't they realize what would happen, were we to displace our inhabitants? They would go to the farms and the houses and the town would have to deal with something far worse than whatever had temporarily slipped out of our grasp.

Now it was my turn to stand before the town. I said all this and perhaps I wasn't as eloquent as my mother and perhaps I have too much of my father's anger in me, but for a brief moment I thought I had convinced them. A sea of bobbing heads stared up at me, nodding faintly as they remembered that things could be so much worse than a few people being poisoned on Halloween. The sheriff stood near the back, arms crossed, his scowl deepening as I talked.

I thought that my parents would be proud of me, were they still alive. Here I was, defending our family line.

I was so close.

Then, as I finished talking, a man I didn't immediately recognize stumbled in through the doors of the town hall. They creaked on their hinges and a hush fell over the room. His footsteps lilted, one landing more heavily than the other, and it was like listening to a bell toll as each step landed, the dragging foot whispering on the wooden floor like a trailing rope. His expression was distant, his eyes cast upwards towards the heavens, and his mouth hung slightly agape.

His arms swung loosely at his sides and one hand clutched the hair of my uncle's severed head. He threw this, when he was halfway down the aisle, and it rolled across the floor and came to a stop at my feet. Then the stranger fell face-down onto the ground and has yet to regain consciousness.

The doctors at the local hospital do not think that he will ever wake up again. They are less complicit than the police, but they understand my campground. They are familiar with the casualties it produces. At some point they will have to contact the man's family and tell them where he is and that he won't wake up. There will be no mention of murder. It's one kindness the police can afford for the man's family.

We *do* have contact information for his relatives. I found it. For while the people in the town hall panicked and screamed or wept I stood there, silent and still, staring down at my uncle's face that was frozen into an expression of mute surprise. I thought about the stranger and wondered why he seemed familiar. I thought on this for a long time, even while a police officer (and I don't recall who, which is strange because I know them all) took me by the arm and led me away and took me back to the campground.

In my office I went through my records until I found the name that felt familiar.

The stranger has camped here every year for almost twenty years. He's one of my regulars. I had his registration from last year on file, including his emergency contact.

I remember something else. The man's shadow, as I walked past his prone body. How the edges were tattered. Fraying, like an old scrap of cloth. I'm not sure anyone else noticed.

My uncle was murdered on the campgrounds. The staff report that the man came by, asking for me, and my uncle said he'd talk to him instead as I wasn't around. They heard a gunshot and by the time they arrived at the scene, the man was gone and my uncle's head was gone with him.

The town reconvened their meeting a few days later. I was not present. I don't recall if I was invited or not and it doesn't seem to matter right now. Very little feels like it matters. The funeral for my uncle is this weekend. I feel like that day is endlessly far away, or perhaps it has already happened and this is merely an echo. I'm struggling to understand *when* I am at any given moment. This is shock, I suppose. I tell myself it will pass.

The sheriff stopped by this morning. I didn't talk much. I'm very tired. I haven't been sleeping much. He said that the town was out of patience and needed proof that we could do what we claimed - that our campground being old land actually did contain the various *other* creatures in this world, rather than act as a beacon to bring them in and let them prey on the innocent.

(I know the secrets of this town. Few of us are innocent)

Look what happened to my uncle, he continued, and I lost what else he said after that. Hatred boiled inside me and it took all of my focus to contain it. It coursed through my veins like molten iron. How *dare* he use my uncle's death against me.

Christmas is coming, he was saying, when I was able to register his words again. Yule. Midwinter. 12th Night. There would be no deaths - no *incidents* - during this time. Think of it as a test, he said and he smiled when he spoke. A trial to regain the town's confidence.

It is nothing more than a pretense. I do not think this it is possible to do as they request. The powers of this world converge in the winter and ancients walk the land and they go where they will and they do as they want.

I need to find out why the sheriff is so determined to destroy my campground. I need to find out how long this has been going on and who else is involved. And I need to find out how long the sheriff has been working with one of my camp's occupants and who exactly is the master in that relationship.

You see, while there are many creatures on my campsite that can influence a person's behavior - perhaps even driving them to murder - there is only one that does so by eating their victim's shadow.

Rule #17 - Be wary of a friendly man that may approach you in shaded areas. Try to convince him to move into the sunlight. If he casts a shadow, you can assume it's another camper and proceed accordingly. Otherwise, end the conversation immediately. He is trying to earn your trust.

I'm a campground manager. I can't protect everyone, not even the members of my own family. This doesn't mean I'm going to stop trying, however. I'll use whatever means are available to me. Most of the time, this means providing people with a list and more recently, telling you about what happens to the people that don't follow the rules, so you understand the importance of them.

One of my campers didn't follow the rules. He allowed the man with no shadow to befriend him and now my uncle is dead.

We haven't contacted the camper's kin yet. We don't *have* to. No one knows he's here. People vanish all the time. I think I will go to the hospital and ask if I could have something of his. He's not going to come out of his coma so I believe they will give me what I want. They don't have to endure the hassle of keeping him on life support if he doesn't have a head anymore, after all.

I will repay the man with no shadow with a gift of my own.

RULE #17 – THE MAN WITH NO SHADOW

Posted Nov 27 2019 21:35:38 GMT-0400

The man with no shadow is why I had no friends growing up. I suppose it was better that way. We're lucky that no one got hurt - at least, not while we were kids.

I don't know when it started. The man with no shadow plans for the long-term. He befriends his victims and then waits, years sometimes, before using their trust to carry out his bidding. He is different from the rest of our campground inhabitants in this respect. The majority of them are creatures of impulse and instinct, acting on their desires as they arise. Few plan. Few think ahead. This difference between them is what makes the man with no shadow dangerous.

It's unnerving to think that he could have had my best friend in his sway for years. What did she tell him? Was there anything of substance he could have learned from me second-hand at such an early age, or did she listen in on my parent's conversations, when they were in the kitchen talking in low voices so that we wouldn't overhear? Did she look through their office when no one was around? My parents questioned her, after it was discovered, but all she would say was that her friend had said not to tell and so she wouldn't.

I remember the end. The last time I had friends over to the campground. Before then, I felt like a normal kid. I was eight. I attended school and while I wasn't popular, I certainly wasn't bullied and my classmates treated me with respect. No doubt there were conversations around the dinner table about how my family was the reason their parents had livelihoods and they were to not hassle my brother and I. Just in case.

I like to believe my parents wouldn't have retaliated. Yet I've told you of the times I've killed a camper or an employee and you know that I *learned* that from someone.

Perhaps I was a bit conceited and I certainly enjoyed the attention of my peers, but I wasn't overtly cruel. I was mean in subtle ways, in how I made those around me feel lesser simply by how I put myself above them, and then I made them love me by deigning to grant them my notice. It netted me a number of loyal friends, girls that responded to this sort of manipulation.

There was only one that I considered my peer. Arrogant and intelligent like me, canny and sharp like a whip, a skinny girl with wild hair and coiled energy nestled inside like a snake ready to strike. Her name was Laura and she became my best friend.

We loved the woods. We'd sneak into the treeline at recess and climb the rocks and trees until the teachers saw us and yelled for us to come out, then we'd go right back in once their backs were turned. We made our own elaborate games of make-believe and Laura and I were both queens of our own lands and all the rest of our friends were our subjects. We'd wage war with sticks and array our armies against each other, until the teachers yelled at us again.

The campground was a much better playground for us. There were no teachers to yell. Just my parents and the staff and during daylight hours, in the well-trafficked parts of the campground, there was little danger. We were just told to not bother the people here to camp.

If you're taken aback at the idea of a bunch of young children playing in the woods of my campground, I should remind you that we see a *lot* of people pass through every year and most of them return home safely. It's only the unwary or the exceedingly unlucky that come to harm. Your perception of my campground is perhaps a little skewed because I've told you the worst of it, because that is what is interesting. None of you read these posts to hear about how someone spent two weeks reading in a hammock and taking naps.

We sometimes split up for our games. It's apparent why the man with no shadow targeted Laura. She was always the leader of the other team, and I the leader of the other. I'm not sure how he separated her from the others - or perhaps he didn't, perhaps they forgot what my parents told them as well - but at some point during our friendship he approached her and they talked and then she belonged to him.

It doesn't take long for the man with no shadow to claim a new servant. One conversation, maybe two, depending on how strong the victim's will is.

If you encounter a stranger, coerce him into the sunlight quickly. Speak as little as possible until you can see if he has a shadow.

He waited until my birthday to use Laura against my family. I wanted a sleepover and since my birthday is close to Christmas, my parents tried to ensure it felt special by letting me do whatever I liked. We were put in the living room with sleeping bags and snacks and my brother was allowed to hide in his room and play video games all night while we watched movies and shrieked and laughed. At some point I fell asleep, along with a handful of my friends. Laura woke them up, careful not to disturb me. She told them to come with her. None of them remembered quite what lie she told them, but it was Laura asking, and they obeyed her as easily as they obeyed me.

I continued to sleep until the cold air creeping in from the front door woke me. I was disoriented and then frightened, realizing that my friends were gone and the front door hung open. I ran to it, terrified that my parents would find out, because they had told us over and over and over that we were to never leave a window or door open overnight.

The little girl sat cross-legged just on the other side of the doorway. I hesitated, reluctant to be so rude as to shut the door in her face. I asked why she hadn't come inside. She told me she couldn't, that only the proper residents of the house could invite her inside by leaving a point of entry open. Then she said that the man with no shadow wanted to see me. He was waiting at the edge of the woods.

I asked her if it was safe. She shrugged and rose, smoothing her white skirt with her palms.

"Nothing is safe," she replied. "You just try to pretend otherwise."

It was only 1 AM. There was still time to find my friends and get back to the house before the beast showed up. This is what I told myself. I thought that if I woke my parents they'd be so angry; at my friends, but especially at me for not keeping them safe. I didn't want any of us to get in trouble and so I resolved to fix this before morning. I left through the front door, shutting it behind me, reasoning that because my friend had opened it instead of me then I would be safe from the little girl. And I was; she stood a short distance away and watched, but I'm not sure if that was because my logic was correct or if she just didn't want to kill me until I was an adult.

I found the man with no shadow out by the trees, just as she'd said. He changes his appearance periodically. At the time, he was dark-haired, tanned, tall and muscular. He crouched as I approached so that I didn't have to stare up at him so much.

"I can take you to your friends," he said.

"My parents said I can't talk to you," I replied.

"Then I won't talk."

This seemed like an acceptable compromise and when he stood and walked away, I followed. I was afraid, but not nearly as afraid as I should have been. Not enough to turn back.

The things in the woods treat children differently. Some of the beasts are mindless things that make no distinction and view all humans as mere meat. But the ones that do understand? There are conditions that have to be met first before they will harm a child. A trial. A rite of passage. A failure to grow.

The man with no shadow *was* my trial, but not at this time. Not until much later. When I was eight, I was merely the tool which he wielded against my parents.

He took me to the grove with the stones. Giant, moss-covered boulders dug up by glaciers hunkered in the middle of a small clearing. This was where the man with no shadow could be typically found. I do not think he has much power outside the grove. Aside from his ability to persuade and thus entrap minds, I've seen him exhibit no other power outside its boundaries.

He stepped aside and let me enter the clearing. My eyes had adjusted to the dim moonlight by that point and I could make out the outline of bodies, seven girls, sitting with their backs against the boulder and their chins drooping to their chests. I went up to Maria and put a hand against her chest to feel that she was still breathing.

"Now run and tell your mother what you've seen," the man with no shadow murmured from behind me. "Tell her that if she wants these released, then I must have something in exchange."

I did as he bid. I turned and ran from that clearing, tears obscuring my vision, stumbling through the darkness with only one desperate thought in my mind - my parents could fix this. The silent, still forms of my friends haunted my mind and I thought - if I'd been *smarter* or more *careful* or maybe if I didn't have friends *at all...* then this wouldn't have happened.

I was incoherent when I woke my mother. She quickly hushed my sobs and extricated herself from the bed, careful to not wake my father as well. Then, in the kitchen, I sat and gasped hysterically, getting my words out one at a time until my mother was able to put the pieces together.

The man with no shadow had my friends.

She told me to stay in the house. She put on shoes and a jacket and went to deal with him. And when she came back, my friends were with her, pale and shaking. Laura, however, was serene and she smiled at me and this didn't escape my mother's notice, for she took Laura aside and questioned her separately from the other girls. Then she took Laura to the car and drove her home.

My parents sat me down the next day, after everyone had gone, and told me I couldn't be friends with Laura anymore. They knew that would be hard because I was close to her, but she belonged to the man with no shadow now, and she wasn't safe.

I wonder what he promised her. We were rivals, sometimes. I saw jealousy in her eyes in a rare moment when she thought I wasn't looking. I wonder if he said he could make her greater than me.

At school on Monday I found that Laura was the only one that would speak to me and I refused to acknowledge her, just as I'd been instructed. When I went to sit with my other friends at lunch, they all got up and left, leaving me sitting alone at the table. That's how it was after that. I think their parents told them to stay away from me, just as I was told to stay away from Laura, and all the rest of the kids followed their example. I was desperately lonely from that point on and spent my recesses in the library, where the librarian took pity on me and gave me her favorite books to read and talked to me when no one else would.

I didn't really interact with Laura again until after our highschool graduation.

My family held a party for me, even though I'd said I didn't want one, because I knew none of my peers would attend. It was just aunts and uncles and so many cousins... and all the campground staff, which was kind of them. Some of them even brought gifts. One brought me a small ironing board and an iron, which I used well past college until the handle of the iron cracked and fell off.

At one point during the party, I stepped outside to get away from the crowd. My parent's house was not made to accommodate that many people. Someone was walking down the path leading from the campground entrance, a person in robes and wearing a cap. For a brief moment I was elated, thinking that perhaps one of my classmates had actually come to my party. I hurried to meet them, then slowed and stopped as I realized who it was.

Laura. Laura was here.

"You still don't trust me?" she asked sadly, as she saw my apprehension. "It's been a long time."

"The man with no shadow never lets go of people," I replied.

"No," a voice said from somewhere just behind me. I had not heard him approach. "I do not."

And he said something else and I don't recall the exact words, for Laura lunged at me, fingers outstretched, reaching for my throat. Her lips were peeled back in a soundless snarl and her eyes were wide and I thought I saw desperation buried inside them. Then there was no time left for contemplation, for we were falling, hitting the packed dirt of the road, and her fingers were around my neck.

I was the stronger one. I spent my evenings and my summers working on the campground. I don't recall exactly how it happened, but I seized her and threw her aside and then I was over top of her, and it was *my* hands around *her* throat.

I held her down while she thrashed beneath me, fingernails clawing at my face, froth speckling her lips, and her feet kicking helplessly at the ground. I hated her in that moment, because she'd betrayed me, because she was the reason I'd been so lonely all these years. Perhaps that isn't fair, but that hatred was strong enough to give me the will to keep pressing down on her windpipe even as her chest convulsed in a desperate attempt to bring in air, even as her struggles subsided and she went still, even as a bluish cast settled into the skin around her mouth and eyes and I held on long after she stopped moving until she was well and truly dead.

Through all of this, the man with no shadow watched impassively.

"Now you are of age," he said, and he walked away.

I said earlier that the creatures of the forest will not harm children unless they fail their test. This was mine. The day I graduated highschool is the day I first killed someone. It's when I realized that my childhood was officially over and nothing was left to protect me from the dangers of this world.

It's the day I finally *understood* that someday the beast and the little girl will be my doom; knew it in my heart and felt it in my bones.

The man with no shadow plays a very long game. He hangs on to people their entire lives. I'm not certain what he's trying to accomplish or even if he has a specific goal in mind. Perhaps he merely takes opportunities as they arise, collecting those foolish enough to fall into his grasp and keeping them until the day comes when he can make use of their naivety.

We evict anyone we catch conversing with the man with no shadow. They're banned from the campsite forever. We can't take risks.

My uncle's funeral was on Sunday. Afterwards, I decided to pay the grove a visit. Turtle insisted on going with me, even though I told her there was no danger. The man with no shadow cannot harm anyone directly. This was not enough to dissuade my employee. Things have been weird around here, she said, and she said it carefully so that I knew she was referring to my uncle. Then she said that there's been other things, too. That the lady with extra eyes has invited her for tea eight times in the past week, which I have to agree is strange.

We waited just outside the boundaries and made the man with no shadow come to us. He's currently lanky with freckles and messy red hair. His smile, however, has not changed. A thin half-smile, smug, condescending. He dipped his head at us in greeting. He speaks sparsely when dealing with people that know what he is. At his feet, the sunlight pooled unbroken.

I asked him what his agreement had been with my mother. I'd never asked until now because it ended with her death and I had no desire to dredge up painful memories. He told me and then I thanked him, dropped the human head I carried at his feet, and walked away. I heard him laughing as we left. He sounded delighted.

My mother was to let him leave the campground, he'd said. Three times, of his choosing. He'd used two of these instances before she died.

This is a dark thought, but it comes to mind unbidden and I cannot put it aside. What if... my mother left the window open deliberately? To deny the man his third request?

I'm a campground manager. My land attracts the things that prey on humanity, like a candle draws moths. I'm realizing that some of them - like the man with no shadow - cannot leave once they are here. I'm not sure why that is, but I understand now that it has fostered enmity between us.

Outside of these woods I am merely a woman in a navy shirt and khaki shorts who sometimes shows up to yell at people for not following the rules and exceeding the allotted land for their campsite. But inside these woods... to certain inhabitants... I am their jailor.

Perhaps not for much longer, however. There's only a few days left before December and then the world will shift and things will come out of dormancy and I will be powerless to stop them.

I ALMOST DROWNED ON TUESDAY

Posted Dec 06 2019 20:50:16 GMT-0400

I am not looking forward to Christmas. How could I, after attending the funeral of one of our own? It was a closed casket, not because the funeral parlor couldn't dress him up and hide the wounds, but because the cleverest of clothing couldn't erase our memories of his head rolling down the aisle of town hall. I pulled my Christmas decorations out of the basement and then left them sitting in the living room in their boxes, because it all felt hollow and pointless.

I spent a lot of time after Thanksgiving holed up in my office, ostensibly trying to figure out a way to counter the bigger creatures of winter. Realistically, I didn't want to talk to anyone. But on Monday I got a phone call from the neighbor. He owns quite a bit of land and over the years I've toyed with the idea of making an offer on it. The lake gives me pause. I'm not sure I want to deal with absorbing a lake into old land. There's a mess of trouble that comes with that. Anyway, he called me up and asked for help containing the Christmas demons for when they show up this year.

They're from northern Russia. We've got a family from that region living around here. They're called shulikun and good luck finding info on them online, I haven't had much luck, and the only reason I even know how to spell it is because in my parent's files is a typed handout with brief summaries of all the various Slavic creatures. Shulikun show up around Christmas by breaking out of frozen lakes using their pointy metal hats and then they ambush Christmas revelers. Mostly they just play pranks. Sometimes they shove people into snow banks or frozen lakes to freeze to death. They're banished by the celebrations leading up to Lent.

Needless to say, they're not a threat in early December. They're not much of a threat the rest of the Christmas season, either, as we don't get deep snow banks and people don't walk home, generally. I thought that perhaps a distraction was warranted, however, as I *had* spent the last few days in my office hardly talking to anyone. My staff have been coming around with bullshit things they need from me as an excuse to check on how I'm doing and I'm suspicious as to who orchestrated that plan.

Turtle.

I gathered some supplies and went over to my neighbor's property. His family are also old landowners, which is how they got a sizable parcel that includes the lake. It's becoming old land as well. The timer got reset at some point through some shady business that caused it to change hands for a few years and then change back - that happened several generations ago and there's not much common knowledge about exactly *what* went down.

We talk every now and then about purchasing the land for the campground. He's willing to sell the lake and some surrounding acres. It's tempting, but I keep thinking of how many rules I'd have to add and I reconsider.

I took the car over and parked in his driveway. He came out to meet me while I popped the back and started unloading my gear. Thanked me for coming over. Told me that the business with my uncle had him frightened and he wanted to try to contain them to the lake this year instead of letting them wander all over town. He was nervous. Kept tripping over his words. I wonder if that should have tipped me off but I attributed it to his lack of experience with non-human entities.

I was trying to be a good neighbor. I regret it.

The lake is quite large. There's a narrow strip of land leading out to an island off one bank. The landmass is too symmetrical to be natural, at least by my judgement, and I do wonder when and why my neighbor's family constructed it. It had to have taken a *lot* of dirt and work, as the pathway is fully big enough to accommodate a car and the island could hold probably twenty campers, depending on the size of their tents.

Yes, I think of things in terms of campground usage. It's a habit.

I circled it once, hanging bundles of warding materials in the branches as I went. I don't know what repels shulikun - if they even *can* be repelled - so I just went with the full assortment of materials known to affect various other creatures from the same region. If you're wondering why my neighbor didn't do this himself, well, the materials aren't easy to get a hold of. It's not like you can buy stones with holes in them en masse at the town hardware store, for example. My family has invested time and money into building a stock and so I have ready access to everything I need and am willing to loan it out on occasion.

I was walking back up the path leading to his house when I was stopped by the sound of something behind me. A noise that shot terror through my blood, ice-cold, freezing my muscles and robbing me of my breath. I stood there in horrified immobility, realizing that it was futile to run. And behind me, the horse walked closer, the thump of its hooves on the packed earth unmistakable.

Then a male voice spoke and I almost wept with relief, before realizing that while it might not be the dappled gray horse, it was still something dangerous. I turned, slowly, weighing what I would say in reply, knowing that my fate hinged on my response.

"It's... a little early, isn't it?" I asked weakly. "I mean, it's only December 2nd."

I suppose I could have done better.

Five shulikun stood on the trail before me. Now, when I said that they prank revelers, perhaps you were imagining something a little more... benign. Mischievous gnomes? Christmas elves? Certainly not a warrior in chainmail with a pointed iron cap mounted on a war horse, right?

He stared down at me, stone-faced, his lips and the corners of his eyes tinted with the blue of frostbite, and his gloved hand rested on the pommel of his sword. His four companions were arrayed similarly, straight-backed in their saddles, their stares cold and unyielding.

The shulikun don't just prank revelers. They are also the enforcers of the Christmas spirit and will drag anyone unfit for the season to a watery grave.

I'm sure a handful of you just looked uncomfortably at the empty corner where the Christmas tree should go, right? I sure as hell hadn't set mine up yet. My uncle just died and the sheriff was threatening to destroy my campground. How could I *possibly* be excited for Christmas?

I offered all of this up as my excuses and when I was finished, the lead shulikun kicked his horse forwards, it rounded past me, and as I turned to follow its course the warrior reached down, grabbed hold of the back of my jacket, and then spurred his horse into a run.

I was yanked off my feet and then I was being dragged, half my body on the ground as the warrior leaned over in his saddle, allowing enough slack so that I didn't tumble under the hooves of his horse. I kicked, trying to get my feet under me - for all the good that would have done with a horse in full gallop - trying to get *away* from the stones and debris that tore at my jeans and bruised my flesh. I twisted in my jacket, clawing at the zipper, choking on the pressure just under my chin.

And then we hit the lake. Their momentum slowed some, the water supported my body and I could breathe, but the warrior did not stop dragging me further out, towards the deeper parts of the lake. I yanked savagely at the zipper of my jacket and the damn thing got *stuck*.

"This isn't fair!" I shrieked. "Do I need to be wearing fucking mistletoe around my neck or something?! Maybe an ugly Christmas sweater?"

The warrior glanced down long enough to give me a disgusted look. I know what he was trying to convey. Christmas is something you hold in your heart.

Make a movie out of *this*, Hallmark. Being carried away to drown by a warrior on horseback for not embracing the holiday spirit is certainly more motivating than watching a jaded CEO move to a small town where she falls in love with Christmas and her hunky neighbor.

The water was to the horse's chest. I began to take deep breaths of air, preparing myself to be pulled under. Maybe I could still break free. Maybe I could swim to the surface. The water churned around me as the four other shulikun surrounded us, and then they plunged forwards in one leap and I was yanked down, sharply, and there was nothing but water around me.

The cold of it almost shocked the air from my lungs. I held my breath through sheer force of will and continued to tug at the zipper, savagely, until it came loose and I tore my jacket open and for one brief, exultant moment, I was free.

A hand closed over my throat instead. And it forced me further down into the water and I could only claw helplessly at those fingers, my gaze locked on the receding sunlight above me. All I could think of was how unfair this was. My uncle died. What reason did I - or any of my family - have to be merry?

Finally, as my body strained to release and inhale, the warrior let go. I immediately started swimming up, towards the distant ball of sunlight that marked the surface. In my heart, I knew it was futile. He wouldn't have released me if I had any hope of survival. Still, I had no intention of dying quietly; I would not so easily resign myself to drowning, and I kicked and pulled myself through the water and then it was too late - I remember red spots dancing in my vision and then agony and then nothing.

I woke with one abrupt convulsion, like my entire body was crawling inside itself, and then I was shoved over onto my side as I began to vomit uncontrollably. I brought up everything in my stomach and then some, coughing and retching until I was spitting blood. I dimly felt comforting hands on my back and voices telling me it was okay, I was going to be okay. And finally it was and I could breathe again.

I began to shiver violently, soaked through and while it was not yet freezing, it was still really damn cold. I looked around me and found that I was flanked on either side. To my left was Turtle. To my right was the man with the skull cup.

I stared at him incredulously.

"Your cousin gave me permission to accompany Turtle on a small errand," he said tonelessly to my unasked question.

I turned to look at Turtle.

"He came and found me and said you were in danger," she said quickly. "And that he'd be needed to save you. So I got one of your cousins to give permission and then he led me here and waded out into the water and pulled you out. I thought you were dead and he said you weren't yet and forced the contents of his cup down your throat and that's when you started coughing."

I took a couple deep breaths. I've done some dangerous things around here but I honestly think this might be the closest I've come to actually dying.

"After what happened at Halloween," I said in a low voice, "what on earth made you think he can be trusted?"

Perhaps that was a little unfair of me to say. But... I don't want people getting hurt over me.

"I, uh, read the comments and people keep saying that maybe he's got a thing for you sooooo."

She looked a little sheepish. I looked back to the man with the skull cup and he didn't say a damn thing about that.

"Your cup is empty," I said uneasily, eyeing it. There were only a few drops left inside. Old blood from what was there before. My blood.

"So it is."

He considered it a moment, then his hand shot out and seized Turtle's wrist. She shrieked, half in fear and half in outrage, then he sliced her palm open with his *thumbnail* and held the open wound out over the cup long enough for a few drops to fall inside. Then he let go of my employee and she clutched her hand to her chest, pale, panting, and visibly relieved. When he turned to me, I obligingly held out my own hand to provide him with 'blood freely given.'

"Surprise counts as taking blood by force?" I asked as I bled into the cup from a small wound on my palm.

He gave me a pained look.

"It does when I'm in a hurry," he said. "Could you not be difficult about this? I'm doing you a favor here."

I told Turtle to head back to the campground and fetch a change of clothes. I'd wait at the neighbor's house so I wouldn't have to get in my car while soaking wet. She seemed happy to leave after that, cradling her injured hand as blood leaked through her clenched fingers. As she left, I told the man that his task was done and that he should be returning to the campground as well. He smiled softly and acknowledged that yes, the terms of his agreement were fulfilled. However...

"There's something else you should consider," he said, shifting slightly from where he knelt beside me.

He produced his knife from *somewhere* (he wears jeans and I swear it looked like he pulled it out of his back pocket which isn't possible, it wouldn't fit) and I tensed at seeing it. But he only leaned forwards and set it on the ground in front of me.

"Do you truly believe your neighbor would have missed them being out of the lake already?" he asked.

He stood and walked away, leaving me alone with his knife. He'd come by the house to retrieve it later, he called back to me. It was only a loan. I stared at it for a long time, feeling anger bubbling inside me, and finally when it was roiling and my blood was hot and I no longer felt the cold around me, I stood and my fingers curled around its hilt as I rose. It weighed nothing in my hand and there was something like warmth ebbing through the weapon, receding each time I exhaled.

I didn't kill my neighbor, if that's what you're expecting. No incidents, the sheriff said. I'll be damned if I play into his trap.

My neighbor was surprised to see me, dripping wet on his doorstep. Courtesy demanded he invite me in. I stood in the entryway while he ran to fetch towels and when he went to hand them to me, I put the knife to his throat, the point angled towards the hollow just under his chin. He backed away and I followed him, my steps even, until he was pressed against the wall and there was nowhere to go.

They know I've killed people before. They all know this. They try to forget, so that they don't have to be afraid of me.

"You knew," was all I said.

He tried to deny it. Made a weak joke about how global warming is why the shulikun are out early, but no, he didn't know - until I pressed the knife harder and a bead of blood appeared on its point. Then he admitted that yes, he knew, and he also knew that so soon after the death of my uncle I'd be easy prey for them.

I asked him who it was that told him to invite me over. He tried. He really did. But the words stopped up in his throat and then he collapsed, like his muscles stopped working all at once, and he hit the floor hard. He began to seize, his body snapping about like it was being shaken, and I called 911 and then tried to interject myself between his body and the wall, so that he didn't hit his head.

The paramedics would stop it, I told myself. They could push drugs. They could stop it - if it was due to natural causes. But the man in front of me was jerking so violently, his head snapping back and forth like a doll, and blood began to leak from between his clenched lips.

I knew in my heart they could not save him. The man with no shadow may not be able to leave the camp, but my neighbor has visited it many times, and he has cast his net wide and snared far more than the sheriff, it seems. And he would not let them betray him.

The man with the skull cup's knife lay nearby where I had dropped it in my haste to assist my neighbor. The blade caught the light and thus my attention.

I'm not sure how I knew what to do. Perhaps all that folklore I've read gave me the idea, all jumbled up there in the back of my head. Sometimes agreements are sealed with a piece of flesh, sometimes a similar sacrifice must be given to break one. Or perhaps it bubbled out of that secret well of the human shared subconscious, that morass from which monsters climb, and with them the answers to their undoing.

Regardless of the source, I grabbed hold of that idea and wrapped my fingers around the hilt of the knife and then I cut off the index and middle finger of my neighbor's right hand.

His convulsions stopped. The hospital kept him for twenty-four hours and then sent him home. They weren't able to reattach the fingers. The sheriff was not informed about this incident by either my neighbor or the hospital staff. I then spent three days laid up with a really terrible cold. Seriously, I've been so so sick.

Yesterday the man with the skull cup returned for his knife and I took the opportunity to ask him why he saved me. He said that I deserve a more momentous death than being drowned because I'm a grumpy person. I feel a little insulted.

Today I finally had enough energy to go visit my neighbor. He doesn't remember anything after I showed up on his doorstep with the knife and he certainly doesn't remember his conversations with the man with no shadow. This doesn't surprise me. I think I will forgive him. He *is* my neighbor and it's important to maintain good relationships with the people closest to me. Besides, I feel that forgiveness is in keeping with the Christmas spirit, far more than putting up a tree or lights. (which I still haven't done yet, because yanno, I've been sick)

However, I am less charitable towards the people that are truly responsible for this incident. I don't know what to do about the man with no shadow, but the fact that the sheriff is one of his pawns deeply concerns me. I've had a *lot* of people saying that I should invite him to the campground and let the creatures here finish him off, but here's the thing. I think that would backfire on me. I think that would turn the rest of the town so completely against me that they'd finish his work even with him dead. I'm not willing to harm the town, either, as they provide the infrastructure that allows my campground to survive. So I need to get rid of him through less violent means.

I'm a campground manager. A lot of things change in the off-season. My campground is closed and I'll be sending a lot of staff home, as I do every year. Sadly, this includes Turtle as she doesn't have any seniority to merit her staying and I can't show favoritism, even if she saved me. But on a less mundane level… these dark days of winter are when the boundaries between our worlds are weakest and the dead walk the earth and the devils and malicious spirits are loosed upon us to roam free until the day of Epiphany. I can use that. After Christmas and before 12th Night is my window. This is when divinations are best performed and what is lost can be found.

It's time to bring back the old sheriff.

YES WE'RE TALKING ABOUT THE LIGHTS AGAIN

Posted Dec 16 2019 20:41:06 GMT-0400

The sheriff vanished six years ago. It was during the early spring when the nights were still cold and we only got the dedicated campers that enjoy that sort of weather. Which is a shame, the campground is pleasant during the early spring. The trees are luminescent in the sunlight, their leaves glow gold, and the spirits of the forest and field are beginning to stir. The queen of spring and fertility might even pass through and we leave out offerings, just in case she graces our campground. It is probably the safest part of the year, provided it isn't the week of Pentecost.

You should strongly consider visiting us in the spring. Just check the rating on your sleeping bag first. I don't want to get panicked phone calls about Rule #19 (While it can get cold at night, you should not see frost forming inside your tent. If you are woken by the cold and see frost, call the camp emergency number. Stay calm and stay in your tent. We will come get you.) at three in the morning just because you didn't pack appropriately for the weather.

Also, don't forget about Rule #16 (Don't eat food you find sitting out around the campsite. It's not yours and worse, it might be an offering and you will offend whatever it is intended for.) There's at least one culture that I know of where the goddess of spring and fertility is also the goddess of fire and while no one wants to die, you *especially* don't want to die that way.

Anyway, six years ago we had some campers that had clearly not read the list of rules or maybe they did and thought they were just some kind of joke... because they broke Rule #3.

Don't follow the lights. I can't believe I even have to say this one. *Don't follow the lights.*

They wound up exiting the campsite without anything bad happening to them, at which point they lost sight of the lights because they were no longer on old land. They were on a road. This is when they called the camp emergency line, as they realized they were lost and weren't wanting to try to figure out the way back so late at night, not when they were on a road and someone could easily come and pick them up. I'm accustomed to being woken up with emergencies so I was able to go from being sound asleep to fully coherent in a matter of seconds. I told them to stay where they were, that I'd get the car and make a lap around the campground and pick them up. I told them what my car looked like and the license plate and sternly told them that under no circumstances should they accept rides from anyone else.

The old sheriff dealt with *that* particular problem many years ago but it's better to be cautious.

Then I put on some jeans and my shoes and got my car keys. Dawn was a long way off, so I estimated that I'd be able to find them and return them to their campsite and still have time to return to the house before the beast arrived. The little girl skipped alongside the car as I eased it out of the garage and down the driveway, but she was also still sobbing while skipping, so it was a bit unnerving.

It started raining as I was pulling through the gate and onto the road that led out of the campgrounds. Inwardly, I groaned. The forecast had said only a 40% chance but it seemed we'd gotten unlucky, for the rain quickly escalated into a downpour, covering my windshield in a sheet of water as I pulled out onto the road that wound along the west side of the campgrounds. At least they weren't *on* campground land, I thought. The rain can be dangerous for people caught out in it, but fortunately people don't go out in the rain because, well, *rain*. They stay under shelter and thus stay safe and the only emergencies we have to respond to is if someone's tent collapses.

I covered the west side of the campsite and was almost to the south road when the lost campers called me back. They were taking shelter on the front porch of a house, they said. There weren't any lights on inside and no one answered when they'd knocked on the door, so they were just going to stay there on the porch until they saw my car. I drove slowly, across the south side and then up the east and then I was at the northern border. They were still on the phone with me and they said they hadn't seen my headlights when I asked.

I thought about it a moment, trying to place where they were. I asked if they could see any landmarks. No, they said. Nothing. Then it occurred to me. The campsite borders a major road to the south and some fields and houses to the east and west. The north is just empty land. They'd come out the north. They were on the ass-end of nowhere and there shouldn't be any houses out there.

I didn't know whose front porch they were standing on.

I opened my mouth to say that I had a bad feeling about this and I'd like them to stay beside the road, please, when the phone call abruptly disconnected.

My family doesn't deal with things that exist outside the campground boundaries. It's not because we can't or won't, but because they're a different sort of threat, one that cannot be contained and endangers everyone in the area. So I called the sheriff. Then I turned onto the north road and drove slowly, peering through the dark and the rain, straining to see a house nestled in among the trees. I drove past it twice and finally, on the third pass, I saw it.

A small, wood building was nestled not far from the road, at the base of a slight slope. The porch covered half the front of the house and the windows were vacant and dark. No one stood outside. No flashlight beams illuminated the interior. I pulled halfway off the road, as far as I could with the nearly non-existent shoulder. I waited in my car until the sheriff arrived and I was deeply relieved to see his headlights appear in my rear-view mirror. Waiting in the dark and the rain like that, with the house hunched ominously in the corner of my vision... while I kept a careful watch on the trees to either side of the road... it was a little stressful, to say the least. At one point a dead branch had fallen from a tree and it felt like my heart was *still* hammering in my chest, even as I got out of the car to go greet the sheriff.

"That house shouldn't be here," he said as I approached, holding his umbrella out so I could duck under it.

"Yeah, no shit," I snapped, which he took with good humor. He was used to my temper when things were going wrong. "Two of my campers followed the lights. They dumped them off around here and their phone disconnected after they took shelter on that porch."

The sheriff said that he'd called for backup already. We'd wait until they got here and then they'd sweep the house and find the bodies of the campers. Too bad about the rain, he said dourly, otherwise we could set the house on fire and take care of it that way.

This is why I liked the old sheriff. He took care of things. While I relied on rituals and appeasements, he believed in assault rifles and gasoline. And sure, gunfire isn't going to kill everything - or most things, if we're being honest - but *nothing*, human or otherwise, likes being shot. It'd knock a lot of things down and after that, well, that's what the gasoline is for.

Fire is far more effective than bullets.

We'd try lighting it up from inside, he continued. Once the bodies were out so they could be returned to their families. They could douse the interior and light it from the doorway and see if the fire took out the support beams and collapsed the roof. He sounded confident it would. I was only half-listening at this point.

Something was moving inside the house.

I tapped the sheriff on the elbow and pointed. He fell silent and then pressed the handle of the umbrella into my palms. He moved towards the house, walking slowly, his hand falling to unclip his pistol in the holster. I followed just behind him, glancing back and forth to watch our flanks. Not that it would have done a lot of good. Have you been out in the country at night? I'm used to the darkness, but I think people forget how *bright* the cities and suburbs are. Out here, in the rain, it's like the world ends outside of the narrow beam of a flashlight.

The sheriff paused just short of the porch. He shone the flashlight into the window and the house swallowed the light up, presenting us with an inky void and nothing more. I wondered if perhaps the windows were covered on the inside.

A body slammed against the window. I screamed and fell backwards, slipping on the mud and falling, landing hard on my ass in a puddle. The umbrella bounced away and the cold rain shocked the panic out of me and I stared up at the house in naked horror as a young man stared back at me. His eyes were wide, the whites vivid in the light of the sheriff's flashlight, his skin pale where his palms pressed against the pane of glass. His mouth was open. He was screaming something, desperately yelling directly at us, his gaze locked onto my face, but I could not hear anything except for the roar of the rain.

Something jerked him backwards. He flew away from us, his hands outstretched towards the window, his mouth open in a shriek, his eyes still fixed on me in mindless desperation. The darkness inside swallowed him, like he vanished behind a cloud, and the interior was an empty void once more.

The sheriff didn't hesitate. He stripped off his rain jacket, wrapped it around his fist a couple times, and then punched the fucking window in. He knocked the glass away and fumbled with the pane, unlocking it and sliding it up. I scrambled to my feet, yelling at him to stop, to wait, that the backup hadn't arrived yet. He glanced back at me, one hand on the gun at his waist.

"They're not going to get here in time," he said calmly. "It never works out that way. We're always too late."

Then he put a leg through and eased the rest of his body into that house and the darkness swallowed him up.

I fretted. There was no way in hell I was following the sheriff inside. I can't even claim that I was doing the sensible thing and waiting to tell the backup what the situation was, because I knew in my heart that the sheriff was right. These entities - all of them, the things on our campground and the things that hunt elsewhere - never let numbers get the better of them. They slip away well before help arrives and yes, this was a *house* we're talking about, but it had somehow gotten here where there had been no house before and I did not doubt that whatever was inside would whisk its lair away before it could be stormed by angry men with guns and cans of gasoline.

These things only yielded up the dead and only on their terms.

So if I'm being honest, I didn't go after the sheriff because I was afraid. And I know there was nothing I could have done at any point to save him, but I didn't even try, and logically I know I would have been lost too if I'd attempted it, but I can't help but hate myself for it.

This next part is hard to write.

The front door was flung open. I saw the sheriff and he seemed *larger*, his eyes shone like an animal's in the light of my flashlight, and his frame filled the doorway. I think this is just my imagination, remembering him as something powerful, something indomitable. I wish it were so. He was just a man caught in the teeth of something terrible. Yet despite the odds... he had the young man with him. One fist was gripped tight on the back of the man's jacket and he was hauling him along, the poor boy almost too terrified to move. Then he threw him forwards, the man stumbled on the steps of the porch and he fell into the mud and I moved to help him.

And the sheriff... he went back inside. For the woman.

I dragged the man away from the house. He was babbling incoherently, something about the darkness and how it never ended, it just kept going and going. I told him to shut up and twisted on his jacket, pulling him along behind me until I reached my car and threw him in the backseat. I regretted my lack of towels as water began to soak into my upholstery.

"Stay put," I said sternly, which I'm quite good at and it's especially effective on the newly-traumatized.

He nodded at me, pale and shivering, and I shut the door on him and returned to stand vigil at the house, waiting for the sheriff's return. He'd gotten one of them out and because of this I allowed myself a faint glimmer of hope.

The door swung slowly back in forth in the wind. I peered into the darkness that my flashlight could not breach, waiting. And the sheriff emerged for a second time, both hands around a woman. She was screaming hysterically and fighting, thrashing and kicking at her rescuer. He had her in a bear hug and was literally carrying her from the building. I stepped forwards, to the very edge of the porch, and reached out a hand to grab her from him.

The darkness boiled out of the house. It was like watching a pot overflow, thick bubbles of inky blackness churned out of the doorframe and around the sheriff, enveloping him in an instant. I saw his arms outstretched, shoving the woman forwards to where I stood waiting. My hand closed over her wrist and I pulled, but the darkness surged forwards, thick pustules rolling over the woman as well and there was a moment of pressure, as it pulled back towards the house and I dug my heels into the mud, felt myself slipping -

- I considered letting go lest I be pulled in too -

- and then it released her. I fell backwards, stumbling wildly and I hit the ground for a second time that night and I stayed there, sitting in a puddle and staring at the wrist still clutched in my fingers. A wrist, an elbow, a shoulder, and part of a ribcage, and nothing more.

The house was gone and with it, the sheriff and the rest of the woman.

We claimed that the woman had an accident in the rain, fell and broke her neck and died in the woods or something. There's wild animals about and that was why we could only recover part of the body. That's the excuse we gave.

The young man we said was separated from her while lost and we recovered him, a little hypothermic but no serious injuries. I lost track of what happened to him after he was released from the hospital. He came back to our town, though, many years later. The police found him dead after a local called in a car crash. We'd have assumed it was a suicide if it weren't for the dashboard camera that I suspect he'd gotten specifically to provide evidence of what he was seeing. He'd driven off the road in an attempt to ram the house with his car. The house vanished before he hit it and he tried to turn but couldn't, not before he smashed into a particularly stout tree. The police let me see the video off the camera and then they destroyed it.

You see, the house is still around. People see it every now and then. Never for long. Only for a handful of seconds, perhaps a minute or two. Long enough to get a second look, sometimes a third, just enough to confirm that it is that tiny wooden house with the porch and the black windows. The door hangs open, barely a foot. It never appears in the same place twice, at least not in the reports I've gathered. I have them marked on a map I keep folded in my desk.

The sheriff is still alive. The woman is not. There was half of her lung in the piece the darkness left behind, after it severed her out of my grasp. She couldn't have survived that. But the sheriff... the lady with extra eyes gave me a candle, not long after he vanished. She told me to light it and when it went out, then I would know that he was dead.

I don't think she was trying to console me. It sits in my bedroom, on top of my dresser. It's been burning for six years now. I feel the weight of my guilt every time I look at it, pressing on my shoulders, and I hear the rain and see that darkness bubbling out of the house and the sheriff's outstretched hands, shoving the woman to safety in a last, futile gesture.

He shouldn't have gone back in. One would have been enough.

Or perhaps I shouldn't have been so frightened, perhaps I should have stepped up on that porch, been closer, had better footing and been able to wrench her free before it was too late and then his sacrifice wouldn't have been in vain.

I think it is more likely that I would have been swallowed up by the house as well.

I'm a campground manager. I deal with monsters and demons but I don't think that's made me particularly brave. As I write this I cannot help but hope that my attempt to locate the house will fail, in the days between Christmas and 12th Night. I don't have a strategy yet. The sheriff got someone out through sheer force of will and I think I will just have to do the same and hope for the best. If I don't come back... maybe one of you can ask the lady with extra eyes if she has a candle for me.

I ACCIDENTALLY HOSTED THE DANCERS' CHRISTMAS PARTY

Posted Dec 28 2019 20:12:14 GMT-0400

Honestly, the dancers are probably the least interesting part of this, but thinking up the occasional amusing title is a rare spot of joy in this bleak and miserable excuse for Christmastime. I don't even care if the shulikun take offense at that. This Christmas sucked.

I've been in jail for a couple days now. Yes, the sheriff is responsible. Yes, it was for bullshit reasons. Yes, I hate him and would shed no tears if something on my campground flayed the skin off his body and made it into a hat.

Obviously, something bad happened. I think we all knew it would. Christmas is a strange time of year when old traditions collide with the new and ancient creatures walk the earth, as is their right. Yet... I hoped that nothing would happen until closer to Epiphany. After all, Christmas is a joyous time and accordingly, the creatures of winter are more mischievous than malicious. Even when Krampus shows up we get one of the more benign versions that merely abducts naughty children, beats them with a switch, and then leaves them behind at dawn far from home.

I once had a classmate that received a visit from Krampus. This pleased me quite a bit, as he'd stuck a piece of bubble gum in my hair that year and it took hours to get it all out, and even with cold water and a lot of patience, Mom still had to resort to using scissors. Seeing him unable to sit comfortably in his chair after the winter break ended felt *right*. It felt like justice.

Anyway, I expected some sort of incident, but not necessarily anything *significant*. Nothing that the sheriff could rightly use against me, much less blame me for as a reason to take me into custody until the judge returned and told him to knock it off.

Let me tell you how this all happened so you can be angry with me.

After my encounter with the shulikun I was trying to embrace the Christmas spirit. I kept an assortment of cookies on a plate in the kitchen and there was a carton of eggnog and a jug of apple cider in the fridge, ready to be warmed up at a moment's notice. Good thing, too, because I did get carolers on Christmas Eve.

The dancers showed up at my house with one of them dressed as the Mari Lwyd. I opened the door and was taken aback at the sight of a horse skull looming in the doorway, green ball ornaments shoved into the eye sockets. A white sheet covered the dancer holding the skull down to their ankles. For a moment I thought my visitors were from town - although no one I knew practiced the Mari Lwyd tradition - and then I saw a familiar face grinning at me impishly from the edge of the crowd. The dancer that had grabbed my shotgun all those years ago. I shifted nervously in the doorway and they began to sing. Then, at the end, they feel eerily silent and waited for my reply so that the battle of wits could begin. We'd go back and forth, answering in rhyme, until finally one side couldn't reply fast enough and either had to leave or had to invite the entire party in for food and drink.

"There is no way I'm winning this one," I sighed. "Just come inside."

And I threw the door open and the entire dancer party stomped inside, tracking snow all the way down my entryway. The musicians, mercifully, were masked and considerately kept their hoods on as well. I focused on the kitchen for a bit, warming up the apple cider in a crockpot and getting out the paper plates while the dancers demolished the cookies.

"I have to ask," I said to the one female dancer, once everyone was occupied with food and beverages. "That skull. Is it... one of *our* horses?"

"We'll put it back," she replied primly. "Rumor has it you're going to rescue the old sheriff."

"Are you reading Reddit?"

She pivoted to face me squarely.

"You're going to die," she said bluntly. "Unless, of course, you prepare yourself. Do you want a hint?"

"It'd be appreciated."

"The rule of three. You have one of the items already."

She nodded towards the bedroom. The candle. The one marking whether the sheriff lived or died.

"And the other two?" I asked desperately.

One would come to me, she said. Indeed, it was already en route. The other I would have to request. Then she flashed me a thin smile and trotted off to make sure she got some of the cookies before they all vanished.

I don't remember much else from that night. I woke up on the sofa the next morning and found that my pantry and refrigerator were empty, my trash was full of wrappers and packages (how do you go through four sticks of butter in one night?), and there was an eviscerated deer on my kitchen table. I have a vague memory of one of the dancers telling my fortune using its entrails, but I don't remember what she said. It was something momentous. I remember being afraid - emotional, I think I cried. I just don't remember the words. I'm not sure if it was some kind of spell or if I was hilariously drunk. They certainly spiked the cider at some point, because my crockpot smelled like the contents of my now-barren liquor cabinet.

I'm starting to be convinced the dancers are fairies again.

I stumbled into the kitchen to get some water, just in case a hangover was the reason I felt like crap, and that's when Bryan burst in through the front door. I guess it wasn't locked from when the dancers left. I had a moment of panic, not sure who was in my house, until I heard Bryan's voice, or at least, as much as he could wheeze out between ragged gasps for air.

"Yule cat," he panted. "Your neighbor."

I got a couple answers out of him. Which neighbor it was. (I have quite a few, on account of owning such a large piece of land) Whether he thought the cat was hunting or not. (it was) And then I was running out the door. I wasn't certain what I could do to *stop* the cat, but I just knew that I had to try, because otherwise the sheriff would get the incident he wanted.

My neighbor's house was a squat one-story of tan brick, set near the top of a low hill. I stopped halfway up the driveway, my tires throwing gravel as it slid from how fast I was going and how hard I had to brake. I got out and ran towards the house, just in time to see a large cat backing out of a broken window.

When I say "large" I'm not talking about something like your grandmother's cat that she swears is a Maine coon but it doesn't have long hair and you're certain it's not actually a Maine coon, just obese. I mean that this was a picture window and the cat was barely making it through. The frame was completely filled with its ass, its hind legs braced against the wall of the house as it ponderously heaved the rest of its body back through the opening, tail aloft to prominently display its butthole in perfect feline fashion.

Which all sounds hilarious, except this is the Yule cat, and the Yule cat is one of a handful of Christmas creatures that roam the world purely for the purpose of brutal murder.

It dropped out of the window and onto all fours. If not for its size, the Yule cat would look like an ordinary fluffy house cat. Its coloration is that of a gray tabby and its coat is long and bushy, giving it a majestic mane around its neck and enveloping its legs and body into a formless mass of fur. In its mouth was my neighbor's arm. He was at least still connected to the arm, a bit bloodied from being pulled through the broken window, but otherwise still alive. Screaming in terror, but alive.

It was far, far too late to do anything to ward off the cat's arrival. The Yule cat hunts only under very specific circumstances. It roams the countryside during Christmastime in search of people that haven't received new clothing before Christmas Eve. (don't worry, I'm pretty sure presents of clothing not opened until Christmas day count) I guess my neighbor hadn't received a new shirt or gloves and hadn't thought to buy any for himself before Christmas came.

The cat released my neighbor and he began to crawl away, struggling to get to his feet, almost senseless with terror. I ran for him, thinking that if we couldn't stop the cat, perhaps we could flee. I could get him into the car. Behind him, the cat dropped low to the ground, tail lashing furiously. It was growing in size - it was bigger each time I blinked - and by the time I crossed the short distance between myself and my neighbor, the tips of its ears were even with the roof of the house.

I seized my neighbor's arm and pulled him to his feet. I screamed at him to run. The car, I said. We just had to get to the car.

The cat pounced right as we reached it. It landed over top of us, the impact knocked both of us off our feet, and there was a screech of twisting metal as one of its paws came down on the front of my car and crushed the hood. I tumbled in one direction and my neighbor in another, then the cat snapped a paw out and slapped him away, sending him tumbling across the yard. It hunkered down to the ground, eyes intent on my neighbor's prone body, waiting for him to get up again.

Panting, I got to my feet. My arm was bleeding from hitting the gravel but I didn't feel *anything* under the adrenaline. The car was ruined. At least the cat was still playing with its prey and as horrific as that is, it at least bought me more time.

I got the shotgun out of the back of the car. I didn't know if this could hurt it and it certainly wouldn't kill it, but perhaps it would make it think this particular morsel wasn't worth the trouble. And since the cat was ignoring me... it lunged at my neighbor again, knocking him back and forth between its paws, stepping over him when he fell and whipping around to bat at him some more. His cries had turned into ragged whimpers, his eyes were wide and I wasn't sure if he could even register my presence anymore, his mind clearly consumed with a primitive instinct to run, to survive.

I walked up to the Yule cat until I could hit it at almost point-blank range. I aimed the gun up, between legs as thick as tree trunks, and fired right into its belly.

The cat yowled and jumped away, spinning and hissing with its ears flattened against its skull. Blood dripped from its stomach like a light spring rain. There was a blur of movement - just a flash, an impression of something dark headed at me, and then I was airborne - I hit the ground on my shoulder and the resulting burst of agony blinded me for a moment. I rolled and wound up on my stomach, dazed from the blow.

I raised my head again just in time to see the cat holding my neighbor down with one paw on his legs. Its teeth were sunk into his torso. I could hear his screams and then the cat simply... raised its head... and the screams were abruptly silenced.

The cat opened its mouth and let the upper half of my neighbor's body fall to the dirt. It sniffed at it, daintily plucked up a loop of intestine and ate that, and then immediately lost interest. I made no effort to stand. It was too late. Someone had died and yes, it wasn't my fault, but did that really matter?

I knew all this time that the sheriff was likely going to get what he wanted, but some part of me had dared hope otherwise. Forgive my cowardice, but I wanted another way out, one that wouldn't force me to find that house and brave its darkness to find the old sheriff.

The cat turned its head and stared down at me. It put its ears back.

"Oh fuck off," I said to it. "I got new clothes, you don't get to eat me."

It dropped to the ground, its belly a mere foot above the grass. It took one slow step forwards. I nervously began to stand.

Had I gotten new clothes? It wasn't like I'd opened my presents yet. Normally I bought myself some new socks, just in case, but I haven't been getting out much this year and my trip into town was a frantic, last-minute ordeal where I just got presents for my family and my Reddit Secret Santa and called it a day. But even without my yearly socks, my aunt always was sure to give us *something*, I desperately thought as the cat continued to stalk closer. It was kind of her *thing*.

My aunt.

The one that just lost her husband.

I couldn't recall her showing up at my house to drop off a package this year.

For as much as I go on and on about the rules, I find it ironic that I would finally forget about one myself. I suppose it's inevitable. I know it seems like such a simple thing - just read the rules and follow them - but there's so many things to remember and life crowds them out and the years blur together and we grow complacent. And eventually, we all make mistakes. My mother left a window open. I... forgot to buy a new pair of socks.

I turned to run. I didn't get far. A massive paw hit me in the back and sent me flying forwards, landing face-first in the gravel, barely getting my arms up in time to shield myself. I scrambled to my feet, slipping on the loose stones, my mind consumed with replaying the memory of the cat *toying* with my neighbor before finally ripping him in two. My chest was so tight with panic it was like my lungs were twisting together and I couldn't even inhale.

A hand seized the back of my jacket. For a moment I was lifted clean off my feet and the world spun as I was twirled around and then something heavy and warm fell over my head and shoulders. A strong arm wrapped around my back and pulled me forwards, burying my face into a thick wool shirt that smelled like pine.

"She has new clothing," a voice boomed over my head.

Whoever this guy was, he was *tall*. I twisted my neck enough to look up and all I could see was a mass of curly white hair.

A shadow fell over us. The cat, looming over me and my rescuer both. I felt a gust of air as it flicked its tail in frustration.

"It's *my* gift to her," my rescuer continued.

And somehow that sounded like a threat. The cat yowled with displeasure, gave a little growl that made the hair on the back of my neck stand on end, and then the shadow over us withdrew. The man holding me let go and I stepped back, glancing fearfully to the side to where the cat had been standing. Nothing. Just the driveway, the house with the shattered window, my crushed car, and the neighbor's corpse.

I stood there for a few moments, stunned into incoherency. Then, as my heart rate slowly began to wind down, I turned my attention to my rescuer. A tall man, dressed in jeans and a red plaid shirt, with a long, white curly beard and hair to match. His expression was stern and his eyes were cold. A simple silver cross hung around his neck.

"Saint... Nicholas?" I ventured.

A faint nod. I was rendered speechless. I'd heard the stories, of course, but I'd never thought...

There are many creatures in this world. Old things and more ancient beings that are both god and not and many that lie somewhere in-between. Not all of them are cruel. Not all of them are predators.

On my shoulders rested a thick wool mantle, hanging almost to my waist. The hood and hem was trimmed in white fur. I fingered it for a moment, then made to take it off and return it to the saint. He shook his head.

"It's a gift," he said firmly. "That's what I *do*."

"You do a lot more than give gifts," I replied. "You *save* people. I didn't think you'd save me, though. I'm not a good person."

"I help the good and the wicked," he said with a smile. "It's why I'm a saint."

There's plenty of saints that punish the wicked, but I felt it would be rude to point that out. Saint Nicholas is known as an embodiment of mercy who helps anyone in their time of dire need and I guess I qualified.

"Can you bring him back?" I asked, pointing at my neighbor.

But Saint Nicholas just patted me gently on the arm and walked away.

91

The sheriff arrested me a few hours later. I called in the death to the local police, of course, and I guess he got word of it from there. I'd barely returned to my house before he showed up on my doorstep, claiming I was responsible for my neighbor's demise. Because my car was there. That's it. My car.

"The Yule cat *stepped* on it," I said, indignant. "This is *bullshit* and you know it."

Anyway, he just grabbed my shoulder after that and threw me against the wall to handcuff me, and I let him, because I didn't want to give him a reason to escalate on the grounds that I was resisting arrest. I spent Christmas day in a jail cell and have been sitting there until early this morning, when the judge returned to town and someone quietly let him know what was going on.

I'm deeply grateful to whoever among my staff cleaned up after the dancers because coming home to days-old disemboweled deer carcass would not have been a pleasant experience. If I find out who it is they're getting a bonus in their next paycheck.

So I'm free now, but it's a little too late. The damage has been done. My employees tell me that while I was incarcerated, the sheriff was stirring up trouble. Blaming my neighbor's death on my campground even though I had *nothing* to do with it. "Collateral damage", he's calling it. Maybe it was. Maybe we do attract more than our fair share of inhuman entities. But I'm starting to think that even if that is the case, is it really such a bad thing? Sure, they're dangerous, but they *can* be lived alongside and humanity has been doing exactly that for a long, long time now.

There was another town meeting. They want me to sell the campground. Reset the timer. The sheriff proposed this plan and is ushering it along. He says he's already got a buyer. Of course, the first thing I thought was 'over my dead body' but maybe that's his backup plan.

That's fine. I have my own plan.

The dancers said I needed three things. I have the candle and now I have the Saint's mantle. I need to find the third item and I need to find out where the house is going to appear next. But when the old year dies and the new begins, the future is close at hand, and it reveals its patterns to us. I've spent my whole life learning about the inhuman and supernatural things in our world and it's time to turn that into a weapon, instead of mere protection.

I'm a campground manager. This isn't just my land - it's also my home. I'm going to fight him and the rest of the town. I can't entirely say why I'm driven to do this. It's just... something I have to do. I won't be the person that lets this land fall out of my family's possession, I won't throw all the creatures that merely need a place to live off it, and I won't be the person that releases the ones that are too dangerous to roam free on the world.

SOMETHING WORSE THAN COAL

Posted Jan 01 2020 20:33:25 GMT-0400

I met the sheriff's "buyer". He came by on New Year's Eve. I'll be honest - I had trouble hating him. I was all set to be rude and angry when he showed up on my doorstep, looking for the camp office. He introduced himself as the person interested in buying the campsite so I told him I wasn't selling and he just looked...bewildered. Hurt, almost. Then he apologized and said the sheriff had told him I was ready to sell at the end of January, that I just needed to wrap a few things up first. And that he had been told he didn't need to be present until then, but he was just… excited. Had some time off and wanted to come down here early and see it when he wouldn't be busy and stressed with the acquisition paperwork.

I felt bad for him. I have no idea how the sheriff dug him up, but clearly he's been duped. So I took him for a tour. Showed him the woods, fields, and even the family cemetery. Nothing out of the ordinary. Then I escorted him off the property and reiterated that I wasn't selling, that the sheriff was a little overzealous. He said that was a shame but he'd stick around a few more days - vacation and all - and if I changed my mind he had the finances all lined up already.

At least now I know the timeline. End of January.

I've also alerted my staff to keep an eye out for him in case he comes back. I do not want him wandering around unescorted.

A half hour from midnight I got out my tarot deck. I laid out a Celtic cross, as someone suggested. I was sitting on the floor of my living room with the guidebook open on my phone, trying to figure out if The Devil represents the sheriff or the man with no shadow and whether there's any significance in so many cards being from the oak suite or if I'm just bad at shuffling. I'd just finished reading up on The Chariot and was thinking, well that's a good sign, when the front door flew open.

It smashed into the entryway wall and hung there, letting in a gust of cold air that stirred the cards on the floor. Framed in the doorway was a woman, beautiful, with pale skin like winter frost and hair like snow.

"Uh, hello?" I said tentatively. "And you are?"

She wasn't inside yet. This was a good sign. All manners of creatures roam the world on the eve of the new year but most of them cannot enter the home without permission. There are stories of even the devil itself being repulsed for lack of an invitation.

"I am Perchta," she replied. "Don't trouble yourself to get up; I'll invite myself in."

She stepped through the open doorway. This was not a good sign. And worse, I knew that name. Another one of our Christmastime... visitors. One that could go wherever she willed, regardless of whether she was welcome or not.

For good children she would leave a silver coin. For the wicked, she would cut open their abdomens, remove their stomach and guts, stuff them full of straw and pebbles, and sew them back together again. So a little bit like Santa Claus, but with 100% more murder.

Perchta has not visited our town for a long time. Not in my lifetime, but she did in my parents', before I was born. They told me of her when I was young and could be frightened into obedience, and then again when I was older and understood that these stories were more real than I believed as a young child. They told me how a young man had done something terribly wicked and one night, in the days leading up to 12th Night, his neighbors had been woken by his screaming. They broke into his house through a window and that entire time he had not stopped screaming. They entered his room to find a beautiful woman with long white hair standing over him, knotting and snipping free her thread. She turned to them, smiled, and vanished.

He died in the hospital. His abdomen had been sewn neatly up in a straight line, the stitches so tiny they were almost invisible, and when the surgeon snipped them open, bloody straw and stones bulged up through the incision and spilled out onto the floor of the operating room.

Now, I stared at Perchta as she stood framed by the lights of my entryway and she held a needle between the pinched fingers in one hand and her thread was wound around the fingers of her other.

I grabbed my deck of tarot cards and scrambled to my feet to run. Some cards fell from my hand as I sprinted towards the kitchen, but I knew better than to stop and grab them. I could hear her footsteps crossing the living room as I fumbled with the deadbolt on the door leading to the garage.

"You've been wicked, haven't you?" Perchta said from behind me, her voice a lilting sing-song. "Saint Nicholas saved you, but I am not *nearly* so kind."

How many did I kill this year? Was it only two? The camper that died in the hospital, writhing and vomiting blood? And Jessie, who died screaming as she burned? I've had worse years.

"I did what was necessary!" I panted, throwing myself through the door, slamming it shut behind me, and locking it.

It jolted as Perchta slammed into it and I was thrown backwards. I dove for the other door, the one leading outside, and got it open just as the other door was ripped off its hinges. It clattered noisily onto the floor of the garage and I ran out into the cold air, letting it fill my lungs, fighting through that initial shock that threatened to rob me of all ability to breath. I was running, down through the yard, towards the edge of the driveway. I had no idea where I could go to get away.

Perchta was once a goddess. Perhaps she still is. I don't know if ancient beings can lose their divinity, or perhaps divinity is merely a *word* that only has meaning for humanity. Her status as a "former" goddess has certainly done nothing to lessen her power.

I reached the end of the drive and at first I thought to cut towards the road; I could try to reach Bryan and his dogs, but there was something standing on the asphalt. Multiple somethings. Their heads hung sideways at odd angles and their limbs swayed in the wind. I veered wide around them, confused, unsure of whether I should go around or go the other direction entirely.

Then my eyes adjusted to the darkness and I realized what they were. Scarecrows.

And their heads snapped up, still hanging sideways on loose necks, but the empty spots where their eyes should go were fixed on where I stood, hesitating, keenly aware of the woman with white hair making her way steadily down the driveway at a confident, unhurried clip. The pace of a predator that knows it is only a matter of time.

I began to back away and then - in the corner of my vision - I saw a large shape lunging at me out of the darkness. From just outside the reach of my porch lights. I dodged to the side, stumbling on the damp grass and almost falling. Its arms passed over my head and I smelled damp straw and a foul stench, the smell of rot, and then I was sprinting across the field and leaving the scarecrows behind me. The treeline rose up before me. The darkness was impenetrable between the trees, but it was the darkness of my childhood and there was a sense of safety hidden inside the forest. I just had to reach it.

And then what? Keep running all night? I didn't know. I couldn't *think*.

My reprieve was short-lived. I heard a noise from behind my right shoulder and I risked a glance backwards.

The scarecrow was racing across the field after me. All of them were. They ran in great, loping strides on all fours like animals and their limbs seemed elongated, thin, more like gangly canines than human forms now. They were rapidly gaining. I kept running, hitting the tree line and the grass gave way to dead leaves. I knew it was hopeless and I couldn't possibly outrun them.

I stumbled through the underbrush and then one hit me, a bodily impact that took me off my feet and I landed on my side, felt a weight fall over top of me, pinning me to the ground. I struggled, kicking and punching, and my fingers clawed straw from the back of its head and my knee connected with something soft, something that came free with a sickly sound, like the last of jam releasing from the bottom of a jar. Something like rope, but slick and wet, landing on my legs and I gagged at the stench of bad meat.

Now I know what Perchta does with the intestines of her victims.

I seized the scarecrow's arm with both hands and *wrenched* and the straw parted and I tore it clean off. The scarecrow's body titled, off-balance, and one last blow to its side knocked it off of me. It writhed on the ground, trying to stand, more intestines spilling out of the hole in its midsection. I rolled and pushed myself up.

Then another blow and this one took me off my feet and *kept* me off my feet, slamming my back against a tree trunk. My chest seized up at the impact and for a moment I could only feel the agony radiating from beneath my ribcage and then that was buried under the ice of terror. Perchta's hand was around my neck and it was she that held me pinned, my feet straining to touch the ground. My tarot cards lay strewn across the forest floor.

"Necessary, perhaps," she said, answering my earlier plea for understanding, "but no less wicked."

A twist of her wrist and her bone needle shone ivory in the moonlight. She pushed my shirt up and out of the way and I felt the point of it against my skin, just above my belly-button. The woman leaned in close to me and her breath on my neck felt like frost.

"What else am I to do?" I whimpered. "I'm trying the best I can but I can't save everyone."

"You *can* save them all," she hissed in my ear.

She released my neck and let my feet hit the ground, but I remained pinned with my back against the tree, the point her needle digging deeper into my stomach. I whimpered low in the back of my throat. She bent over languidly, the needle immobile against my skin, and her thin fingers plucked one of the fallen tarot cards from the ground. She held it up in front of my face. Justice, questioning my rules, examining it for its triumphs and its flaws.

"I don't know what it's trying to tell me," I whispered. "I don't know what I'm doing."

"Figure it out," she replied grimly.

And the needle pierced my skin - I yelped with pain - but it wasn't as bad as I'd expected, and then it exited, two bright points just above my bellybutton, and she was knotting the thread and she snapped it with a jerk, eliciting another brief moment of blinding agony as the stitch pulled tight against the wounds.

She left. And I pulled my shirt up and stared at my stomach in the moonlight and saw a faint line of white against my skin, the single stitch that she'd sewn into my flesh with her needle. I fell on my hands and knees and vomited. When I recovered, I sat back on my knees and looked aside, panting, waiting to stand until after my dizziness passed. Then I gathered up my scattered cards and returned to my house.

I broke the stitch once I was home and cleaned and bandaged the wound. I tried to sit at the table and try the tarot once more, but I couldn't focus. I drew one card... and then stopped.

This was ridiculous. I didn't know what I was doing. Even if this did mean something, I didn't have the knowledge to interpret it. I was looking for answers from the tarot because I thought that was the *expected* method of divination, but it wasn't the only one. There are patterns to these creatures I deal with, patterns to the stories, and all I do is pick the one that fits the best.

The tarot cards weren't *fitting*. I'm too unfamiliar with them. I'm shit at shuffling. Fortunately, just as there are many variations of the Cinderella story, there are many variations of how to divine the future.

So here's what I did. An older method. I took the candle from my bedroom - the sheriff's candle - and poured some of the wax into a spoon. I then poured that into a cup of cold water and stared down at the resulting image. It coalesced into a blob with two empty spaces like eyes.

A skull. Floating in a cup of water.

I have the third item. I wandered the campsite for hours and just before sunup I found him. The man with the skull cup. I told him I was here to claim my favor and he held very still while I spoke. Then he smiled, when I said what it was I wanted.

"To save the sheriff," he murmured, running a finger along the rim of the cup contemplatively.

"Do *you* read Reddit?" I demanded. "Or do you gossip with the dancers?"

His eyes flicked up to stare at me in unspoken reproach. The man with the skull cup merely *tolerates* my sarcasm. The silence between us stretched on until my nerve broke and I coughed and awkwardly changed the subject.

"So what am I going to find inside that house?" I asked.

"I cannot tell you. I have no more ability to read the future than you. I see patterns and possibilities and perhaps I see ones that you miss while you struggle in this web not of your own making, but even I do not know what the house's master is."

"I'm getting tired of puzzles," I muttered. "What web?"

He sighed softly and shoved the cup into my hands.

"You continually disappoint me. The man with no shadow has you ensnared and you focus on a single strand of his plans."

"Would you help me fight him?"

A question asked on impulse, born of a wild hope that the man with the skull cup had no fondness for his... neighbor. His expression went carefully blank and while he only displayed the emotions he chose to - disdain, usually - this felt even more controlled than usual.

"This is all the help I will give you," he said dismissively. "Our agreement is concluded."

He told me I could have the cup until the next full moon. I must be careful not to spill it, he said sternly, for it would take a heavy cost to fill it again.

The cup sits on my dresser, between the candle and the folded mantle.

As for finding the house? Well, I wasn't able to divine its next appearance, but maybe I don't need to. Remember the young man that the old sheriff rescued? He found it. It vanished because he *attacked* it with his car, but he still found it. He didn't have any knowledge of divination to help him. He just... drove until it appeared. Brute force may be inefficient, but it worked.

I've got a route planned through all the places it tends to appear. And every day until the new moon I'm going to go looking for it until I find it. My aunt has agreed to drive, since I don't have a car right now. She needs something to distract her, she says. The house is lonely without her husband.

I'm a campground manager. I can't read the future. I don't know what Perchta - or anyone else, for that matter - expects out of me. I can only understand what I think is right and what must be done and maybe I'm missing something, maybe there's a bigger picture here and the man with the skull cup is right - I'm thrashing in a web I can't even see - but I gotta be honest. I really hate the sheriff. Anything that ruins his day is a win in my book. So that's what I'm going to focus on because I'm only human and I'm not that clever and I'm just doing the best I can.

I will say this, though. I've commented in the past that we have bad years where our deaths and injuries are significantly increased and that I start looking for signs early in the year.

I think I've seen a sign already. The bloodied piece of string I ripped out of my own flesh.

This is going to be one of the bad years.

THE VANISHING HOUSE

Posted Jan 09 2020 21:34:38 GMT-0400

So about those rules. I don't believe anything should be an absolute, because intent is more important than the letter of the rule. A rule is meant to coerce a desired outcome, after all, and if there's a way to get that outcome that might not be exactly within the confines of the rules... well, what's more important? Dogma or results?

I did what I said you shouldn't do. Rule #3. The one I keep saying over and over because it's something that everyone should know, if not from folklore, than *at least* from watching Lord of the Rings.

Don't follow the lights.

I followed them.

Thanks to one of my readers for the idea. I like my aunt but days of quality time with her in the car was getting to be a bit much. She mostly talked about my uncle - her late husband - and while I think this was part of her grieving process, I was woefully unqualified and mostly just sat there saying "uh-huh" occasionally and hoping to god the vanishing house showed up and rescued me from the conversation.

But I started trying to find the lights each night after that suggestion and finally, they showed up. And I went after them. They tried to lead me into danger a handful of times before we reached the edge of my property. They took me to the mound where the thing in the darkness lies sleeping but I went around and waited until the lights began moving again, reluctantly, in another direction. They took me to the people with no faces but as I have said before, they will not harm me. I felt them looking at the mantle I wore and the cup and candle I carried and one of them asked me in a low voice where I was going. To the vanishing house, I told them. I asked if they knew the way, hoping to circumvent having to follow the damned lights all over the campground. They did not, they said. They would make a sacrifice for me, however, in the hopes that some power would smile upon me. I think they offered because it was the polite thing to do.

I declined. I know what kind of sacrifice they would make and with no campers on site, it would be one of my staff. Besides, I had the mantle of Saint Nicholas. A power has already given me its favor.

After that, the lights took me to where frost hung on the leaves and coated the ground, but I wore the mantle and the cold could not touch me and I passed by unscathed. They took me past the children with no wagon but I ignored their offers of ice for sale and they, too, I passed by. Finally, they took me to the edge of the property.

They stopped just shy of the border, marked only by my memory and a few scattered "no trespassing" signs. Part of my land is fenced, but not here. Not on this edge of the campground where the road is some distance away, across neglected and empty land. I figure that few people are going to be willing to haul their gear this far in order to sneak into the campground and those that are physically able to are likely backpackers who are respectful enough of the land to pay for its usage.

I phoned my aunt and told her where I was. She'd bring the car around with the rest of the supplies. Let's just say I had a backup plan... that involved gasoline and matches. If I couldn't rescue the sheriff I at least wanted to eliminate one of the dangers around here.

The house sat before me on the other side of the road, a squat thing of wood and shingles with that front porch and the barely open door. Inviting me in.

I won't lie - I was afraid. I did not want to go inside. I'm not entirely sure how I forced myself to move. The mantle was heavy on my shoulders and that was some comfort, it and the light cast by the candle and the feel of the skull cup in my hand. Were the heroes frightened, in the stories? I think they were. Yes, they were. Of course they were. But they had their protection, their three items, their rules, their helpers, or whatever it was that would see them to safety. They only had to trust and do as they were told.

I didn't have any rules to follow. Not here, on the threshold of the vanishing house. All I had was my three items and my courage, which was sadly lacking. But I went inside. I said a prayer to Saint Nicholas (because if any of the benevolent powers would be listening, surely it would be him) and stepped across the threshold.

The door swung open at my touch. The world ended at the edge of the candlelight. Within the bubble of its glow I could see weathered wooden floors, covered with a layer of dust, and wooden walls devoid of ornamentation. There were squares where the color of the wood was darker, untouched by the sun's light, where pictures had once hung. After that... nothing. Just a darkness so deep it was as if nothing existed at all and I had reached the end of reality. I felt a tinge of panic merely looking at it, the instinctive terror you experience when you stand on a precipice. I tore my eyes away and focused instead on what was directly in front of me, what was *real* and stable.

The door swung shut behind me. Gently. I heard the latch catch.

"I'm here for the sheriff," I said to the empty house.

Nothing. If the house had a master, it wasn't inclined to converse. I took a shallow breath and pressed forwards. The house unfolded before me as the candlelight touched it. I took the first doorway, resolving to follow the left-hand rule. I entered the living room. Two windows were against the front wall, the very same windows that the young man had stared out at me from all those years ago. There were dark rectangles on the floor, clear of dust, where furniture had once sat. Only a single sitting chair remained, shoved into a corner. A woman sat in it, naked and limp, her head lolling to the side so that her ear almost touched her elbow. Black blood coated her side and pooled on the floor, having poured out of her missing arm and the gaping cavity that was once her lung. It'd long since dried into something resembling ink.

"Do you remember my name?" she asked as I entered the room.

She raised her head and it flopped over to the missing shoulder. Black bile dribbled out of the corner of her mouth and her nose. It fell in viscous drops to the floor.

"I'm afraid not," I said. "I think I learned it, but I've since forgotten. Sorry."

"It's okay. You've seen so many die, I imagine. What's one more name?"

I walked around the edge of the room, to the windows on one wall, covered with heavy curtains of a pale brown loose knit. I looked outside and saw my aunt's car parked on the shoulder of the road, but there was a pall over the scene, as if a black mist had settled over her vehicle.

"Are you dead?" I asked the woman, if only to hear my own voice.

"Quite. You feel guilty, don't you?"

"I wish I could have saved you."

"You tried. You did more than most people would have."

Her words sounded hollow. The polite thing to say, but not something that either of us actually believed.

"Can you tell me where the sheriff is?"

"I cannot. He was dragged away from me, cursing, fighting to get to me the entire time. The house took him and I was left to die alone. I was so scared. I was choking on my own blood and I just wanted someone to be there, to hold my head up so I didn't have to taste it in my mouth, to tell me it was all going to be okay."

She paused for a moment, a thin stream of black liquid trickling down her chin through pale lips.

"I suppose it wouldn't have mattered," she said contemplatively. "We all die alone and afraid, don't we? Someone being there is no comfort when you can feel your body failing all around you."

I thought of my father, dragging the little girl by her hair out into the yard. I thought of my aunt, stabbing the faceless person with their own scalpel. We die alone and afraid… or angry. Angry was also an option.

I walked past the young woman towards the next doorway. I couldn't help her. I had to keep moving. We had no idea how long the house would remain in one spot and I didn't want to risk being trapped in here simply because I took too long.

The next room was a kitchen. Cupboards and cabinets were along the far wall. All their doors were removed and the shelves were barren. The stove was an empty spot of torn linoleum, stained with rust and grease. A table with no chairs was shoved against the other wall and the young woman lay upon it. She was on her back with her remaining limbs splayed and dangling limply over the edge. Her head also dangled, her long hair almost touching the floor.

I glanced back into the first room. She was still there, sprawled in the chair. And she was here, sprawled on the table.

"Is this the house's doing?" I asked. "Are you here to distract me? Or… are you the master of the house?"

She laughed and black liquid frothed at her lips until it filled her mouth and she began to choke on it. She spat a thick clump like a clot out onto the floor and regained her voice.

"I'm not the master," she said bitterly. "The master took the sheriff and left me to die alone."

"Yes, we covered that already," I replied.

I edged past her. I pressed my back against the edge of the cabinets, not wanting to get any closer to the dead woman than I had to. Her eyes tracked my every movement. She spoke again when we were directly even with each other.

"I died." More black liquid dribbled down her chin, bubbling forth every time her lips moved. "You killed me."

"I tried to *save* you."

I continued edging past her, my heart hammering. I watched her remaining arm. If it so much as *twitched* I was going to bolt.

"You could have done more. You've *always* been able to do more."

Now that just wasn't fair. First Perchta and now this… dead girl.

"Like *what?*" I snarled.

"You could sell the campground."

A giggle, punctuated by the rasp of liquid obscuring her throat.

"Like hell I will," I muttered.

I continued down the left side of the kitchen wall, letting out a deep sigh of relief once I was out of reach. She stretched out her hands towards me as I reached the next doorway, rolling on the table so that she stared at me from her side, the swell of her broken ribcage luminescent white in the light of my candle.

I stared into the next room - a hallway with a staircase at the end.

"Is it pride?" she whispered from behind me, almost to herself. "I think it is. You're too proud to admit that *you're killing all of us.*"

I'd had enough. I whirled on her, stalked back through the kitchen to where she lay, and plunged the candle flame into her body. I'm not sure what I thought would happen. I was blinded by anger and acting on instinct.

She caught like paper, her skin curled and blackened and burned and she screamed, the remains of her body thrashing and that black liquid fountained sluggishly out. It swallowed up the candlelight and the flame both and all light vanished just as she finally fell silent. I realized what I'd done too late, panic seized at my chest as I strained to see *anything.*

Then I felt the lap of cold liquid, like watery mud, at my feet. I moved, quickly. I put one hand out, the hand with the candle, and stretched out two fingers to feel for a wall. There were stairs. I remembered seeing stairs. I had to find them.

The liquid was at my ankle. It was so cold.

I stumbled forwards. A wall. I had to find a wall. My hands touched something fibrous, like the surface of a dry leaf. I desperately traced along it, running my hand up and down its height to see if it turned into a staircase at any point. It continued on and then it turned sharply. I stretched out my other hand, trying to find the other wall to indicate a doorway. Nothing.

At my knee. I was beginning to shiver and I clenched my teeth together to keep them from chattering. I followed the wall and it turned again, and again. This exceeded the bounds of the house, I realized. I'd been walking for too long. I'd made too many turns. Where the fuck *was I?*

And then the water was at my waist and I struggled to move, for its consistency was akin to mud and it dragged at my body, pulling me back. All I could think was forwards, forwards. Keep moving, keep feeling for a wall with trembling fingertips.

The water was at my chest. I remembered what it felt like, when the shulikun pulled me under. When I almost drowned. And I began to panic, my lungs fluttered and my breath came so fast I was dizzy and I stumbled and staggered, consumed with the desperate thought that I just had to keep going because there was nothing else I could do.

The water got to my chin and that was when the floor vanished. I began to tread water, trying to keep my head above the surface, but it began to rise so quickly and the consistency was thick, like it was *pulling* me down and I was dragged under. It felt like falling, like I was tumbling in a current that was taking me deeper into the morass, and I curled around the cup I still had clutched in my hands. I clamped my fingers over the improvised cover for it - layers of plastic wrap and rubber bands - because that was all I could think to do in my panic. I couldn't spill the cup. He would be so angry. I couldn't let it spill.

Then I remember nothing else until I woke in a strange place, wrapped in blankets and lying next to a fireplace.

THE MASTER OF THE VANISHING HOUSE

Posted Jan 10 2020 22:39:38 GMT-0500

I woke in a room with wooden floors and beige striped wallpaper. The fireplace was brick and a handful of logs burned heartily inside its mouth. An iron poker and shovel hung on a squat stand next to it. I sat up, slowly, letting the faded quilt fall off my shoulders and onto the floor. The cup was still clutched in my hands and Saint Nicholas's mantle was over my shoulders, the clasp securely fastened between my collarbones.

"You were caught out in the rain," a voice from behind me said. It felt familiar. "Do you remember?"

"I do," I whispered.

It'd been raining. The campers had taken shelter on the front porch and I'd gone looking for them.

"You were out in the cold so long you were hypothermic," the voice continued gently. "Just sit by the fire a bit longer. I'm here for you. I'll always protect you."

Something stirred in the back of my mind. Never in my life had anyone said they'd protect me. I remember my own mother, the strength of her arms, the lines of her muscles as she held something down against the ground, her grip taut on a knife handle.

"We can't protect you," she'd said. "You'll have to learn to do this on your own."

And she'd slit the monster's throat and let it bleed out into the dirt.

I wondered who this voice was, then, that it would make such a promise to me. It no longer felt as familiar as it did, more like a voice I'd heard in a dream. I could feel the edges of my memories fraying the more I tried to examine them, trying to place who it was that was behind me.

"You were so cold and exhausted when I brought you inside," it continued. Its tone was soothing. I felt heavy, listening to it, and it was an effort to keep my eyes open. "Do you want to sleep some more? You can sleep as much as you want. You don't have to fight anymore, not in my house. You can finally rest."

I slumped to the ground, laying down on my side and I stared at the fire. It blurred before my eyes and I teetered there on the verge of sleep, but then I shifted, trying to get my head into a more comfortable angle, and the pin of Saint Nicholas's mantle pricked my collarbone.

The voice was *over* me. I couldn't see it, it remained just out of my eyeshot, but I felt its presence hovering over my body like a shroud. I felt it draw the blanket up and lay it against my shoulder. Its touch reminded me of dry leaves.

"Do you love me?" the voice whispered.

Something felt off. I fingered the edge of the mantle I wore. It was the source of my warmth, I realized. Not the fire. I stretched out my fingers towards the flames and felt no heat.

"You don't want my love," I murmured. "Everyone I love dies."

A hiss and the presence recoiled. I continued reaching out, until my fingers touched the flames and then my entire hand was in the fire and it licked at my skin and I felt nothing but cold air. I felt the drowsiness slipping away and I pushed myself up, then I stood, taking the skull cup as I did.

I turned. The room vanished into darkness beyond the edge of the firelight and I heard a creaking noise, like a strained rope swaying back and forth, and ragged, uneven breathing. It paused, I heard the catch in the back of its throat, and it spoke again.

"If you will not love me," it hissed, "will you worship me?"

I reached to the side and my hand closed on the handle of the iron poker. It felt real enough. I took it with me and stepped forwards, to the edge of the light.

"I worship no god and no power," I murmured mechanically. "Worship demands obedience and the only obligations I will carry is to my land and my family."

I stepped into the darkness. I no longer heard the creak of the wooden floor as I pressed forwards, straining to place the movement of the rope and the ragged breathing. Somewhere above me. I hefted my improvised weapon uneasily.

"Do you *fear* me?"

The fire sputtered and died. I felt its breath stir the hair on the back of my head.

"I fear death," I snarled. I whirled and swung and the poker passed through empty air. I backed up. "I fear failure. But I don't fear *you!* Show yourself, master of the vanishing house!"

The quality of the air changed. It thinned. It left a faint, metallic taste on my lips and then I could see. There was no light source, merely a lifting of the darkness and before me hung the master of the house. A human torso with the legs and head of a deer, hanging limp from the rope bound tightly around its legs. The fur was stained with black blood from where its bonds cut through its flesh. Its eyes were empty, black hollows where they once were, and dead moss hung off its antlers. Its wrists were bound together, the arms dangling lifelessly before it. It rotated slowly on the rope that held it aloft.

A line bisected its belly. Then it split open, the upper body tipping back to reveal the insides - a mouth with a black throat and a tongue and white teeth slick with something like ink. The liquid dribbled down its torso as it spoke, ran along the grooves of its antlers, and dripped onto the floor.

"Do you fear me now?" it rasped.

"Buddy, you are asking the wrong person," I replied. "I have a dead girl knocking on my window every single night and every morning I get to listen to her be dragged off by a monstrous beast. And that's probably among the *least* of the horrific things I've witnessed. Now *where is the sheriff?!*"

I brandished my iron poker for effect. I'm not sure it made a difference.

"He didn't love me," the mouth said. "He wouldn't worship me. And he *certainly* didn't fear me."

"He's alive, though."

The candle was still burning, up until the moment I set someone on fire with it. I didn't think that extinguishing the candle would actually kill him; it was a representation of his life, not his life itself.

"I kept him. I keep *all* of them. Even the ones that die."

"For *what?*"

It told me, its words rolling out of its mouth like the toll of a bell. They echoed in my ears, sharp like needles, and I scratched futilely at my own skin to dislodge them. The inhuman things of this world can die, it said. We kill them. But there are always more - another river spirit to drown the unwary, another hunter to stalk the lonely caught out after sundown. They exist because at some point, long ago, someone made them *persist*. So that they would not fade away when the sun rose and banished the terrors of the night like the morning fog.

Someone loved them, like the saints. Or someone worshipped them, like the gods. Or someone feared them, like the monsters.

"It is so hard," the creature lamented and its sorrow was like a wave. I might have wept, if I hadn't come to kill it. "So hard to move my house. So hard to make you humans find it."

The rope continued to twist until the mouth rotated to face me. It stared at me with dead eyes in the deer's tattered skull. The rope stopped twisting. It hung there, immobile, until the belly split open again, the torso bobbing with every word.

"I will *make* you fear me."

It began to sway, the body jerked on the rope, and the line curved as it reached for me, those bound hands suddenly full of life and it stretched its fingers out to where I stood. The mouth gaped, the tongue running across its oily teeth, and more liquid spilled forth to land in thick clots on the ground like tar.

The darkness closed in again, robbing me of my only advantage: mobility. I swung wildly into empty air, turned, swung again. Keep moving, I thought, because while I could no longer see the monster perhaps I could keep it at bay if I just kept *moving*. I felt the brush of air touch my cheek, I swung and the iron poker continued its arc without ever meeting resistance. The creak of a rope, from somewhere to my right. I turned abruptly, swung again, stumbling because panic had not given me the presence of mind to catch my balance first.

A hand closed on my hair. A jerk - sudden bright agony - and I was suspended in midair. My feet kicked wildly at empty air; I clutched at the fingers holding me, gripped the ropes that were bound around its wrist, trying to get purchase enough to take the strain off the back of my head and give me leverage to fight. My fingers slipped off the ropes, wet with black blood, fastened so tight that it was like they were simply part of its skin. I felt liquid splatter on my forehead and slide down past my eyebrows and I closed my eyes tight, desperately hoping it wouldn't get in my eyes. My skin was numb along the path it traced. More fell onto my shoulders, like rain on the mantle I wore. The pin stabbed into my collarbone.

"Fear me," it hissed, more black liquid splattering on my neck and face. "*Fear me.*"

I let go of its fingers and my hand closed on the pin of Saint Nicholas's mantle instead. It came loose at my touch. I stabbed the heavy metal needle into the creature's wrist.

It shrieked. Its arms went slack and I fell, landing hard on the ground. My left foot struck the iron poker and I seized it and scrambled to my feet. From all around me came the frenzied shrieks of the creature and the groan of the rope as it struggled to support its frantic writhing.

The darkness lifted a fraction. Enough that I could see its writhing silhouette, jerking like a fish on a line. It was weak. It'd admitted as much. The house was so much to maintain and it wasn't getting the prey it needed. And while it suffered here in the darkness, starving and desperate, the sun continued to rise each morning and banish the terrors of the night once more. It knew its end was near.

Back when I decided to rescue the sheriff I swore that I would bring him out, even if I had nothing but my own will to drag him free with. It seemed that the time had come.

I am my mother's daughter, after all.

I said nothing. I felt nothing but a cold, smoldering rage. An old anger that was kindled to life long ago, perhaps when I watched my aunt choose her death, or perhaps when I helped my father bury his horses, or perhaps when I came of age by strangling my childhood friend. I hefted the iron poker in one hand and walked up to the master of the vanishing house. I raised it, let it fall, throwing my shoulder and hip into its path to lend it the mass of my body.

The meaty impact of each blow traveled up my arm, past my elbow and into my shoulder. I felt the resistance of bone and then the softness of when they shattered, the sickening crunch echoing through the chamber. The pin fell free from its shattered arms and landed at my feet.

"Fear me," it gasped and this time, it sounded like it was begging.

I continued to swing until my arms ached and I was panting, covered in sweat, and still the monstrosity made its demands, even as its head caved in and its body split and splattered like overripe fruit. Its legs and pelvis dangled from the ropes and the rest of it lay in a puddle of meat and blood and bone at my feet and still it cried out, barely a wet gurgle, but a cry nonetheless. And while it could no longer speak intelligibly, its words still echoed in my mind.

Love me.

Worship me.

Fear me.

Make me *last*.

I don't think that what I did next came from my own mind. I think I was guided and considering the source, I'm okay with that. I knelt beside its broken form. I whispered to it, gently, that it was okay, that this was the end and that it was time to go. The mantle had slipped from my shoulders and I picked it up and draped it out over the creature's body. The white fur flattened, melted into a single strip of cloth, and the whole of it elongated into a thin white sheet. A shroud. A funeral shroud. It fell over the monster's body, black bile soaking into the cloth, and then it was still and silent. And the words I spoke over it were not my own but they were a blessing, a rite, and then it was dead.

The house shook around me. It went still a few seconds later, groaning ponderously, and then another tremor shook it. I glanced around me in panic. An attic. The roof was close by overhead and the floors were roughly hewn wooden slats.

In the corner lay the sheriff.

I ran to him, dropping to my knees. He was breathing but he did not stir as I shook him. Around me, the house creaked and moaned and another shudder sent a shower of dust and wood splinters over my head and shoulders.

The cup. The last item.

I hastily jerked off the covering and forced it up to his lips. Tipped it and most of the liquid ran out and onto his chest, but some of it went into his mouth and I saw the movement of his throat as he swallowed. I gave him all of it - I had to - just to get some inside him. Still, he did not move, and behind me a beam collapsed, taking part of the floor with it as the house shook yet again.

The liquid alone wasn't enough. There had to be something else ingested before the poison activated. So I found a broken beam - easy enough, with the house collapsing around us - and I cut my palm open on a jagged splinter of wood.

I fed him my own blood.

And he came to and vomited black liquid onto the wooden floor. I threw his arm under my shoulders and yelled that we had to go, we had to move. He was dazed, but my words stirred him into action and he stood, shakily, and staggered along with me even as his body continued to convulse and bring up more and more of that sickly liquid, thick as tar.

We made it outside and were halfway to my aunt's car when the house collapsed behind us. I put the sheriff on the ground by the road and he continued to vomit into the grass. He'd be fine, I thought, and I went to the trunk of the car. I got one of the cans of gasoline out. And my aunt and I, we soaked the remains of the house and then burned it into ash.

I confess I'm a little disappointed that the current sheriff wasn't called out by someone reporting the blaze. The downside of the house appearing in remote areas, I suppose.

I should clarify the timeline real quick - the rescue occurred a few days ago. I rested a bit before typing all this out and the sheriff wanted to reconnect with his kids. He lost his wife to breast cancer some years before he vanished, but his kids are still in town. He doesn't remember much of the time that passed between when he entered the house and when I woke him up. For him, he walked into that house only a few days ago. It's going to be a challenge adjusting to the changes. That's why he's not going to take up his old job. He's a grandfather now and while he missed the birth of his eldest's child, he's determined to make up for it. I can't really blame him. I envy his children. I know what it's like to lose a father.

We've had some long talks, the sheriff and I, since the rescue.

This morning, however, we were ready to make the visit we'd been planning. We went to meet with the current sheriff.

We'd been keeping a low profile about the rescue so he had no idea what had happened. It was a hell of a shock when the old sheriff walked in the door behind me. One minute, the sheriff is wearing a shit-eating grin seeing me walk in, thinking that I was here to talk about selling the land, and the next minute he's white as a sheet, thinking he's seeing a ghost. Which is a reasonable thing to think. But no, the old sheriff was back, and he sat himself down in the only chair opposite the sheriff's desk and I stood at his shoulder.

And the old sheriff went on a lecture. Real calm and collected about it. Gently explained that the campground brought in a lot of money for a lot of people around here. That my family were upright citizens and an asset to the community and he'd done us a real disservice by bad-mouthing our names. The sheriff's job, he explained, was to make our lives easier by lending his assistance. Sometimes that was mere paperwork, sometimes it was cleaning up a body or two, and sometimes it meant a little more - like risking one's life to drag someone out of a vanishing house.

The sheriff squirmed uncomfortably at that. We all know that he wasn't the type to risk his life. Then the old sheriff leaned forwards and got to the most important part of his talk.

The threats.

"You're gonna be up for re-election at some point," the old sheriff said. "You know if I run against you, you gonna lose. So if you want to keep your job, you keep your head down and stop stirring up the town. And if you want to keep your life, you stay the hell away from Kate."

"My life?" he asked dumbly.

The sheriff continued on just as he had before. No smile. No change in tone. Just that matter-of-fact way of talking that impressed upon the recipient that he was a man that said what he meant and wasn't here to impress or intimidate - just here to state how things were going to go.

"You set foot on that campsite ever again to do anything but your damn job," the old sheriff said, "and I'll show up at your office and blow your brains out. And I'll just tell the town that you were working with some nasty evil thing and maybe you are or maybe you aren't but the town isn't going to question it, not if I'm the one saying it."

Then he leaned back, glanced up at me, and asked if I was happy with this arrangement.

"I'm not satisfied yet," I replied grimly.

I walked around the desk to where the sheriff sat. He recoiled from me. I slammed the skull cup down on the desk in front of him.

"Blood from what was already there," I said. "Blood freely given. And blood taken by force."

He didn't have much time to react. I knew what I was going to do and I moved quick, jabbing a thin pocket knife blade into his neck. I jerked it sideways and then blood gushed forth and I yanked it free, grabbed his hair, and held his head over the cup.

I didn't get much. Not before the old sheriff grabbed the back of my shirt and threw me off, slamming me into the wall of the office. He grabbed the sheriff's radio and started yelling for an ambulance to be sent. Then he yelled at me to *get out*.

So I did. I took the cup with me.

The sheriff didn't die. Amazingly, the ambulance arrived in time and they were helped by the fact that the old sheriff managed to reach *inside* the man's neck and pinch the artery shut and hold it shut until they arrived. It's incredible he didn't bleed to death. I'm a little disappointed. I'd intended for him to die, as the man with the skull cup had said that it would take a high cost to refill it. The lifeblood of my enemy seemed like it would suffice.

The old sheriff is a better person than I am.

Sadly, they expect the sheriff to recover. He took a couple transfusions but apparently you can survive with only one carotid artery intact. I didn't know that. The old sheriff updated me on his condition a few hours ago, along with a lecture on how I didn't need to solve *everything* with violence and I was too much like my mother. There's not going to be any further backlash for what I did. The old sheriff knows he owes me his life and the current sheriff knows I'm now untouchable by him.

I keep thinking of the master of the vanishing house. I deal with a lot of old beings but not all of them come out of humanity's history. Some are younger, crawling out of our collective cultural morass, slinking out of our shared subconscious and into our world. I guess that thing in there was just trying to hold on long enough to become a fixture in our world. I wonder how many others are trying to do the same and how many fail every day and vanish back into the night mist from which they were formed.

Now, I'm sure some of you are wondering if maybe I'm mistaken and the vanishing house will return or maybe it'll show up somewhere else.

I am not mistaken. I am certain of what I did.

It. Is. Dead.

And nothing can bring it back.

I'm a campground manager. It's been a rough Christmas season but with the old sheriff back I think I've gotten myself an ally - and hopefully some time. I could really use a bit of peace around here. Take some naps. Paint some more; I like painting. Tell you all about more of the rules. That sort of thing. I think I deserve a brief reprise. I've had a great victory, after all. I killed the master of the vanishing house.

Next on my list: the man with no shadow.

RULE #5 - THE GRAY WORLD

Posted Jan 21 2020 22:44:23 GMT-0400

I've been thinking about alternate worlds a bit, for obvious reasons. They're hardly a new occurrence. The old stories are riddled with them; fantastic worlds of wonder and danger into which the unwary can fall or through which the heroic must journey to reach the object of their quest. Narnia was hardly original. And yet what *is* new in our modern era is these worlds that lie nestled within our own are losing their wonder, bit by bit, until only danger remains.

Like they're decaying.

I don't know why this is. Things change. Old creatures dwindle and new creations are born and I'm at a loss to explain how or why. Perhaps now that we've explored our world and named all the continents and dived into the ocean's depths and even now peer at our skies with a cold, cynical rationality, we've lost the wonder of the unknown. The wardrobe is nothing but a dusty wardrobe and our Narnias are tattered remnants declining into forgotten graveyards for the creatures they still house.

I suppose I do pity the master of the vanishing house, even if I do not regret what I did. That is my father's influence.

Some of you have expressed interest in rule #5. If you think you're lost, stop and look at your surroundings. If the everything appears a little gray, like the color has seeped from the world, then you're no longer in the campsite. Seek out the highest hill and beg whatever you find there to return you to the camp. Pray it is in a benevolent mood.

Why or how a world came to exist inside my campground is beyond my understanding. I can't claim to comprehend most of the creatures on my land - I know some things about them, but there is still so much that eludes me. I don't know how they came to be or why the wound up here. I just deal with them as best as I can.

I have not been inside the gray world, myself. I first heard about it from my uncle. Yes, the uncle that the man with no shadow murdered. (while it wasn't his hand that severed my uncle's head, the person that did was merely a tool, and so I consider him solely responsible) My uncle liked to tell stories. He embellished liberally and it was often hard to distinguish where the truth ended and the fiction began, so I did not consider him a reliable source of information about the creatures on our land.

When I began to write my rules he came to the house and said I should include something about the gray world. He then told me about his own encounter with it and the creatures within and I listened with the interest of someone that is too old for ghost stories and had something better to be doing at the time. However, the name of the campers in his story seemed familiar and when I consulted the records (the real ones, not the ones the police keep) they did turn up as missing persons. Presumed dead, but still labeled as missing only because we never found the bodies.

I began to dig through more accounts, searching for campers that had come back alive, found wandering the woods, deeply shaken and reluctant to share their experiences. From some of them we only got fragments. Others were more willing to divulge, once given a token of confidence that the interviewer (always one of my family) would believe them. These accounts go back to my grandparent's generation, which is when we started keeping better records. After sorting them into themes and setting aside the ones that weren't relevant I was forced to admit that there was some truth to what my uncle said.

The gray world was real.

I added it to the rules.

It is a rare occurrence, but I am uneasy with it, as it feels *bigger* than most of the other things on the campground. We can deal with monsters or vengeful spirits or the like. But there is a weight to the gray world and much like the creature in the darkness... I would prefer my campers to cross its path as little as possible.

Let me tell you what happened to my uncle. I'm afraid I'm not as boisterous as he was and will be stripping out some of the 'flair' that I could not corroborate.

I wish you all could have met my uncle and heard the story from him directly. Maybe I should have written it down while he was still alive and the personality he lent his storytelling wasn't down in the grave with his corpse.

We all have our regrets, I suppose.

Before cellphones were commonplace we had to find alternatives for responding to emergencies within the campgrounds. By emergency I mean things like bee stings resulting in an allergic reaction or severe dehydration requiring medical attention or noise from the repaver on the nearby road triggering a seizure in someone. We started patrolling the campsite with four-wheelers and radios. For our really large events we have a volunteer secondary patrol, comprised of the campers themselves. They get a golf cart and a radio. They help with what they can (usually that's just giving directions) and can radio back to the command staff in the case of a real emergency. Cellphones have reduced the need, but we still run the patrols.

This all works fairly well but sometimes things go awry, such as the infamous incident where a volunteer left their golf cart unattended with the keys in the ignition and it was stolen and taken on a joyride before being deposited in my neighbor's lake. He was not happy about it. Nor were we. Anyway, this is what my uncle assumed had happened again when he got a call about a patrol cart that had stopped responding. He went out to scour the area they were supposed to be in.

He didn't notice that something was amiss until his four-wheeler's engine died. It was daylight and he wasn't being very observant, as it was a relatively safe time of day. He looked around with a growing sense of unease after his four-wheeler went silent and rolled to a halt, however. The world had a strange quality to it, an ashen cast, and the ground seemed darker - thicker, like it was saturated with the weight of all the color that had drained from the sky and the trees. There was no sound. No wind, no distant lull of voices from nearby campsites. Just the faint crunch of dry leaves under his feet as he got off the vehicle and even that was muted.

He went ahead on foot. The ground in front of him sloped upwards and he quickly realized that the hill should have crested long before this, that it was steep but short and it would have leveled out before his legs started to cramp with exhaustion. He paused for a moment to catch his wind.

He felt disoriented, he'd say. Confused, mostly, and perhaps a little scared.

And that fear kept him moving, because if he stayed in one place for too long it'd grow and grow until it ate him up from the inside. This is how he came across the missing volunteers. They were further up the hill, standing beside their golf cart. Two women. The younger one was crying silently. The older was trying to get the radio to work. They both looked relieved at my uncle's arrival. They'd been trying to get the golf cart to start again, the older woman said. They'd gone up the hill a little bit and realized they were lost, because their camp should be just on the right after the treeline ended, but the treeline wasn't ending. Which was crazy, the woman continued, because she *recognized* this hill and they were in the right place.

So my uncle confirmed what they both feared but didn't dare say. They weren't in the campground anymore. The younger woman stopped crying at that and suggested they all go back and retrace their steps and try to find a way out.

This is where I doubt my uncle's narrative. No one else reported there being something in the trees, following them. People either make it to the top of the hill and come back or they don't. But my uncle swears that this is what happened - they heard the branches above them creak and then snap and something came crashing down towards them. My uncle had only seconds to react - he grabbed the person nearest him, the older woman, and threw her aside. Then he was knocked off his feet and hit the ground hard, his shoulder absorbing the impact.

Close by crouched a creature, a bit larger than a human with the skull of a monstrous bird, a thick neck of glossy black feathers, and wings that ended in human hands at the joint. Its body ended at its midsection, the feathers and skin hanging in rough tatters and the remnants of its spine dragged along the ground. Beneath its bulk lay the young woman and my uncle could hear her faint whimpering, the only sound she could make in her terror. The creature's hand was against the back of her head, holding her to the dirt.

My uncle scrambled to his feet. He seized the older woman's arm. Pulled her away, urging her to run. And she did, for a minute or less, before some sort of reason overcame her terror. She snatched her arm out of my uncle's grip.

Not without her friend, she said. She wasn't leaving without her friend.

And she went back.

My uncle yelled at her to stop, that it was too late - always too late - that they can't save everyone.

Hah. Our family motto, I suppose.

My uncle left them both behind and continued up the hill. He half-ran, half-walked, his lungs burning for oxygen as the hill stretched on and on. It was growing steeper. His progress was tortured; by now the angle was such that he could put his hands out and touch the dirt and his progress was on all fours, clawing his way up the packed earth.

Behind him came the whisper of feathers, of something brittle dragging against the ground.

Then the treeline broke and there was nothing but mute gray sky in front of him. He stumbled, swaying with exhaustion, almost sobbing with relief that his feet were on level ground once more.

He risked one backwards glance. He could see the bottom of the hill, perhaps thirty feet away, and his four-wheeler sat at the base and not far from it was the missing golf cart.

We never got that four-wheeler or the golf cart back. I suppose they're still in the gray world.

Here is where he would end the story with only a brief footnote for how he escaped. The creature at the top permitted him to leave, he'd say, with the vagueness of someone that doesn't want to talk about what they experienced. I attributed the scarcity of details to an impediment to the memory, as it seemed odd that someone who would gleefully recount the creature's severed spine would suddenly stop with their descriptions. It mirrored the other campers' accounts as well. That unease, that sudden reluctance when relating what they found at the top of the hill.

My aunt talked a lot about my uncle while we were searching for the vanishing house. She told me things that he'd never spoken about to anyone but her. Of the top of the hill and the tree and what its branches contained. How it spoke to him and then asked if he still wanted to return to his own world.

How he considered it for a long time and then made his decision.

He didn't tell her everything of what the being at the top of the hill said. Better she not know, he insisted. Better they live like the day would never come.

He'd learned the date and manner of his death, my aunt said. And the being in the tree had asked if he wished to remain, so that his death would not find him.

I miss my uncle. Maybe this story is how I'm grieving for him.

I want to kill the man with no shadow for what he did but I don't think I can do it on my own. I've been searching for the lady with extra eyes but her house remains hidden. She can only be found when she wants visitors. It is not unusual for her to go missing for some length of time, but it is certainly inconvenient. And the man with the skull cup… well, I don't really know what to make of *that* situation.

Let me just make this real clear: I am not in love with him. I am intrigued by his assistance but please remember that he put a knife to my throat and made me believe he was going to kill me and so while his help is appreciated, I am still quite terrified of him.

You see, I returned the cup as I had promised I would. I explained that I'd emptied it while rescuing the sheriff but had refilled it with my blood, freely given, and the blood of my enemy, forcefully taken. He accepted the cup without saying a word. It was after sunset and his face was hidden in shadow so I could not see his expression. I only felt the weight of his gaze. He left in silence and took the cup with him. I haven't seen him since.

So I really have no idea if he's okay with all of this or if he's going to exact some kind of revenge at a later time. I'm just going to avoid him for a little bit, *just in case*.

I'm a campground manager. I'm not doing this alone, however. I've called a family meeting. Everyone that is on the family tree. I've explained the situation and told them that this is going to be one of the bad years. I've seen signs. And we're going to prepare for it in any way we can. I'll keep doing this - telling you about the campground and maybe it'll help or maybe it'll just be an outlet for my own purposes… but I'll take whatever I can at this point.

I CAN'T BELIEVE WE'RE TALKING ABOUT THE LIGHTS YET AGAIN

Posted Jan 28 2020 22:41:08 GMT-0400

What the hell, people. How is this so hard to understand? I have a set of rules to ensure everyone stays safe and initially I didn't think I even needed to include #3 because it's so obvious but apparently it *isn't* because here we are talking about them. Again.

Maybe you can tell me what I'm doing wrong because clearly people aren't capable of figuring this one out.

Okay, the lights aside, I've mostly been focused on how to deal with the man with no shadow. We've been taking some precautions. Bryan has set the dogs to patrolling the campground. I wanted to have them guard the grove itself, but Bryan refused as he didn't want them getting too close. We don't know his capabilities. He didn't want to endanger his animals. Our hope was that by making the *rest* of the campground hostile to his presence, we could trap him inside his grove anyway and limit his access to new servants. I've also instructed my winter staff to work in pairs - which is typical procedure for a bad year - but I've also started rotating the pairs so that two people aren't together for too long. Finally, anyone that enters the campground is accompanied by a staff member.

I have to resolve this before we reopen in March.

I've been looking through our records to see if there's anything that can be gleaned about the man with no shadow. There's not much. His actions are less overt than our more violent inhabitants and he is careful to avoid my staff. I did find one thing of interest, however, in my mother's journals. She didn't write a lot down. Tidbits of things she found important to remember in a disjointed notation that surely made sense to her. I've been through them a handful of times now and the pain of seeing her handwriting is not worth the information I've gained. This time, however, I knew what I was looking for. I found it in three lines. "The man with no shadow" followed by two dates.

They were meaningless for me, but I shared them with the old sheriff. He noticed something interesting about one of them. It was the first year that the new sheriff ran against him for office. He didn't win, not until the old sheriff vanished, but he ran every year after that. It struck the old sheriff as odd at the time, because he'd never really thought that the current sheriff was someone that would ever want the job.

He's going to look into what was happening in the area around the time of the other date. As I feared, the man with no shadow appears to have been planning for this for some time now.

And he has certainly not been idle after the loss of the current sheriff as one of his pawns.

We had a delivery at the campground earlier this week. Our old propane tank was dangerously rusted and I'd ordered a replacement. This is not a propane tank you can pick up at your local hardware store to fuel your grill. It is large. They sent it via a truck. My cousin radioed me that the truck was here, sitting next to where the tank was to go, but the driver was nowhere to be seen. None of my staff knew where he was or how long he'd been missing.

I got my jacket and told my staff I was going to check the glade. The clearing with the stones covered in moss, where the man with no shadow resides. It didn't have to be said why. One of them softly told me to be careful. I'm not sure which it was.

The man with no shadow was waiting for me. He stood tall and willowy next to the missing truck driver, his red hair brilliant in the sunlight. His arm was draped over the man's shoulder, as if they were friends, but his nails dug into flesh and a thin bead of blood trickled down the truck driver's chest. He was stripped to the waist, his skin reddened from the cold in the early stages of frostbite. Five holes bled slowly on his chest, clogged with congealing blood, the black-crimson of a deep wound. They were arrayed around where his heart was, like fingers had been thrust through his flesh.

From the dried blood on the man with no shadow's fingers I have to believe that was exactly what happened.

"Speak *sparingly*," I hissed, "or I walk away."

A thin smile of acknowledgement. Amusement that I would abandon his captive to save myself.

"How did you get him here?" I asked.

"The lights can be... *coerced*, sometimes," he replied carefully.

Seriously, how fucking hard is it to not follow the lights? You shouldn't even have to read the rules to realize this. It was a whole *thing* in Lord of the Rings and everyone has watched Lord of the Rings, right?

"You don't release people without asking for something in return," I said grimly. "Name your price."

"Oh no, you can have this one for free," he purred.

He shoved the truck driver forwards. The man stumbled across the boundary of the man with no shadow's lair. His eyes cleared and he looked about him, startled, bewildered by his surroundings. He stared down at the wounds on his chest.

"You don't let go of anyone," I said, gently pulling the truck driver to stand behind me. He moved as I directed, made passive by his disorientation.

"I do when they're useless. And this one is no good anymore, on account of the mark I put on him. You know. The one that taints his soul with my presence. Gives him my *scent*."

He turned abruptly, laughing, and walked off. I grabbed the truck driver's arm and drew him away from the glade, back towards the house. He needed to get into some warmth, I reasoned. It wasn't bitterly cold, not like some other winters we've had, but he'd clearly been outside for too long. I could figure out what the man with no shadow had done - and why - later. He tried to ask me what was happening and who that man was, but I told him I'd explain it once we were inside.

We didn't make it to the house before I heard the baying of the hounds.

When I hired Bryan his dogs came with him. It was simply understood that they were part of him, that he wasn't whole unless they were nearby. I remember growing up with him, how he was a quiet, reclusive boy and how the dogs would wait outside the school. At recess he would play chase with them, far from the other children, eschewing human company. He rarely spoke.

I never paid him much attention, not until he showed up at my campsite inquiring about a job opening. His dogs sat behind him during the interview, staring at me and wagging their tails.

They should have died of old age long ago but I think we all know they are not normal dogs.

They remind me of wolfhounds, tall and shaggy, but they are muscular instead of lean and there is a sharpness to their muzzles that is more akin to a wolf. Their coats are gray-black, the color of soot, deepening to charcoal in dim light. Their voices can be heard across the entire campground.

Now they echoed from all around us.

The truck driver paused uneasily and I hesitated, my mind screaming at me the last thing the man with no shadow had said.

The marks on the driver's chest.

His *scent*.

We were halfway between the grove and the house. There was no other shelter easily available. I tightened my grip on the man's arm, digging my nails into his frozen flesh, and I yelled at him to run. It was hard to get him to move. I pulled him along, breaking into a sprint myself, and after a handful of stumbling, reluctant steps he fell into a trot.

Not fast enough. Not nearly fast enough.

"The dogs!" I yelled at him. "They'll kill you!"

That got him moving. Some primal instinct finally shook itself free in his mind and he began to outpace me, drawing ahead with his longer legs and my lungs burned as I sucked in cold air in an effort to keep pace.

I caught a glimpse of a large shape in my peripheral vision - black-gray - and then it slammed into my side.

The hound threw itself between us. I was knocked bodily aside by a mass of fur and muscle and then the dog was over top of me, legs splayed, its head lowered and a growl rumbling deep in its chest. I clawed at its fur, searching for a collar, but it would not be moved.

It had to protect me from the man with no shadow, after all.

I opened the channel on my radio.

"Bryan!" I screamed. "Recall your dogs! Recall your FUCKING dogs!"

The truck driver had managed to stay on his feet and he was continuing to run, across the stretch of grass that led to the house. Another black-gray shape peeled out of the forest, another came from the other direction, and then the entire pack was bearing down on him and I knew it was too late.

They surrounded him, running to either side, snapping ivory teeth at his legs. Searching for an opening. I could only watch in horror, helpless to stop this, my radio clutched uselessly between my fingers.

One lunged for his leg. The man leapt away, twisting his body out its reach - and putting his back to another one of the dogs. It stretched out its head and its jaws clamped down on his calf. It spun its hindquarters, bracing against the ground, halting its forward momentum in one fluid gesture and the man's leg bent sharply sideways at the knee. His body jerked like a whip cracking, tumbling towards the ground, and then he vanished from sight under a mass of bodies. His screams did not last long. At least they gave him the mercy of a quick death by tearing out his throat first.

Only then did the dog standing over me move. I walked slowly towards where the rest of the pack were still dismembering the poor man's remains. On the radio, Bryan was frantically calling my name. I told him it was okay, I was safe, but I needed him to meet me at my house.

I covered the body with a tarp before he got there. Bryan still saw the blood on the muzzles of his dogs that were waiting patiently in the yard and he entered my house uneasily, warily watching me and surely noticing the pained, resigned expression I bore.

I had him sit down and then I told him what had happened.

Bryan was inconsolable. He'd recalled them, he said, sitting in my living room with his head bowed. His eyes were wide with shock and his voice shook. He'd recalled them and they'd *heard* him, but they had their quarry and they would not be dissuaded.

But they're your *dogs*, I insisted. Aren't you their master? And he just shook his head, vehemently, and then he stood and went to the door. He whispered that he was sorry. And that he'd remove them from the campgrounds.

I watched him leave from the window. His dogs crowded around him and he started to pet one on the head in reflex and then he hesitated. He lifted his hand, stuffed it in his pocket, and continued walking without touching any of them. They followed him, uncomprehending.

I regret calling them his 'fucking dogs'. I think he feels this is his failure to bear. But I'm the one that told him to set them to patrolling the campsite, to chase down and kill the man with no shadow if they caught his scent. I'm the one that knows the folklore, the stories of how the guise or essence of another can be transferred through symbolic acts - a piece of clothing, an ointment, or in this case: a mark over the heart.

I just didn't make the connection. This possible outcome eluded me.

Some of you have said I should try to outwit the man with no shadow. I am not nearly so clever. I know things, but I don't always see the patterns, and I lack the cunning malice necessary for navigating the man with no shadow's web.

More of its strands are visible. Too late, however. It feels like I don't notice them until they're wrapped around my neck.

I like getting things in the mail. I suspect that my kickstarter habit is in part fueled by the excitement of getting small packages and not being entirely sure what their contents are until they're opened. For this reason, I am typically highly aware of whether the mailman has come today or not and what time he generally arrives. Yesterday, he sat at my mailbox for a good four minutes and I finally went out to his truck to see what the matter was.

He nervously gave me a piece of mail that was not mine. A flyer, addressed to someone in town. He'd been delivering them all day, he said, and he knew he shouldn't be doing this but he wanted me to see what it was people were receiving all across town.

He likes us. We make his job easy when our big events happen by setting up a camp "post office" where he can dump all the packages of things people forgot and ordered off Amazon and then we handle distributing them to the campers that come to collect.

He drove off before I could open the flyer. I read it, went inside, read it again. Maybe screamed some profanity for a little bit. Calmed down enough to take a photo, considered texting everyone I knew in outrage, realized that would be a *terrible* idea and sent it to the old sheriff instead.

So. Initial thoughts. It's a real nice flyer. Good use of stock art for the background. And I really just want to stab whoever made it in the neck except some of you have pointed out that maybe I shouldn't resort to violence to silence my enemies and the old sheriff has also said something along those lines so I guess there's nothing I can really do right now except be really fucking pissed off.

The emblem in the lower left concerns me, however. I circled it. A black sheep. My current theory is that this is a calling-card of sorts and if it is, there's a sinister message in it.

A family member made this flyer. A "black sheep" who disagrees with us keeping the land within the family.

This is a delicate situation, both in how to handle it and my own emotions. You see, there's one person that comes to mind as the black sheep. While they haven't been vocal, they've never been comfortable with the campground in its current state and they have a very strong outside influence to turn them against us.

My brother's wife is pregnant. He called me recently, from his car as he was running errands. He fears she will divorce him after the baby is born. She is afraid that their child will be pressured to carry on the family business. I adamantly denied that. It was a choice, I said. If she wasn't interested, there were plenty of cousins and they had children of their own. We were a big family. *Someone* would step up.

Then he confessed his own fear. Perhaps she *should* take their child and go, he said. Perhaps they should keep their child away from the campground because he wasn't afraid that the child would feel obligated, he was afraid it would *want* to be the next owner of our land.

If she asks for a divorce he said, his voice breaking, he wasn't going to contest it.

Or perhaps he could coerce me to sell the campground and then he could keep his wife *and* child.

I haven't decided what to do yet. This is just a hunch. It could be someone under the control of the man with no shadow and it doesn't necessarily have to be family; just someone masquerading as them.

I wish I were closer to my brother. I wish I could be certain.

I'm a campground manager. I'm not sure who I can trust anymore. Even with the current sheriff... *dealt with*... someone is still trying to turn the town against me and they may be someone I love. I cannot even trust my own defenses for the man with no shadow has demonstrated that he can subvert them and turn them against me.

At least. I think he's safe. He resisted the master of the vanishing house, after all. And I just... need *someone*. I need just *one* person on my side.

I'm not sure I can do this, otherwise.

RULE #15 – THE LADY WITH EXTRA EYES

Posted Feb 05 2020 20:56:55 GMT-0400

To start with, I feel I need to update everyone on the dog situation because it was alarming and understandably upsetting to most of you. Yes, Bryan still loves them. He's just deeply unnerved by what they did and it's taking a little time before he can trust them again. They *are* back on the campground. They're not allowed to go off on their own anymore. They have to stay with Bryan. That's the compromise we came to so that he could feel safe again, knowing they couldn't hurt anyone else while under his watchful eye.

Anyway.

Many of you have asked about the lady with extra eyes. I've known her since I was a child. I don't remember how we first met. She's always been a presence in my life. When I was in school and able to understand that our land was different from the land of my classmates, I asked where she'd come from and why she was here.

She has been on our land for a long time, my father said. That's all he knew. We could visit her whenever we wanted, so long as we returned to the house before sundown. My brother went with me for a while, but after the horse incident he lost interest which I suppose is understandable. He would stay inside, doing his homework or reading a book while sitting next to the fireplace. She would serve him tea and cookies and then bring a plate out to me, as I liked to spend my time up in the branches of a large oak that grew in her front yard. It wasn't a yard like we think of one, with cut grass and flower beds with carefully defined boundaries. The ground was covered with dead leaves, delineated from the rest of the forest by a short wooden fence. The entire area was carpeted with bloodroot and I had to pick my way carefully to the tree, not wanting to trample the delicate flowers.

The tree is gone now. Only a shallow depression remains to mark where it once stood. It died during my freshman year of college. I came home for spring break and found it gone. The woman with extra eyes said that it was sad that I no longer sat in its branches - for I had stopped in highschool - and my departure had convinced it that it's time had come. Its sap grew sluggish, it didn't put out new leaves, and then it died. I didn't quite understand her words at the time, but I think I do now.

I think the tree was someone I once knew.

I know that sounds ominous, but the lady with extra eyes has not harmed anyone on my campground. Why is she taking up one of my precious rule slots, then? I have said over and over that I only put the most dangerous threats on my list, so that my campers are not overwhelmed and discard the rules entirely. Why waste space on someone that is not going to hurt anyone?

I need my campers to trust the people that are here to keep them safe. That is why my staff all wear the same uniform; to make them easily recognizable as a figure of authority and safety.

They need to trust the lady with extra eyes as well.

About a year after I first published the rules we had one of the lesser threats appear on the campground. These are the creatures that aren't on the list because we can typically clear them out before they harm anyone. We spotted the signs pretty quickly. Perhaps you've seen the same indications when you've been out in the woods. Have you ever come across a patch of a substance like yellow-white snot, lying in thick globs on the floor of the forest?

Sometimes it's just jelly fungus.

Sometimes it's not.

This is how you can tell the difference. Prick your finger and let a few drops of blood fall onto it. If the mass swallows it, contracting around the blood and absorbing it, taking on a fleshy, pink color; then it is not fungus and you should return to your home and not go into the woods after dark.

I do not know if there is an official name for these things. They fit a number of descriptions, but only in fragments. Or perhaps I simply haven't found the right name. My expertise *is* limited.

At the campground, we call them 'yarn balls'. It sounds less terrifying than the more accurate description of 'arm balls' and we can reference them freely in front of campers without anyone being alarmed.

They're formed from a central gelatinous mass of flesh. Initially, they start with only two or three arms, but they seek out more by finding human victims and ripping their limbs off. They attach these stolen arms to their own body until they are all you can see, sticking out haphazardly from its core. They are fast, clawing their way across the ground, half-skittering and half-rolling as their multitude of arms drag them along. The more arms they have, the faster they are, and the more dangerous.

When they run out of room for more arms, they start disemboweling their victims and adding the loops of intestine to their core so that they can grow larger and have more surface area for arms. My parent's notes say that if we start finding victims missing both their insides *and* their arms, that the campsite needs to close and teams of five need to sweep the area until the yarn ball is found and dispatched.

A staff member found evidence of their presence and brought it to me, wrapped carefully in a handkerchief. It quivered like a piece of fat, cut fresh from the haunch of a pig, and it convulsed around the drop of blood I dripped onto its surface. I told my staff to watch the roads leading into the forest, to keep track of what campers went down from the fields, and to ensure they were out by nightfall. We had an event at the campground but it was a small one and they'd contained their campers to the plain where there are no trees.

The rest of my staff were to check in on the campers themselves and tell them to stay out of the woods after dark. A mountain lion was spotted in the area, they said. Nothing to worry about, they'd stay away from people, but don't go wondering about on your own. It might be willing to attack an isolated individual.

This was not entirely a lie. Yarn balls do avoid large groups of people. They prefer to pick off solitary individuals who are far from the safety of others.

Then, at sundown, five of my staff and myself got our gear and headed out into the woods. We went off singly, for one person is enough to deal with a yarn ball given the right equipment. All of us carried a radio on a dedicated channel with one person remaining at the office to help coordinate between the six of us. I had my shotgun. The others had guns as well, whatever they felt comfortable with. And all of us carried a primary source of light with a couple backups - just in case.

Yarn balls are repulsed by light. Shine a flashlight on them and they'll scatter, but they're agile, and will promptly try to attack you from another angle. Our solution is a heavy-duty lantern light, mounted on a pole so we can hold it above our heads and encompass the entire area around us in light. It works *very* well and if you attach the pole to a harness you can still carry a gun, allowing us to hunt them with almost no risk to ourselves.

If you see a light bobbing through the woods, well above the height of a human head, it might be one of us. I don't recommend following it, though. It might also be *the* lights. Just go back to your campsite and stay there until morning.

No, I'm not adding this to the rules. I have enough trouble with getting people to follow the much simpler "don't follow the lights" one.

I was investigating a white clump of some congealed mass, trying to determine if it was part of a yarn ball, a kind of mushroom, or leftover vomit from a camper that had drank too much in previous evenings when my radio crackled. A camper had slipped off into the woods. They'd not taken any of the roads, thereby eluding my sentries. One of their friends had informed my staff, telling them that he'd decided he wanted to look for the mountain lion, because he was - in her words - "a damn fucking idiot".

This is what I have to deal with. I know some people have expressed concern about visiting my campground for fear of running afoul of the rules but honestly, unless you're this willfully stupid, you should be fine.

I swore and straightened, my circle of light swaying erratically around me. We'd prioritize finding him first, I instructed my hunters grimly, and then we could resume searching for the yarn ball.

I was the one that found the man. He wasn't hard to locate, on account of how he was noisily crashing through the forest, breaking branches and stumbling over the uneven terrain with every step. Certainly, he'd tried for stealth by leaving his flashlight behind, but if there *was* a mountain lion in the area the racket he was making would have hopefully scared it off.

It had also attracted the yarn ball.

He wasn't *stumbling* like a drunk through the woods because he was clumsy - he was trying to *flee*. I heard his panicked half-cries as I approached and saw him running, flailing, trying to fight his way through the forest, blinded by the darkness, as a rolling, tumbling ball the size of a large dog continued to gain on him. It clawed its way forwards, each arm snapping out and seizing the soft earth with its fingers, yanking it forwards and then another hand latched onto the soil and another and another.

I broke into a run, yelling here, to me, to me. I got his attention. I saw his face, pale white in the scant moonlight, and saw the pink mass of flesh behind him and knew he wouldn't make it.

Then the lady appeared, like she'd stepped out of the night, like it was a curtain that had been drawn across her and she'd merely shrugged it aside. She touched his shoulder, grabbed his arm just above the elbow, and spun him about and pulled him close to her. The yarn ball stopped where it was, dragging its fingers into the dirt to halt its momentum, and then it reversed its course and... fled.

I considered going after it. Perhaps I should have. But my first priority was to my campers and so I went to him, to where he stood with his hands on his knees, doubled over, wheezing and coughing. The lady had her hand on his back and all those eyes furrowed in concern over the camper in front of her.

"So the mountain lion story is bullshit," I said as I approached. "But you're safe now. I can take you back to camp."

He looked up at me in abject relief. Then he turned to face his rescuer.

She smiled at him, her cheeks dimpling around the eyes set closest to her lips. They all blinked in unison.

And the man screamed, turned, and ran back into the woods, out of the circle of light that would have kept him safe.

I took one step to follow, yelling at him to stop. The lady gently put a hand on my arm to restrain me. I knew better than to shrug her off and I waited by her side as he ran further and further into the woods, until a mass fell from the trees overhead and onto his back, dragging him to the ground. Another skittered out of the darkness, and then a third, and I understood why the lady had kept me from going after him.

We were dealing with a nest.

They quarreled over their prey, grabbing at each other as much as they grabbed at his limbs, until finally he wiggled forwards enough on the ground to free his upper body while two clawed at each other by his legs, and the third seized the opportunity. It grabbed his shoulders, then his elbows, and ripped both arms free with a sickeningly wet sound of meat tearing, almost drowned out by the man's shrill, agonized shriek. Then the yarn ball tore off into the darkness, quickly followed by the other two, intent on stealing its prize from it.

I tried to stop the bleeding long enough for the ambulance to arrive, for whatever that's worth.

We told his friend that he had found the mountain lion after all and sent his maimed corpse back home for burial. We couldn't recover the arms, we told them. It was a closed casket funeral. And for the rest of the event, we kept people out of the woods and then closed the campsite for a few days until we could hunt out their nest.

We found it and we burned it. It was a mass of fallen trees, some freshly uprooted no doubt by the yarn balls themselves. We went to it in daylight, cleared out the surrounding brush, and emptied gasoline over top of it. Then we set it on fire and watched as four yarn balls tried to drag themselves out, flesh melting like wax, dying in silence with no mouths with which to scream as they burned.

One made it further than the rest. It reached the edge of the cleared dirt, dragging itself forwards by only one arm, the rest trailing limp behind it with cracked black skin that wept clear liquid. It stretched quivering fingers out towards me and then collapsed and went still.

The lady with extra eyes came walking out of the woods to stand next to me. She stared down at the dead monstrosity, gave a small sigh, and knelt. She produced a pair of shears and grimly cut the arm free from the fleshy core.

"I'll take care of him," she murmured, stroking the blistered flesh of the arm's wrist. "I couldn't save him that night but I can do this much for him."

She took the arm with her when she left.

I looked for her after that, but it wasn't until a few months had passed that I finally was allowed to find her house. She invited me in for scones and tea. Near the end of my visit, I gently inquired about the deceased man. She took me out to her garden in the backyard with the carpet of small white flowers that were eternally in bloom, no matter the season. A tree overshadowed them now, spreading its branches with vivid green maple leaves that shone in the sunlight.

She told me that the camper could finish out his life now, perhaps not as he'd wished, but it was a life nonetheless. The least she could do. I placed my palm on the bark and wondered if it was a heart that I felt beating beneath my palm or if it was merely a trick of my mind.

I asked if he was suffering. She shook her head and said that he was different now, that he thought as a tree thought, though perhaps a little more. He felt the wind and the sun and drank deep of the earth. When he was tired of this life and ready to pass on to the next, he would wither and his leaves would fall and he would die, as is the nature of all things. She said if I was truly concerned about him, I could always bring her a bit of tree fertilizer, from time to time.

Just some from the local hardware store would be fine, she said. I'm glad she clarified. I get a little nervous whenever something that's not human starts talking about fertilizing a garden.

I asked if I could add her to the list of rules. She agreed.

Rule #15 - The woman with extra eyes will help you. You can trust her. If she invites you to her house for tea, accept. I think she's a bit lonely.

I didn't tell her what the exact wording would be.

A day ago I found her. I've been wandering the woods with a satchel of tea and spices. I'd ordered online from a small seller of spice blends that also visits our campgrounds and the tea was from a variety of sources. She invited me in, brewed some nettle tea, and told me my gift was appreciated but it was not the reason she'd sought me out today.

"The man with no shadow," I said.

She smiled sadly and said she would help me defeat him and then she would never help me again. Was this a price I was willing to pay?

Would she still help my campers, I asked. Yes. She would. But I... I would be on my own.

I don't know why this was the cost. I don't know why these creatures make the demands they do. I could only consider my options, weigh the more immediate threat against a future that has never been certain of anything except the little girl and the beast, and then decide.

Forgive me, but I said yes.

I'm a campground manager. In my pantry is nettle tea, mixed with the earth from around the roots of the tree in her backyard. If I drink it each morning I will be immune for that day from the man with no shadow's silver tongue. This magic will only work for me. In my right eye is a splinter, carefully placed just below the lower lid and I can feel it when I blink. It doesn't hurt much. It is like a grain of sand and it will allow me to see clearly the thing that will hunt for me in the days to come.

My not-brother, she said, has returned to the campground. And he has a master.

THREE EXCITING THINGS

Posted Feb 11 2020 20:48:01 GMT-0400

Three interesting things have happened since my last update.

Do you remember the person who wanted to buy my campground? A pleasant young man that I pitied, for being duped by the current sheriff? He's still in town. Staying at a long-term housing unit about an hour out from here. The old sheriff has been looking into where he came from and why he's still here. He didn't want to tell me initially, as he was acting on a hunch, but now he has proof that something strange is going on. He showed up at my house the other day with a packet of papers detailing houses being sold, birth records, etc. The paper trail of a woman's life.

He found only one event of any significance around the second date that the man with no shadow was allowed outside of the campground. It was shortly after my mother made the bargain. The event itself was so insignificant that the old sheriff didn't pay much attention to it at first, not until he failed to find any more promising leads and followed up on it out of a sense of diligence.

A woman moved away. She wasn't even *that* local, she lived closer to the larger town a few hours from here. The old sheriff found the record of the sale of her house and since it went on the market the day after the man with no shadow was permitted to leave the campground, he dutifully tracked down what happened to her after that.

She went to another state. And three months after leaving she gave birth to a boy and raised him all by herself.

The buyer is younger than me. The old sheriff put on his old uniform and borrowed a police cruiser from an officer he was friends with and pulled him over for a speeding ticket. Checked his license to confirm the birthdate and then "let him off" with a warning.

The name matches. The birthdate matches. The buyer is the son of the woman that moved away.

So that was the first exciting development. I'm not really sure why that's important, but the old sheriff is going to keep digging.

The second exciting thing that happened was an angry mob showed up at the entrance to my campground.

I've installed a security camera at the front gate. There's also a motion sensor that pushes a text message to my phone whenever it triggers, which is far more often than I'd like, to be honest. However, I dutifully check the feed (also accessible from my phone, which is convenient) and I almost dismissed it with barely a glance out of reflex. Thankfully, the array of colors from the mob's shirts registered as unusual in some part of my brain and I looked at my phone again. Then I radioed my staff and told them to get in contact with the police while I went to the gate.

I think the mob didn't expect me to actually show up. They'd brought a reporter from the local newspaper (easily recognizable on account of there are only a handful of people on staff) and he was busy taking photos from angles where the signs would block the view and make the crowd seem larger than it was. There were perhaps a dozen people present. The signs were about what you'd expect. "The camp must go" and "Kate is the real monster."

Not gonna lie, that second one made me a bit angry. After all, they had a literal monster leading them.

He stood in the front of the mob, well-dressed with his hands in his pockets and a smile on his lean face. At least, that's what I saw with my left eye. Through my right, the one that itches under my lower eyelid, I saw a cavernous abdomen and the bone of his spine. The mob unconsciously formed around him, clinging tight as if he pulled them into his orbit.

I walked to the gate and leaned on it, staring him in the eyes.

"You wouldn't be the first monster I've killed with my own hands," I mused, keeping my voice low so that the others wouldn't hear.

He leaned in so that we were face-to-face. My focus was entirely on him, my heart hammering, knowing that this was dangerous, that I was mere inches from a predator. Behind him, the mindless shouting of the mob fell away, meaningless in my ears.

"In front of all these witnesses?" he chided. "You'd really show them your true colors?"

"Everyone will see what *you* are when you're dead. You know what they call people that kill monsters? Heroes."

He straightened, still smiling, but I saw hostility in his eyes. One of us was going to end up dead before this was done.

"What did I *ever* do to piss you off?" I hissed.

"You exist." His eyes flickered to just over my shoulder, studying the road leading into the campground in calculation. "And I want what is yours. Perhaps I won't be the master of it… but access will suffice."

A campground full of ignorant campers with organs for the harvesting? Of course he'd want it.

The police arrived shortly after. One cruiser with one officer and he didn't have much luck dispersing the crowd, as they were too riled up. It didn't help that my not-brother kept murmuring under his breath and while I couldn't hear his words, they seemed to have an effect on the crowd, for they surged forwards and hit the gate, shaking it violently and I was suddenly grateful for the heavy iron chain that held it closed.

They didn't leave until the sheriff turned up to disperse them. Yes, the current sheriff. The one I stabbed.

Let me tell you, that was real awkward. He stood on the other side of the gate after everyone was gone and I went over there to thank him, because I felt obligated to, and he just looked at me with undisguised loathing.

"I wouldn't even *be* sheriff if it weren't for your damn campground," he growled after a minute of uncomfortable silence.

"I'm sorry," I said. "I didn't realize you were under *his* control."

It didn't have to be said who we were talking about. He looked away, down at the ground, and the line of his jaw tightened as he clenched his teeth in helpless anger.

"Yeah, well," he muttered, "I think I'd still hate you. You're not a very likable person."

"So you can talk about him now?"

A terse nod.

"It's like having someone whispering in your ear," he said. "And even when they're silent, you know they're there, just about to speak. He's always there. Always. I've had him in my head for a long time now. I don't think he'll like me telling you this, but I guess… I don't care. Almost dying gives you a weird sort of courage."

I asked him if he knew what the man with no shadow was planning. He did not. He only knew what his instructions were, to force me into a position where I had to sell the campground. Then the old sheriff showed back up and the man with no shadow stopped giving him instructions, because he knew the sheriff was no longer a viable pawn.

I warned him about the not-brother. Similar to the man with no shadow, I said, but disguises itself as someone trustworthy through which to work its deceit. He grimaced and said nothing and in that silence it felt as if he were waiting for something.

"I'm sorry for what I did," I said. "I had to refill the cup somehow, but I shouldn't have gone for an artery."

Then, because we were being honest, I asked him if he thought I should sell the campground. He thought about it for a long time, it felt like, and my heart pounded in my chest, afraid to hear his response. Honesty is terrifying like that. It strips away our excuses and our lies and leaves us adrift in a world that is no longer familiar.

"I don't," he finally said. "This town… needs the campground. Losing it would throw a lot of people straight into poverty, we'd be ripe for the drug mills to move in, and then all those creatures you harbor would be set loose into our community to prey on the weak and vulnerable. But Kate, this whole thing-"

He gestured in at the road, in the direction the angry mob had dispersed.

"- is not entirely the fault of the man with no shadow. The town is realizing they've made a deal with the devil and they're not liking what they see when they look in the mirror."

Then he added that I was the devil, in case I didn't realize that, and I said I'd figured that out all on my own, thank you very much. He said the town needed more industry, more business, something else to bring in revenue and when his term as sheriff was over he was going to run for a position on the council and try to make that happen. Make me... unnecessary. Which, honestly, I feel that's a fair position to take. It may be inconvenient for me but I can understand why he'd do that.

Then he said one more thing before he left. He said that he *did* blame me for not trying harder to kill the things that lived here. It wasn't enough to contain them. Some of them needed to be destroyed. Then he gave me a gift - a pistol - and told me to aim where the man's shadow *should* be.

And that leads us to the third exciting thing.

The man with no shadow was waiting for me on the road. He stood well away from the trees lining the edge so that full sunlight fell upon him and his red hair shone like fire. His expression was smug.

I held one hand behind my waist, keeping the gun out of sight.

"This is a fun game, isn't it?" he said as I approached. "I'm enjoying it."

"I'm going to take a crowbar to your friend's head," I snarled, "just like I killed the master of the vanishing house."

His smile faltered. His eyes narrowed, his confidence melting into wary calculation.

"You feel... distant. My words can't find a foothold. What did you do?"

I remained silent, not trusting myself to not give anything away. It didn't matter. His expression shifted once more, twisting into an ugly sneer.

"The lady in the woods," he snarled. "That treacherous bitch. I'll have to deal with her once you're out of the way."

I wish you could have heard his tone. The condescension. The certainty in his victory. The naked disdain he had for the one entity on this campground that I *trust*, the one that has been with me since I was a child.

"You'll leave her alone," I said evenly, raising the gun and pointing it at his chest.

"That won't hurt me," he said mockingly. "You think you have us under control, with your etiquette and your rules. You've deluded yourself. The lady isn't your friend. *None* of us are. I at least have the *decency* to be honest about how I will *take* your campground from you-"

Something in me snapped and I took the sheriff's advice.

To be fair, it wasn't bad advice. The man with no shadow does need to die.

I've just been underestimating his capabilities.

I shot him in the space where his shadow should go, just as the sheriff suggested. The bullet hit the ground in a cloud of dust. And the man with no shadow shrieked in agony, his body spasmed and he fell heavily to his hands and knees, one hand clutching at his ribs. Blood leaked between his fingers and fell in beads to the dusty ground beneath him.

And I aimed for where I approximated his head to be and then I hesitated.

I'm not sure why. Maybe I was surprised that this actually worked. Or maybe I am my father's daughter as well and something inside me balked at the thought of killing someone - for while he isn't human, the man with no shadow is still a *someone* - in cold, remote detachment. There was no anger to push me forwards, no hatred to blind me. It wasn't like the master of the vanishing house where I was fighting for my life. It wasn't like the sheriff, where my anger simmered so low for so long that it only took a small push to send me over that edge and then there was no more time to think about it. Perhaps hatred had made me pull the trigger but then... with him crumpled in front of me, making small, mewling noises of pain - noises that *I* have made before - I felt the full weight of what I was about to do. There was nothing hiding it from me. There was nothing to bind my reason and let me act out of mindless instinct. I knew what this was.

It would be an execution.

And I hesitated long enough for him to save himself.

He twisted, face contorted in rage and agony, and he raised his bloodstained hand in my direction. Gripped the air tight, his knuckles white, and I *felt* something grab hold of my shadow. Like a shiver up my spine, but sharp as a knife.

He pulled. Something *gave*. And white agony blinded me, drove me to the ground, and all I could do was scream, digging my fingers into my shoulder as my body told me that my arm was *gone*, that there was nothing there, even as my fingernails clutched at numb flesh.

I'm not sure how long it took for me to regain my wits. Agony has a way of distorting time, narrowing your thoughts so that it is all you know, so that you forget yourself and everything is driven from your mind except a desperate desire to be free of it. I next remember being on my knees, my forehead pressed against the ground, my fingers clutching a shoulder that I could barely feel.

My shadow's arm was gone. Only a tattered end remained behind. And the man with no shadow was also gone. I found a trail of blood that led into the woods. I didn't dare follow it, not with my right arm hanging limp at my side.

I suppose I'm lucky that he didn't do worse. That his priority was to get the gun out of my hand and taking the arm was the fastest way to do it.

I feel there is something wrong with me. I'm slowly regaining the use of my arm as my shadow heals, but the world seems *off*. The shadows stretch long and in the corner of my vision it seems like they are reaching for me. I catch myself jumping, startled, at the slightest noise. At night the shadows feel oppressive, like a blanket covering me up and I lay in my bed, my breathing shallow, and I sleep fitfully and I dream of a dark shape rushing at me out of the darkness and I wake with a cry when its shadow covers me up.

I'm doing my best to function. I keep telling myself that this injury will heal. I don't want to leave my house though, not with my arm in a sling like this. My most trusted staff are managing the campgrounds and really, with it still being closed for the winter, there's not much to do. Bryan says the man with no shadow hasn't been seen since I shot him. Likely in his grove, recovering from his own injury. Just as I am, enclosed in my house. In the morning I have my tea and then I call the old sheriff to see what he's found out and then I wait. I just... wait. Wait and watch the shadows.

The old sheriff is asking about the not-brother. The answers were all over the place. That's James, just finished his service with the army. That's Peter, the factory he was working at closed down and he's back home looking for a new start. That's Mark... the details hardly matter anymore. But they all had something in common. He's my best friend, I trust him. He's my best friend, I'd trust him with anything.

He's my best friend.

I'd trust him with my life.

It seems like the not-brother has learned his lesson from the dogs *too* well. He's not going to come at me directly.

He's going to get the town to do it.

I'm a campground manager. I know some of you will be relieved that I didn't kill the man with no shadow like that, that you hope that this halts my descent into becoming a monster myself. Others will say it would be justified - and it *is*, I suppose, with all the people he's killed - and that I should have done what is necessary and finished the job. Perhaps this is my weakness, that I am only strong when I'm angry. I wish I'd known this about myself before I let my rage pull that trigger and start something that I wasn't able to finish.

My arm still hurts. It comes and goes, sharp, twisting pain that leaves me winded. In those moments I remember something, a moment I saw and heard but only distantly, to be replayed as if in a dream. I remember the man with no shadow, huddled with his back to me, crouching low to the ground. The guttural sound of eating as he consumed the stolen piece of my shadow. Then he rose and staggered away into the woods.

Next time, there can be no hesitation.

I SAVED SOMEONE. SORT OF.

Posted Feb 18 2020 18:12:53 GMT-0400

Holy hell did I disappoint pretty much everyone by not killing the man with no shadow when I had the opportunity. Have I hesitated in the past? Perhaps? It's hard to remember. Anger does that to you and I have spent a lot of time angry at people, for putting others in danger, for getting in my way. If I hesitated then, it was only for a few seconds and I pushed past them and found my anger again. But with things that aren't human... a few seconds of uncertainty was all it took and I'm currently paying the price for that. It's part of why the rules exist. We're weak, fallible things, and so it is better if we never get into a situation where we may fail and die - or get others killed - to begin with.

I've been doing a lot of introspection. I don't have much else to do, cooped up in my house like this. The incident with Perchta has been rattling around in my head for some time now. She said I could save them all and handed me the card for Justice, questioning my rules. The subjugation of the self for an orderly, safe, society.

There is an old anger inside of me. I can't remember when it was first kindled but it is an anger born of helplessness and that is the worst anger to harbor. It has no target, no direction, and it can smolder for a lifetime until the coals are white hot and all they lack is a scrap of fuel with which to ignite and scorch everything to ash.

I pretend I am the master of my anger. That my rules are there to keep everyone safe, that I do what I can, and if someone breaks them - if someone talks to the children with no wagon or is disrespectful of one of the entities on this land - that they deserve my anger. These are the consequences after all, the results of a world that is both cruel and unfair.

It is a false justice.

The thread that Perchta stitched into my abdomen is on my dresser. Brittle, stained crimson with my blood. Perhaps her sense of justice is similarly skewed (keeping a messy house is deserving of death, in her book) but I cannot help but wonder about her warning. Certainly, the people that broke my rules invited a greater danger upon my campground, but I wonder...

Have I been taking the easy way out?

I don't know.

I think... if you'd asked me this when I wrote the first post, I would have said that it was necessary. That I'd seen what happens when people try to evade their fate and there is *always* collateral damage. The innocent suffer alongside the culprit. I merely choose the lesser of two evils and that is the closest I will ever get to virtue.

I don't feel so confident anymore. Perhaps it was Perchta's thread or perhaps it was from wearing the mantle of a saint, but I've begun to doubt. Silently, insidiously, and then that seed finally bloomed at the *worst fucking moment possible.*

This is what happens when I'm indoors by myself for too long. I spend too much time thinking. But at least the old sheriff showed up to break the monotony.

I'd kept him appraised of the situation with my shadow. Well, just that I was injured. I didn't give him any details. But he needed to know that I wouldn't be outside my house much, not until it healed and I got my mobility back. It's been improving. I can wiggle my fingers now and can type somewhat normally again. Let me tell you, the last post was a *challenge.* I'm just glad I've got some help with these.

Anyway, the old sheriff showed up on my doorstep. He invited himself in and then started asking how this had happened, anyway, conspicuously eyeing my sling. It's a lot harder to evade someone's questions in person, so I reluctantly filled in the rest and admitted that I was feeling lost and confused. He sighed and said that he'd seen people have a crisis of confidence before, but that this was not the time for it and I needed to suck it up and do my damn job.

There's work to do, he said, gesturing for me to follow him outside. And he'd be damned if he was going to let me sit around feeling sorry for myself.

And somehow, his gruff rebuke did make me feel more normal.

He led me out to his car and he popped the trunk open. I'll be honest - I was not expecting who was inside. Are you thinking right now that it was the buyer? That the old sheriff had finally figured out what his game was and thought it was time to make him vanish for good? Yeah, that was kind of what I was expecting too.

Well, you're just as wrong as I was.

Inside was the sheriff. His wrists were handcuffed behind his back and his ankles were tied together with rope. His knees were tied as well but despite this he continued to struggle, a strangely rhythmic rocking back and forth as his hips shifted and his knees tried to bend. Dried blood crusted his face from a gash directly in the middle of his forehead. His eyes were heavy with exhaustion and fear and he weakly turned his head towards us, squinting at the sudden sunlight.

"Help me," he gasped.

And for a moment I was bewildered as to why he would ask *me* to save him from the old sheriff. I turned to the man beside me, who only stared grimly down at his captive, one hand still on the lid of the trunk.

"So… are you looking for somewhere to dump a body?" I asked. "Because honestly we could just drop him in my neighbor's lake and blame it on the shulikun. Lent hasn't started yet. I don't think they've been banished for the year."

Look, I may be reconsidering *my* actions, but I trust the old sheriff's judgement and if he says someone needs to be disposed of I ain't questioning it for an instant.

The old sheriff only sighed softly and reached down, grabbing the sheriff's arm and hauling him out of the vehicle. He asked for help and I took the man's other arm as best as I could and together we dragged him from the car and into my house.

Then the old sheriff pulled a sizable pocket knife out and set to sawing through the ropes that bound the sheriff's legs. Surprisingly, the sheriff began to fight back, shaking his head violently and saying no, no, don't. *Begging* him not to release him. The old sheriff refused to be dissuaded and the ropes snapped free, leaving the man on the floor with only his hands handcuffed behind me. And he began to weep. It was a broken sort of crying, deep within the chest, and there were no tears. It was paroxysms of despair, the hopeless weeping of a man that had nothing in him with which to fight.

He stood. His legs jerked mechanically, as if they were on strings. And he began to walk in a straight line and didn't stop when he hit the sofa, just continued to go forwards and slowly, slowly, the piece of furniture began to budge. Inch by inch, being resolutely shoved forwards and to the side with each impact of the sheriff's knees. After a minute of this, the old sheriff intervened by taking the man by his shoulders and forcibly turning him to another direction.

And off went the sheriff, like a mindless toy, and it was only the old sheriff's intervention that kept him from walking straight into the wall of my living room.

"I have an idea," I said. And I went to the garage.

I don't keep pets. After the horse incident we decided they were just a bad idea to have around. However, at some point I acquired a dog tie-out - a long spiral stake that went into the ground with a swivel on the end with a long wire lead. I don't remember how I got it and why I still have it. Probably left behind by a camper. At my suggestion, we took the sheriff out into the backyard and put the stake in the ground and the lead around one elbow. He walked in one direction until he was out of slack and then, tugged to the side by the off-center pull of the lead, he began to walk in a long circle.

"Well, that's *a* solution," the sheriff sighed. "He's going to walk himself to death though if this keeps up. He's been at this for hours and he's telling me he's exhausted and I'm afraid he's going to keep going until he simply drops dead."

"The man with no shadow?" I asked, watching the sheriff make his slow, torturous lap around my yard.

A faint nod. "I guess he's decided that he's done with him."

Or more likely he was angry that the sheriff revealed his weakness.

They found the sheriff caught on a fence. We have a little bit of farmland around here and one of those landowners saw a figure struggling at the far end of his field. He went out there to investigate - armed, of course, that's just how we are around here - and was surprised to find the sheriff. Walking. Just... walking. Straight ahead, directly into the wooden fence. He must have been out there for some time, for there were furrows dug into the soft earth from his feet repeating the same steps over and over and over.

The landowner took him inside and called the old sheriff. He's one of the many around here that still use a landline though and while he was in the kitchen, explaining the situation, the sheriff proceeded to walk into a wall and keep walking into it until he'd bashed his head enough times to split the skin open. That was where the head injury came from. The landowner hung up and returned to the living room to find the sheriff moaning in pain with blood running down his face, and still his legs continued to carry him forwards.

After that, the landowner tackled the sheriff and held him down until help arrived. That's when they tied him up and the old sheriff brought him to me.

I went out to the sheriff, once I was caught up on what was happening. I matched pace with him as he continued walking in his long circle.

"What did the man with no shadow tell you to do?" I asked.

"Walk," he panted. "Just... keep walking."

Without turning or stopping. Just walk until his heart gave out or he blundered into something deadly - like the highway. My heart sank. I freed my neighbor from the man with no shadow's influence by removing some fingers, but nothing was coming to me now. Perhaps it was because I didn't have an artifact of some inhuman creature at hand, perhaps there was no connection that would offer up the knowledge I needed to save the sheriff. There was just me and my frail human understanding.

I told him I'd think of something. He stared hopelessly straight ahead and replied that I shouldn't bother, that he knew something like this could happen when he gave me the gun. He suggested I go inside and bring it out here, just to speed things along a little. He was so tired. He just wanted all this to stop.

I went back to the house but I did not get the pistol. I stood with the old sheriff on the back porch and we watched for a little bit in silence. I suggested taking him to the hospital and having them sedate him. He agreed that we could try that, if there weren't any other options. It could buy us a little time. Or the drugs would simply not work, subsumed by whatever foul power was keeping his body moving. He asked if there was any other remedy I knew of. Something that wasn't *normal* medicine.

I knew some things, I said. Ways to protect against powers and ways to banish powers. The problem was that a lot of them didn't work against the greater entities on my campground, like the man with no shadow, or I would have gotten rid of him already. And worse, a lot of what I know is focused on *protection*. There wasn't too much in my repertoire to undo the damage, once done.

And the stories? What happened to people that were cursed in the stories?

Well, I explained, they usually had to have some other being of power intervene. And the old sheriff just looked at me for a moment until I realized what I had said.

So we took the sheriff into the woods. I walked to his right and the old sheriff walked to his left; we each held one his arms to guide him between us, so that he wouldn't keep going straight into a tree. He didn't speak. He was beyond exhaustion, nearly senseless, but unable to do anything about it, not with the man with no shadow's words coursing through his body. I told the sheriff that we were taking him to see the lady with extra eyes and that while she wouldn't help me anymore, I hoped that she'd be willing to help him. I'd stay outside. I wasn't certain if I'd be welcome anymore, after our bargain (and no, I don't know anything else about why that was the price) and I didn't want to risk her refusal. The old sheriff would do the asking.

We didn't find the lady.

We found the dancers.

The young woman that has always been the one to speak to me greeted us on the road. She stood in the middle of the path, barefoot, wearing jeans and a garish hot pink bikini top. Please keep in mind that while it is an unseasonably warm winter it is still too cold to go out without a jacket. We had to adjust our path to go around her and she fell in beside me as we walked.

"You're looking for me," she said.

"I'm looking for the lady with extra eyes," I replied somewhat tersely. I was not in the mood to deal with the dancers today.

"No, you're looking for a *cure*," she corrected.

"Bargains with fairies always have a price."

"Did I say I was a fairy?"

I stopped cold. I let go of the sheriff's arm and let him continue on. I would catch up in a minute. This needed my full attention. I stared at the woman in front of me with her round face and her black hair and that faint smile on her lips.

"You *dance*," I said slowly. "There's some beliefs that a group dancing in a circle around an afflicted person will remove a curse."

"Give him to us. You will not get him back. He will join our company and live as long as he chooses to."

I ran to the sheriff. Took him by the elbow and turned him around. I told him I had a solution, that he had to go with the dancers. They'd make him one of their own and that would save him. It would break the man with no shadow's hold. He'd be free. He couldn't fight back, his body no longer under his control, just as he'd been unable to even raise his arms to stop himself from slamming his head into the wall, over and over until he bled. All he could do was beg, as his legs carried him inevitably forwards towards the waiting dancer. She watched him with bright, eager eyes.

"They *kill* people," he cried weakly. "I can't do that! I'm not - like - *you!*"

My chest felt tight at hearing his cries of protest. But I kept going. He screamed that he would rather die as a human than be one of the monsters on my campground. That he hated me - my whole damn family was evil. That I didn't have the *right* to make this choice for him. But he couldn't stop me. The man with no shadow had told him to walk and so he did, straight towards the dancer that stretched out her arms to take him from me.

I delivered him into her waiting hands. He wept and the lady shushed him, telling him that he'd fought hard but now his fight was done. There were others that would see this through. And she glanced backwards at where I stood with the old sheriff on the road.

This was a few days ago. The old sheriff hasn't said much about it, other then he would try to head off the fallout when people notice the sheriff is missing. Keep them from blaming it on me. He didn't sound very hopeful - everyone knows we had bad blood, what with the stabbing in the neck and all - but I appreciate him trying. I guess this means he thinks I made the right choice, although he hasn't said as much.

Last night, at sundown, one of my staff was making the final rounds through the campground to make sure all our protections were in place. We're going to be taking extra measures this year, even when we don't have campers, on account of the signs of it being one of the bad years. He saw a group of people in the woods and stopped at the edge of the road to see if they were trespassers or something else.

The dancers. They were setting up wood for the bonfire. The sheriff was there, stuffing dead leaves and small branches in at the base in preparation for lighting it. One of the dancers touched his shoulder and he looked up, to where my staff sat on their four-wheeler, and he waved. Then he went back to work.

The dancer said he could choose to die, so I guess he's okay with this for now.

I keep telling myself that maybe this is a good thing. He never wanted to be sheriff. I don't know what the sheriff actually wanted, but it wasn't that. Certainly not that. The man with no shadow dictated his future for him, took hold of his life and discarded whatever hopes and dreams he'd once harbored.

And then I took him by the arm and delivered him to another fate that he hadn't chosen.

I hope he's content with them. I hope he someday stops hating me.

I hope he never has to kill anyone.

I'm a campground manager. I think a few months ago I would have simply killed the sheriff and justified it as a necessary evil. Putting someone out of their misery. Removing a pawn from the man with no shadow's grasp. Perhaps even blamed the sheriff for his predicament even though the man with no shadow had sought him out in that one day he was free from the campground's borders.

A freedom my mother granted him. To save my friends.

I can't blame him for hating my family.

I wish there had been a better way to save him. But when an opportunity to save yourself presents itself, it is often the *only* opportunity. This is a cruel world and mercy is a rare commodity, doled out reluctantly, and to reject the dancer's offer very well could have meant there would be no other. The lady with extra eyes perhaps wouldn't intervene. Other rituals could fail. Sedatives could have done nothing or left him with only a half-life spent sleeping until the day he died. Or we'd walk in search of an alternative, in vain, until he dropped dead or until my resolve cracked and I fetched the pistol to put a quick end to it.

But I was wrong when I tried to kill him the first time. I don't want to be wrong again.

Perchta said I could save them all. So I guess I'm trying that.

I'm not sure I like the results.

THE MAN WITH THE SKULL CUP KISSED ME

Posted Mar 05 2020 18:05:36 GMT-0400

Obviously I read the comments. Obviously I know some of you are, in the vernacular of the internet, "shipping" myself and the man with the skull cup. And obviously I've found that amusing because I've cracked a couple jokes in response. So while I'm sure some of you are inwardly celebrating at the title of this particular update I am afraid I must crush your hopes and tell you that it's not what you think.

This starts with the assholes that want to destroy my campground.

The mailman remains my ally. He brought me another flyer. This one advertised a rally. It was to take place on the town green. The old sheriff thought there was a silver lining to this when I called him. Firstly, it meant that the town was *not* unified against me. Why hold a rally unless you were still trying to bolster your following? He'd show up at it along with the police to help keep order and hopefully his scowling presence might shame some of the undecided folks into going home. He wasn't officially the sheriff anymore but he has his legacy. We all remember him. We all know what he did by going into that house all those years ago.

I wish they'd give more credit to the part *I* played in bringing him back out. The old sheriff has told people I'm the one that saved him. I certainly didn't do it for glory... but maybe they wouldn't be holding a rally at *all* if people paid more attention to the sacrifices I've made.

I'm a little resentful.

People aren't rational. I know this from school. Even when presented with evidence to the contrary, people that have the social support of other like-minded people will instead seek to resolve their cognitive dissonance by reaffirming their erroneous beliefs. And then they'll recruit *more* people to the same beliefs, as if strength in numbers can disprove reality.

It still hurts, seeing the words on the flyer.

The old sheriff, at least, saw an opportunity here. My arm is still not fully healed but I have mobility back, if not strength. He suggested that I go to the courthouse records while the entire town was distracted with the rally. The police would all be at the green. Most of the town population would be there as well. I could slip in without anyone asking questions about what I was looking for.

It wasn't that we were looking for anything *bad*. It's just that we don't know who to trust. We don't know who the man with no shadow has under their control. We want to stay ahead of him and that means doing some things in secrecy.

Such as locating some old court documents about a custody case that didn't quite make it to trial.

The old sheriff thinks we might be able to find out who the buyer's father is.

I think this means that the old sheriff is running out of ideas again, but he knows more about detective work than I do and if he thinks this is important then I'm not going to argue. So around the time the rally was scheduled to start I got in my car and drove into town.

The streets were empty but I took the side road to the courthouse. It wasn't far from the town green so I intended to go in through the back. Our courthouse is connected to the town hall building and across the street is the library. There's a handful of stores - some places to eat, a general store, and a hardware store. And that's it. That's downtown.

I let myself in through the back entrance and took an immediate left down the stairs leading to the basement. They creaked on every step and the building seemed to sigh with the aging wood, like the entire structure was vibrating with my presence. I knew this was a quirk of the old building, but after the experience with the vanishing house I was unnerved by the sound. The basement was dark but I did not dare turn on the lights. I wanted to get in, get the file, and get out totally unseen. So I descended into the darkness and it swallowed me up.

I told myself it wasn't the same. It wasn't the vanishing house. My heart still hammered in my chest until finally, my feet touched concrete and I felt safe turning on my flashlight.

I went up and down the rows of cabinets, searching for the year of the aborted court case. I found it just as I heard the creak of footsteps on the stairs and someone flipped on the lights. Fortunately, my years of dealing with dangerous monsters has given me *some* capacity to think quickly in urgent situations, and I snatched the documents out of their folder, folded them a couple times, and stuffed them inside my bra. Then I grabbed the documents out of the folder *next* to it, folded them, and stuffed them in my back pocket.

Then I shut the file cabinet and turned around just as the not-brother came around the row of cabinets. With him were two locals. I knew them both and while we're not friends (which is unsurprising, I don't have many friends), I won't begrudge them for being entrapped by the not-brother's lies. They stood in the aisle, blocking my path to the stairs. The not-brother's abdomen was like a pit in the dim lighting, the pale ghost of his spine barely visible to connect the two halves of his body. It was like his chest was floating in the gloom. I reluctantly tore my eyes away from it to look him in the eyes.

He *smirked* at me. I detested the sight of that smug smile.

"Shouldn't you be hiding at home?" he asked, showing his teeth.

"Needed some fresh air," I replied. "Shouldn't you be running along to your rally before your master finds out you're neglecting your job?"

"Don't need a rally if we can force you to sign over the campground right here."

One of the men held up a pile of documents and a pen. I eyed them and then carefully spat on the ground at his feet.

And the second man hit me. Right on the side of my mouth. I just remember the impact of when I hit the floor - so sudden that I didn't even register the pain until I was on the ground, watching blood splatter on the cement from a split lip. I was dazed and I didn't comprehend that they'd surrounded me, not until one of the men hoisted me back to my feet. The not-brother took the files out of my back pocket and studied them a moment before tucking them away on his person with a thin smile. My heart pounded in my chest with what little elation I could afford, given the circumstances. They'd taken the decoy, at least.

Not that it would save me. With my arms pinned like that I couldn't exactly fight back when the other man hit me again. And again.

"Does it really count if I sign that under duress?" I finally said, spitting again but this time to clear a thick clot of blood from my mouth.

"It does," the not-brother hissed. "Maybe not in your courts, but the intention matters for *us* and we don't care if the intention is that you wish for the pain to stop."

He considered for a moment. The man holding the paper remained emotionlessly still. I wondered if it was the man with no shadow's influence, or if the not-brother had his own hold over people if given enough time to solidify it.

"I think I'll start breaking your bones," the not-brother said thoughtfully. "We'll see how many I can get through before you sign. I'll leave your right hand alone, of course. You need to be able to hold the pen."

I shifted slightly as he stepped closer. Slid my feet further apart. Widening my stance. And then I twisted, hooking the man that held me by his ankle, and I threw.

People don't realize how strong I really am. They forget I do a lot more than just management. They forget that I do manual labor as well, that I don't sit at home all day letting my staff do *all* the hard work. I dig holes. I carry things. I clear brush and trees. I build.

I kill monsters.

And the man behind me was surprised by my sudden show of defiance and he tumbled forwards and into the gaping abdomen of the not-brother.

He went in head-first and the not-brother's face registered first with shock, and then with outrage and then... hunger. He shuddered, throwing his head back, and his throat bulged as a ripple ran through his entire body. Then he doubled over, clamping his chest down on the man, who was trapped halfway inside the not-brother's body. His legs kicked in the air futility and the not-brother wrapped his arms around the man's waist, greedily shoving him further inside his empty abdomen. The skin of his back began to distend, stretching outwards as his victim frantically tried to claw his way free. I heard muffled screams.

And the other man dropped the paper and the pen, his eyes clearing, and he stumbled away from the not-brother in horror.

I didn't waste any time. I grabbed his arm as I ran past the not-brother and dragged him along with me towards the stairs. He didn't need much encouragement. He was right behind me when I risked only one backwards glance to ensure he was following. Past him, I could see the not-brother still doubled over, the man almost entirely engulfed now. Only his ankles protruded and the not-brother's abdomen was horribly distended, like a tick, and his struggles were growing slower. I looked ahead at the stairway and kept going.

I could at least save one of them.

He followed me to the car. I yelled at him to get in and he did, almost falling into the passenger seat. I demanded to know how they knew I was in the basement. In a daze, he replied that there were people watching the roads into town. I needed to get out of here.

"No shit," I muttered, turning the key in the ignition and peeling out of the parking spot.

I'm not sure how absolute the not-brother's influence is. It's not the only means of control that they're using, however. I was driving back towards the campground, figuring it would be safe there, when the man in the passenger seat reached over and grabbed the steering wheel. I only had a few seconds in which to process what was happening and I used those to slam on the brakes.

"Killing you would work too," he hissed. "Your brother may be more tractable."

And he jerked the wheel to the side. I fought it, but he had his whole body weight to put in it, and the car spun sideways. It went off the road and I remember what I *felt* but nothing else, for it was like my vision shut off as my brain blocked out all else, and then it was like I was floating. Then nothing else.

Like the lights had been turned off.

They switched back on when the paramedics were pulling the door to the car open. I didn't understand how they'd gotten here so fast, not until much later when I was sitting in a bed at the ER and the concussion symptoms showed up. Then I understood that there was a gap in my memories because I'd been knocked unconscious. The car had rolled and there'd been stuff in my backseat, so some debris probably struck me in the head. They scanned my brain and didn't find any bleeding. A concussion, the doctor said, and put me on 'brain rest'. Lying around in a dark room doing nothing, basically. They assumed the bruises and cuts on my face were from the crash. I didn't correct them.

My passenger died, they told me. He wasn't wearing his seat belt and was ejected from the vehicle. Such a polite way of saying it. Ejected. Like I haven't seen worse.

I called the old sheriff and asked him to pick me up. I didn't want to stay at the hospital any longer than I had to.

"You got lucky," the doctor told me as he was finishing up my discharge paperwork. "That accident could have killed you. I have to admit we'd always figured it'd be one of those things on your campground that'd do you in."

The hospital is not part of our town, but they see enough of the victims of our land that they know who I am. I did not appreciate his dry humor about the situation. I snatched the script for painkillers out of his hand and let the sheriff escort me to his car.

We stopped by the pharmacy to fill my meds on the way home. I took the first dose straight away. Neither of us talked much. I told him that the man with no shadow had clearly been recruiting people from town. The not-brother might be helping with that, he suggested. Coercing them onto my land. There were plenty of ways onto it through the woods, as not all of it is fenced. We both agreed that the not-brother needed to be eliminated. Quickly.

"But not until you're off brain rest," the old sheriff said as he pulled the car into my driveway. "Concussions are serious."

I didn't answer. I was staring at the man with the skull cup who stood on the walkway leading up to my front porch.

The old sheriff stayed with the car and let me approach on my own to see what he wanted. I have not described the man with the skull cup initially, because I did not want to give you an impression of his appearance that might mislead you should you ever visit. He is different for everyone, after all, and even his gender may change. However, I think that you all have been reading long enough to recognize his mannerisms and the cup he carries. I feel comfortable tainting your minds with my own version of how he looks.

He appears to be in his mid-thirties, lean but not gaunt, wearing jeans and a hoodie with the hood drawn over his bald head. He wears plain metal rings on most of his fingers. His ears are pierced repeatedly with rings of that same dull metal, as are his eyebrows, nose, and lip. He has a stud in his tongue.

"I am concussed and on pain meds," I said wearily as he approached. "Please make this quick. Why are you here?"

"You refilled the cup," he said slowly.

"Yeah, and? Did I do it right?"

For a brief moment he looked exasperated and then his expression went cool and unreadable again.

"I knew you were injured," he said. "I came to see how bad it is."

He reached out and grabbed my chin, turning my head to the side to inspect the bruises darkening one side of my face. I whined in the back of my throat so that he knew he was hurting me, that his thumb was pressing into the bruises.

"Poor thing," he murmured. "Here. Drink."

Maybe it was the drugs or maybe it was the concussion, but I broke one of my rules.

I refused. I *resisted*.

His grip on my chin tightened and when I opened my mouth with a cry of pain, he forced the cup up to my lips and poured the contents down my throat. I choked on it, swallowed on reflex, and only then did he release me. I coughed up everything I didn't swallow.

"What the hell!?" I demanded weakly, wiping at my lips with the back of my hand. "I can't take my pain meds now!"

"Yes. The medication."

His eyes narrowed, he looked at me with naked calculation for a moment, then he grabbed my throat. I cried out, instinctively, as fresh pain blossomed as his fingers tightened in my bruised flesh.

Then he kissed me.

Due to the nature of my upbringing I am not really "into" other people. I made a half-hearted attempt at boyfriends in college, briefly dated a girl, and once made out with a stranger in a nightclub in a vain attempt to understand what I was missing out on. His lips on mine were awkward, I was repulsed by his tongue, and his gum falling out of his mouth and sticking to my blouse finalized my opinion that the answer to my question was "not much."

This experience was more terrifying than awkward and instead of mint, I tasted the metal of his tongue piercing.

Then he released me and I collapsed at his feet as my stomach convulsed and I vomited repeatedly onto the grass of my front yard. I suppose swapping spit counts as ingesting something.

After my stomach was empty I sat there, crying, until the old sheriff came over and gently urged me inside. I think he also told the man with the skull cup to "fuck off" but maybe that's wishful thinking. I don't know.

I was a bit delirious from everything that had happened. So the old sheriff dumped me on the sofa inside and I eventually cried myself to sleep.

He was gone when I woke up. Bryan was on the front porch with his dogs, standing guard. There was a note from the old sheriff that he'd come back after dinner to take the night shift. Until then... brain rest. Dark room. No reading. And especially no phone usage.

It wasn't until much later that I noticed he'd stolen the bottle of pain medicine I'd gotten from the pharmacy. And a while after that he texted me. He learned about texting last week. He's a big fan.

"Pills came up positive on toxicology screening," it said. "You should be fine though. One dose isn't dangerous on its own and you probably threw it up before it had fully dissolved in your stomach. Police are on their way to arrest the person that filled your script."

Yes, he really does type everything out with proper punctuation and no abbreviations. We should all learn from his example.

And then when I replied back with, "wtf I hate this town", he reminded me that I was on brain rest and now that I've checked my messages I needed to put the phone away.

I must admit that I cheated a little. I still had the court documents on me. I turned the lights on and read them. The old sheriff's gamble paid off. It listed the name of the man suing for custody of the child that would grow up to be our buyer.

His father is my late uncle. I guess there was an affair going on and I suspect that's the reason the custody case was dropped before it really got started. But now I know why the man with no shadow was interested in this woman and her son. He's family. The buyer is my cousin.

The man with no shadow isn't trying to destroy my campground. He's trying to take it away from *me*. Specifically, me.

And put it in the hands of someone that is naive and ill-prepared to deal with what he would inherit.

I'll be *damned* if I let that happen.

I'm the campground manager. It's been a shit couple of weeks, lying around in a dark room all day. The sheriff's disappearance hasn't gone unnoticed and they're whispering that I'm behind it (technically true) and that I'll do the same to anyone else that opposes me - unless I'm stopped. I'm sure the not-brother is the one fueling those rumors. The old sheriff is doing what he can to help, but even he is finding that the town's mood is quickly turning against him. He fears that more and more people are falling into the hands of the man with no shadow, especially since he currently has a pawn that is not bound to my land.

The not-brother needs to die. I have a plan. It might be a little early to go off brain rest, but I'm running out of time. My camp needs to open soon. I can be up for a couple hours, at the very least. Enough time to kill him and in the process, remind the town that maybe they've made a deal with the devil... but the devil is the only thing capable of saving them from the monsters.

Hopefully they'll stop trying to murder me after that.

BLOOD FORCIBLY TAKEN

Posted Mar 11 2020 23:38:25 GMT-0400

The old sheriff came up with a plan to kill the not-brother. He sent it to me via text so that he wouldn't be seen at my house too much and so he couldn't be overheard on the phone. He doesn't trust hardly *anyone* right now, which I think is prudent. This is one advantage we have over the man with no shadow: technology.

For the first step, we needed to convince the man with no shadow that he had me cornered. That I was too afraid to leave my campground and that my fear was causing me to drive people away. The concussion had already helped with that, as I was still largely confined to my home and was relying on the old sheriff and Bryan to bring me things I needed, like groceries. The sheriff's idea was to stage a highly visible blow-up at one of my staff. Yell at them over something trivial. Make it look like I was stressed to the point that any little thing would set off a collapse. I was still considering which staff member to target - who would be the most resilient to being unexpectedly yelled at - when my brother came over to check on how I was doing.

It wasn't an intentional change of plans. It just… sort of happened.

I don't like making our internal drama public. Due to the nature of what we do around here we tend to keep our problems to ourselves and we certainly don't involve outsiders. But I've told you some personal things already and maybe it's only fair that I tell you this as well, no matter how ashamed I am.

I accused my brother of being the black sheep. The one distributing the flyers.

Stupid, I know, but I wasn't thinking straight or maybe it was the pain meds. We finally got some that were safe from another town. Anyway, the comment that the man with no shadow's proxy had made was eating at me, how he insinuated my brother would be willing to sell the campground. I was feeling a little testy when he visited - not at him, just at the situation in general - but he wound up being the person I blew up at and things escalated and I made the accusation.

I wasn't even *pretending* to be angry.

It hurt him pretty bad, I think. Of course it would. Your own sister saying that you're behind stirring up the town to the point it's trying to kill her?

Yeah. I fucked up.

There were a couple other incidents we orchestrated, nice and visible, to demonstrate that perhaps Kate wasn't keeping it together after all. The old sheriff was convinced that I was being watched - the man with no shadow would be a fool not to - and so after a few more "meltdowns" we could be confident that word had gotten back to him. One of those scenes was at the old sheriff and after we staged *that* fight Bryan took over running errands for me.

I wasn't as confident in our plan as the old sheriff was. There was one additional assurance that I wanted. I didn't tell him what I planned to do. He would deem it too risky. He might have tried to stop me.

We would have fought for real, if that happened. I will sometimes listen to suggestions but I do not take kindly to being told what to do.

I went to see the man with no shadow.

A significant risk, especially after he tried to kill me with the car accident. I admit that I was afraid. The only reason I tried was because I believed that killing me meant that he'd have to convince my brother to sell instead. I guess I don't *actually* believe he's the black sheep. It's just my brother's resolve is an unknown quality, even to me. If the man with no shadow thought I was on the edge of collapse... then leaving me alive would be the fastest and easiest route to what he wanted.

The weather was mild that day, so I wore a shirt with a low collar so that the discoloration on my neck was clearly visible. It's purple and yellow with spots of magenta-red, blotches that cover the entirety of one side of my neck, down onto my collarbones, with lingering patches on my jaw. The blood under my skin is slowly dispersing, traveling down my body from the pull of gravity. It's tender but it doesn't hurt like it did. The swelling has come down immensely.

I skipped my pain meds that morning. The less acting I had to do, the better. Then I took my shotgun and went out into the woods. I went to the grove where the man with no shadow lives.

He watched me approach, sitting on a large stone, one bare foot tucked up close to his body, the other stretched out to touch the grass. He conspicuously eyed my gun a moment and then lazily glanced up to meet my gaze.

"Fancy another try at me?" he asked. "Good timing - I was feeling peckish."

He dropped his eyes down to the shadow at my feet and slowly smiled.

"I'm here to negotiate," I replied.

I dredged up the memory of the pain of having my shadow torn apart. How I'd collapsed, screaming. I let my voice tremble. His smile deepened.

"You want off this land," I continued. "I'll release you if you promise to leave. And to take the not-brother with you."

The man with no shadow laughed.

"Kate," he sighed, hopping off the stone. "Oh Kate. I thought you were smarter than this."

He walked towards me. I hoisted my shotgun, letting my hands shake, and he hesitated only briefly at the edge of his grove. Then slowly, deliberately, he stepped out of his territory and continued to advance towards me. I pointed the gun at him and he paused, barely a foot away from the barrel.

"That's not what I want," he murmured.

Then he jerked a hand up, so quickly I might not have been able to react if I weren't expecting it. It was an effort to not squeeze the trigger. I almost did. My hand twitched reflexively but I fought the urge down and let him grab the gun and rip it out of my hands. He tossed it aside onto the forest floor.

I cried out in surprise and stepped backwards but he wasn't letting me escape. He lunged forwards, grabbed the front of my shirt, twisting the fabric between his fingers, and he pulled me close. I was forced to tilt my head back to look up into his eyes and the bruises on my neck were clearly visible. He traced them, with one finger of his free hand, and I did not have to pretend as I trembled in fear.

"Or maybe you're not being stupid," he said, his finger stopping just at the edge of the cut across my lower lip. "Maybe you're *desperate*."

"The not-brother almost killed me," I whispered.

"Is that the closest you've come to dying? Poor thing. Humans aren't really cut out for this sort of thing. Wouldn't it be a relief to let it all go? Is your family's legacy worth this?"

He gently brushed a lock of my hair behind my ear, the tenderness of the gesture offset by how tightly he still held my shirt, pinning me in place. I shuddered and he seemed pleased by my reaction.

"I have... some... authority over the not-brother," he said, studying my face. I dropped my head and avoided eye contact. "I can tell him to stop trying to kill you. Give you a little peace in which to make your decision. But Kate... he is my subordinate, not my slave. Wait too long and I may not be able to restrain him entirely, nor the town. They won't kill you, but neither will they leave you... intact."

The threat was not unexpected. Even though I'd mentally prepared myself for this, on the walk to the grove, I still felt sick hearing the words and understanding their full implication. My words stuck in my throat and I was unable to reply. The man with no shadow took this to mean I was truly cowed - and perhaps in that moment I was - and said that he would tell the not-brother to spare my life. As a gesture of kindness. He didn't *actually* want me dead, after all. That wasn't necessary.

It all sounded very convincing and I think without the lady's tea, I would have believed every word.

"I still don't understand why you want to destroy my campground," I said, finally finding my voice again.

"You don't have to understand. You just have to do what I want."

He smiled broadly and patted me on the check. Then he let go of my shirt and briskly walked away, casually putting his back to me. I eyed the distance between myself and the shotgun. I admit it was *very* tempting. I wasn't sure I wanted to gamble all of this on having better reflexes than him, though.

"This was a good talk," he called back to me. "It was nice to have an actual conversation for once. Maybe I'll visit the lady in the woods and give her my thanks for supplying you with the tea. And then I'll kill her, of course."

He laughed. That was enough for me. I couldn't stay any longer. I scooped up the shotgun and turned to leave, walking quickly, eager to put the sound of his laughter behind me.

And then a townhall meeting was called, just as I expected.

I'm starting to think that the not-brother is actually not that clever on its own and the man with no shadow is the real brains of the operation here. After all, it tried to integrate itself with my campground directly first, thereby putting it in close proximity to the people most familiar with monsters. (though if a commenter hadn't pointed out the discrepancies, I wonder if it would have succeeded) Regardless, for how easily it seems to have taken over the town, I feel it would have had more luck with... whatever its goals are... by starting there.

The rally had stirred up the town enough to ensure a good turnout at the meeting. It was likely that almost everyone would be there. All the not-brother had to do was go out in front of them and introduce himself and they would all be his. Everyone in town that was undecided or still on my side - they would be his.

Unless, of course, someone killed him.

What a shame that would be.

Since I was without a car the plan was that Bryan would pick me up shortly before the meeting was scheduled to start. The old sheriff was already in position. I'm not sure what it says about him that he knows how to get a good angle on the town hall with a scoped rifle, but I'm glad he's on our side. I was armed with the pistol and shotgun. Certainly, they hadn't done a whole lot to the not-brother the first time, but I only needed to make a symbolic gesture.

There was a knock at my door as I sat waiting. Startled, I grabbed my shotgun and hurried to answer, surprised that I hadn't heard Bryan's truck pull up.

The man with the skull cup was on my doorstep.

"Uh, this is a bad time," I finally said after a long moment of awkward silence. "Can we talk about that kiss some other day?"

"What makes you think I came here to talk about that? Perhaps I am here because of how you tried to refuse my offer of a drink."

I froze, like every muscle in my body was shot through with ice, locked up in terror. Some part of my brain gibbered that I was going to die - horribly - and while I heard what he said next, I didn't register the words. Not until he said my name to get my attention and repeated himself. He wasn't going to kill me, not after all he'd done to keep me alive. But I *would* have to atone for my mistakes - and there had been many as of late.

He sighed and traced the rim of the cup with one finger, his eyes half-closed.

"I told you not to empty the cup," he murmured. "It is easy enough to refill when it runs low. Refilling it when it is emptied is another matter. I honestly would have preferred you have returned it empty and let *me* refill it, as I could have managed it properly. But what's done is done and now you need to finish what you started."

His voice sounded weary and this time, it wasn't the condescending exhaustion he adopted when I was - in his opinion - being dense. I peered at him intently, noting how stark his cheekbones were and the shadows under his eyes. He looked... gaunt. Pale. Like he's sick.

Did I do this to him?

He looked me dead in the eyes and with a flat, emotionless stare that never wavered from my face, he turned the cup sideways until the liquid spilled out and puddled on the porch. He tilted the cup upright before the last few drops fell. Blood from what was already there. Then he lifted his hand to his mouth and bit carefully down on a knuckle. The skin split open and brilliant drops of blood beaded up. He tipped his hand so that they collected together and spilled out and into the cup. Blood freely given.

The man with the skull cup handed it to me, along with his knife.

"Blood of an enemy, forcibly taken," he said. "Don't screw it up this time."

I had the right idea but the wrong source. The sheriff was never my enemy.

But the not-brother sure as hell is.

I called up the old sheriff and told him there was a change in the plan. He didn't like it, but grudgingly agreed.

"The town isn't going to like how you're handling this," he said.

"My family isn't here to be their friends," I replied. "We're here to protect them."

And then Bryan was there, the back of his pickup truck loaded with large dogs, and I climbed into the passenger side and buckled myself in. He asked where my gun was and I told him about the change in plans.

"This is going to be messy," he sighed, backing the car out of the driveway. "I can't promise the dogs won't help."

Messy was fine. Maybe a veritable bloodbath would remind the town exactly what they were dealing with. Both what my campground was... and what *I* was.

Yes, I'm trying to save people now instead of letting them suffer the consequences of their choices, but that doesn't mean they can just forget that I'm willing to slit my share of throats.

I hate the sight of the town hall, after my uncle's death. My heart sped up as Bryan parked within eyeshot of the building. I took a shallow breath and let it out slowly, trying to calm myself, and then gave up on that. Screw it. I didn't need to be calm. I needed to be angry. Anger had carried me through every hard thing I'd done, whether it was just or not, and it would carry me through this as well.

I slammed the door of the pickup truck behind me. The dogs watched me go, lined up at the edge of the pickup's bed with their tongues hanging out. I walked alone to the closed doors of the town hall, took a breath, and then shouldered them bodily open.

Kicking them open would have made a more impressive entrance, sure, but I didn't want to risk spilling the contents of the cup I carried.

The not-brother stood behind the podium at the fore of the room. Beside him was the buyer. My unwitting cousin looked nervous, his eyes wide and his forehead shining with sweat. He seemed ready to bolt at any moment and for a brief second he looked relieved for the interruption. Then he saw the knife in my hand and he went pale. Opened his mouth to say something, perhaps to yell for someone to call the police, and then that died when he realized that no one else was moving - like this was *normal*.

Maybe it is, around here.

I don't think he's under the control of the man with no shadow. It's a hunch, but I feel pretty good about it. He looked too afraid there, standing at the front of the room and realizing that someone was bearing down on them with murder in her eyes and not a soul was lifting a finger to stop me.

I stopped halfway to the not-brother, who had not moved from the podium. He stared at me in shock. Clearly our gamble had paid off, for he did not expect me to be here. I raised the knife and pointed the tip at him.

"That is *not* your friend," I said in a clear voice that carried easily throughout the room. "That is an abomination, not much different from all the other monsters that I keep trapped on my land so that you all can sleep safely in your beds at night."

"Kate," the not-brother sighed. "Didn't you get a *concussion* recently? Maybe you should see your doctor about these... outbursts you've been having lately. Is your brother speaking to you again yet?"

The old sheriff had picked up some things during his tenure. Things about surveillance. And he'd wired up the podium so that he could listen in to what was being said while he was in his sniper position. At the moment when the not-brother paused, before anyone in the room could react, a bullet came through the window and into the side of the not-brother's head.

The force of it knocked him over. My cousin - the buyer - shrieked and threw himself to the ground. The rest of the room stirred, some stood, and the police that were present to maintain general order put their hands on their guns, their attention fixed on where I stood waiting. Then everyone went still and silent again as the not-brother slowly picked himself up.

See? Stupid. He could have just played dead long enough for the police to escort me out.

But now…

They all saw him for what he was.

"Fine," he snarled, blood dripping down from the bullet hole in the side of his head. "FINE. This plan was annoying, anyways. I don't *like* being around humans. I don't *like* pretending to be your friend. I just… want… to FEED."

He knocked the podium aside with one sweep of his arm. It smashed sideways to the floor. People were on their feet now, someone screamed, and they bolted to the edges of the room, crowding near the walls, desperate to get away from the creature that was stalking down the aisle to where I stood. His empty abdomen stretched wide, ribs dripping with fluid, and I saw raw hunger in his eyes.

I felt elated. They saw him for what he was.

And it didn't matter.

He called to them and they came, turning over chairs in their haste, eyes maddened and empty. I saw the intention in their mindless stares as they rolled across the room in a wave of human flesh. They would tear me apart and feed me to their master, whose words poisoned their minds and overrode their senses and turned them into monsters.

I've dealt with plenty of monsters on my land. We have a simple strategy.

Guns and dogs.

And Bryan's hounds came in through the door, throwing them fully open with the impact of their body weight, and they rolled past me in a black, angry pack of fur and fangs. They hit the line of people closing in on me, a heavy collision of muscle and fur into flesh and they all went down, a veritable barricade of flailing and fighting. There were screams - I couldn't tell if it was rage or pain - for the dogs had cleared a pathway between me and the not-brother and I was running forwards. They'd stopped the mob just short of the aisle.

The not-brother ran to meet me, arms spread low to his side, ready to pull me into the void of his abdomen. I gripped the knife tight. And just before we collided, the old sheriff took his second shot, and the not-brother's knee exploded into red ruin.

The knife went up and into his chin as he fell. He landed hard in front of me, his body held up by one knee and the strength of my arm, his head twisted back as he dangled from the blade, gurgling as blood flooded his mouth and throat.

The room went quiet. Even the people that were on the ground, pinned under the weight of the dogs, subsided into muffled whimpering. They stopped trying to get to me. They just stared, wide-eyed, breathing fast, and anything they might have said to one another was drowned out by the desperate choking of the not-brother. Then that, too, went quiet, replaced by the steady drip of blood onto the wooden floor.

I held the cup under the wound until it was full. Blood of my enemy, forcibly taken.

Then I ripped the knife free and let his body fall to the ground. And I left. Behind me, the dogs turned their attention to the corpse. They savaged it, ripping into it and tearing the skin from muscle, severing tendons, pulling the bones free. Someone was quietly sick in the corner of the room. I didn't care.

They'd made a deal with the devil. They shouldn't be surprised by the results.

I'm a campground manager. I'm not very clever and there's a lot going on that I don't understand. I think the man with no shadow has underestimated me, however. He only trusts what he can control and this leads him to use people as tools and then to discard them as soon as they aren't useful. I wonder if the not-brother realized this or if he thought he could stay useful for as long as it took to get what the man with no shadow had promised him. The campground as his own personal hunting grounds, no doubt, once it was no longer in my possession. I wonder if the man with no shadow would have betrayed him before that happened.

I guess it doesn't matter now.

I trust the old sheriff. I trust Bryan. And though I question his motives… I trust that the man with the skull cup will help to keep me alive. I returned his knife and cup. He took them and then raised the cup to his lips and drank. Then he nodded at me, faintly, and walked away. So I guess I did it right this time and I guess he's going to be okay.

I don't think I'll be able to trick the man with no shadow again. He'll be wise to it now, realizing that I'm not such a simple creature; that I, too, am capable of deceit. I'm okay with this. I'm not interested in playing his game. I'm bad at it. We're going to play my game instead and that game is just good old fashioned violence. The family specialty.

COGNITIVE DISSONANCE IS A HELL OF A DRUG

Posted Mar 18 2020 13:05:49 GMT-0400

Many of you have speculated on why the town would turn on me so quickly when I'm standing between them and the monsters. How they could be so foolish as to let themselves become the pawns of a creature like the not-brother. Now, I do have an update about the man with no shadow situation, but I'm still working out what exactly I can share from the most recent development. So in the meantime, I'd like to tell you some things about the town. I don't think it'll make any of you more sympathetic towards them… but maybe you'll understand my situation better. I'll tell you about the bridge and how my parents got to know each other.

Before I get too much further, I know some of you don't like to hear about animals being killed, so consider this your warning. The wildlife suffers alongside the rest of us, sometimes.

The town has seen its share of troubles over the years. My campground is hardly the only danger that we've dealt with and they have their own share of the blame. You'd think they'd learn, but these are not stories they tell to their children and so each generation has to start over and make the same mistakes. Do you know the Bible verse about how the children will be punished for the sins of their parents, down to the third and fourth generation? I think this is what it means. They condemn us to repeat their mistakes through our ignorance.

Perhaps the town is ashamed. They buried Louisa's parents deep, after all, and when trees sprouted and grew all in the course of one spring and blanketed the town in their petals, they cut those down and burned them so that they couldn't be reminded of what they did. And then Louisa died under the hooves of the dapple gray stallion and her land belongs to new owners now. Outsiders. We never told them its history. Hopefully they'll never own horses.

My family knows everything that's happened. My parents told me about them all, when I was a child and thought they were nothing more than ghost stories. Then one day, when the stories were starting to feel real, I went to the landmarks. There are a handful. The bridge is one of them.

It is a mere overpass. The road is narrow with barely any shoulder. The bridge is for trains. Small plants grow on the metal crossbeams underneath the tracks. It is wholly unremarkable save for it is the closest bridge to the nursing home.

The bloodstains have long since worn away - or perhaps they merely faded to the same color as the rust - and the asphalt has been repaved. Sometimes our mistakes hide themselves.

The story goes like this. I'll tell you like my mother told me.

Something ancient came to our town. It happens on occasion. Already I have told you of Perchta, the Yule Cat, and Saint Nicholas. All ancient things. Perhaps they are drawn to my campground or perhaps they pass through *all* of our towns more often than we realize and my town knows how to recognize the signs while the rest of the world remains ignorant. I think it is the latter, personally. You laugh off the primal terror that a sudden strong wind invokes but my town looks at the sky, looks to the birds, and looks for the other signs that might mark the arrival of something new.

This is important. If I'm right, ancient beings pass through more often than we realize. Whenever there is a strange storm or an unexpected shift to the weather, be wary of strangers. Someone in your town or city may be approached by an ancient being and not recognize it for what it is. It could be you that it comes to.

For my mother, the first sign that an ancient was present was the deer stuck in the fence around the nursing home. She volunteered there in highschool. She started doing it because her friend asked her and then when her friend lost interest, she continued on, merely because she believed in finishing what she started. There was no other real reason. But one day after school she drove to the nursing home and found two of the staff out by the fence. It is not a proper fence. Decorative. The deer can jump over it. This one, however, had somehow managed to catch its back legs on the top rung and then wrapped its body *through* and around. Like it'd been tied in a knot. It's stomach had split open from the pressure and its intestines lay in a pile on the ground.

They mistook it for a doe. My mother, however, was willing to look closer at the mess and saw the bloody holes in its skull where antlers had been torn free.

She finished her volunteer shift without saying a word to anyone about the deer. Then once she was home, she called my grandfather. She didn't know my father at that time, except by reputation as the next person in line to inherit the notorious campground. That was the first time they talked, when he picked up the campground's office phone and the only thing she said to him was that she would like to speak to his father, please, because he would know what to do.

My father says he was a little offended by the implication that *he* didn't know what to do, at the time.

My grandfather wasn't much help. He was mean even back then and told my mother it was nothing unusual and hung up on her. Then he went into the woods and hung wards all around the border to stave off whatever had come into our town. My father, however, had listened in on the conversation. He found my mother the next day and told her what she should watch for.

Not dangerous on its own, he said. It would pass by peacefully, so long as no one invited it indoors.

There are many ancient things like this. They're less of a threat these days because we as a society no longer practice hospitality. A stranger in the evening can simply find a hotel like everyone else and does not need to even have the door opened for them, much less invited inside. In the past, the person being asked would have to scrutinize the stranger for some deformity - the ear of a sheep or the tail of a goat. And then they would be turned away.

I would not be telling you this story if the ancient had simply passed through the town. We all know these things. We pick them up in tidbits here and there, from our peers at school, from our aunts and uncles. And someone knew them and saw the sign and invited the stranger inside regardless.

He wanted something. A bargain was made.

And the residents of the nursing home began to die. This was not unexpected. It *was* a nursing home, after all. However, my mother was watching for more signs - as my father had warned her to do - and she found them. A resident complained about hearing a bird hitting the window and so she went to check and found that it had not hit the window after all. It had been sitting on the windowsill when the open window slipped in its frame, fell, and crushed it. Fortunately the occupant of the room was elsewhere at the time and so she could remove its broken body without alarming anyone. The next day, however, the resident was gone. Died in his sleep, the staff told her when she asked.

A month passed. Things felt *off* around town. Small things. Little accidents, a fall that twisted an ankle or a shelf in a store collapsing and destroying everything that was on it. People were uneasy and could not explain why. Some would cry for no reason and be bewildered for days at their outburst.

We know when an ancient thing is nearby. Somehow, we know, even if we cannot admit it to ourselves.

The next time it was a cat. It got inside and then expired on the end of the bed in a resident's room. She woke that morning to find a dead cat on her legs and was inconsolable for a better part of the day. It was a stray, the staff told my mother. Probably already dying when it found a way to crawl inside and was looking for a warm place to lie down one last time. They pitied it. And they pitied the woman, when she died the next night as well.

Another month and another death, forewarned by the demise of a small animal close by. My mother spent as much time as she could at the nursing home, watching to see if anyone was acting suspiciously. She was named "volunteer of the month" for all her activity, but she remembered that she just threw the certificate on her desk when she got home and then lost it the next time she cleaned her bedroom. The only thing that mattered was figuring out who was marking the residents for death and how they were accomplishing it.

It was clear what was happening. Someone had made a deal with the ancient thing and the price was paid with lives. The nursing home was an easy target because, well, people die there. In highschool *I* volunteered there, once, as a class activity, and someone died. Just silently passed away in the middle of the dinner we were serving and no one from my class realized it until the rumors spread, because they wheeled him out so quickly and quietly. So to lose a resident every month? At one of the few nursing homes that served all the surrounding towns? Hardly remarkable. The only reason my mother noticed was because she was *looking* for signs.

My mother, however, was limited in her ability to investigate. She quickly ruled out her fellow volunteers and then that was the extent of what she could do, as she had to leave in the evening. She didn't think the police would believe her yet, and perhaps she doubted herself a little too. She wanted to be *certain*. The deaths all occurred on the same day of the month, so on that day she had a friend drop her off at the nursing home so her car wouldn't be in the parking lot. After she finished playing board games with the residents she said goodbye to the staff, but instead of leaving, hid in the closet of an unused room. She waited until the home shut down for the evening and then, with only the night staff present, she lurked by the door and waited. Whenever she heard footsteps in the hallway she peeked out through the cracked doorway to see who it was. For the most part, it was staff. Then, around 2 am, it wasn't.

It was one of the residents. A man whose son was one of her teachers in middle school. At first she was going to dismiss him as just someone wandering the halls at night, but then he crouched besides a closed door not far from where she knelt. There was a scratching sound, like wood on wood, and then he stood and walked away. In his hand was the antler of a young deer. At the bottom of the doorframe was a tiny mark, almost indistinguishable in the darkness.

My mother scratched it out with her house key before she slipped out a back door and called a friend to pick her up nearby. It didn't matter. The signal had been given during those few minutes it was in existence and the next morning the staff found that a rat had slipped into the resident's room, gotten tangled in the cord for the blinds, and hung itself. And the following night, the resident also died.

My mother was a lot more impulsive when she was younger. Furious, she confronted the old man. Told him that she knew he'd made a bargain with an ancient being and if he didn't tell her how to reverse it, she would go to the police. He swore that he'd done no such thing and my mother stormed off. A few hours later, once she was home, she got a call from the volunteer coordinator. They didn't want her to come back. One of the residents had complained that she was in the habit of using "foul language" and they expected better behavior out of their volunteers.

My mother did no such thing, but she sure used plenty of profanity after that call ended, she said. And that also was what convinced her to resolve the situation herself - if the nursing home would so easily side against her on one complaint, then what hope did she have of convincing the police?

She turned to my father for more help - and by then she knew to ask him in the hallways at school rather than calling the campground phone line. He didn't want to help, not at first. My mother can be quite persuasive, however. She waited until the hallway had cleared out a bit and then slammed him into the lockers and threatened to smash the windshield of his car. And she did, when he still refused. That's when he gave in. He said that he figured if she was determined enough to take a baseball bat to his car while it was in the school parking lot then maybe she was a match for an ancient being.

That night she snuck out of her house. She went to a nearby farm and stole one of their chickens out of the coop. She had to run with it clutched under one arm, her hand clamped around its beak to stop it from screeching. The owners were slow to react to the commotion. She was in her car and fleeing by the time they got to the yard to confront the intruder. Then she drove to one of the empty fields that border the nursing home and that's where she killed the chicken and removed its heart. She only had a pair of scissors and they weren't strong enough to cut bone so she had to snap the ribcage open with her bare hands and by then she was covered in blood up to her wrists and figured it was just as well to pull the heart out with her fingers.

That's when the ancient being arrived. Some are evil. Most of them are neutral, indifferent fragments of gods that pay little attention to the affairs of humans. Some, like Saint Nicholas, are benevolent. Some swing between the two extremes, helping one person, harming another. This was one of the evil ones. A passive evil, however, one that was fueled by human initiative and merely reacted to our world instead of trying to shape it.

My mother never turned around. She only felt its presence behind her, a weight, a smell she was never able to place. She felt its malice - but it was restrained. It was there not just because she called, but because it was curious.

She asked why it was here. The ancient being laughed and it sounded like branches breaking under the weight of winter ice. It'd been *invited* in, it said. It would not leave this town and the misfortune and suffering would only deepen so long as it was here. Not just at the nursing home, but the entire town would suffer from the pall it cast over every inhabitant. It sounded delighted at the prospect of the misery to come.

My mother asked what it would take to satisfy it. Not banish - that's a dangerous question. She sought appeasement. The ancient considered and then, still amused, told her what it wanted her to do. She would deliver the life of the middle school teacher to the ancient before the night was over or her own would be forfeit and it would stay. The death of a relative would be a delicious enough betrayal to sate its desire for misery and it would move on to find another town foolish enough to let it in.

Perhaps the ancient hoped that my mother would fail, given such a short timeframe. It misjudged her determination. My mother says she wasn't even sure why she was doing any of this. At some point, while she was driving her car with her hands sticky with drying chicken blood, she realized how insane all of this was. It was like she'd thrown herself down a cliff, however, and she couldn't stop falling until she hit the bottom.

She drove to the teacher's house and broke in through a window. She had no plans. She was acting on impulse and sudden desperation. She picked up a lamp on her way to the bedroom and when the man came stumbling out, she smashed it on his head and he dropped. Then she tied him up with some rope she found in the garage and loaded him - and a bunch of other supplies from the garage - into the back of her car.

She took him to the bridge. The one near the nursing home. The ancient had been specific in how it wanted its offering presented. And he, conscious now, begged her to spare his life as she hoisted him up by his ankles from the bridge's beams and then he could only scream as she drove nails into his eyes and cut out his tongue.

The ancient came to claim what was left of him, after that. She didn't see any of it. She was off to the side of the road, vomiting. My mother was not raised with violence, as I was. She made it her own.

Perhaps this explains a little of why I am... as some of you have said... a borderline psychopath.

Yes it is very uncomfortable to write that word out.

They found the teacher's body the next day and cut it down from the bridge. The skin around his neck was blackened in places and flaked like ash to reveal cooked meat underneath. It almost looked like the mark of hands, like something had wrapped its fingers around his neck.

If you're thinking - what about the broken window from my mother's hurried kidnapping? Surely there was an investigation. How did she not get caught by the police? Well... while my mother's prints were all over the house, they didn't have them on record to match them to. There were also no connections between my mother and her former teacher. She hadn't interacted with him since middle school, after all. A seemingly random break-in and ritualistic murder committed by someone with *no record whatsoever* is quite hard to track down. Honestly, she might have gotten away with it if not for the stolen chicken. She hadn't quite been quick enough getting back to her car and the owners reported her license plate to the police. A stolen chicken is enough to connect someone to a bizarre death around here, especially when they occur on the same night.

My mother had a reputation for being a troublemaker, but murder? The police were astonished and stalled on arresting her and then my father got word of it, because the police gossip with my family, and he went to the station. He lied about being there on behalf of his father, and told them it was campground business. Someone had made a deal with an ancient being and she'd elected to deal with it personally, in order to convince his family that she was capable. They were dating, you see, but of course dad didn't approve of it because he didn't approve of anything these days.

The police had already recognized the signs that an ancient being was lingering in town. They stopped the investigation right there and let it remain unsolved.

But then my parents had to *actually* go out on dates for a while to make the lie believable and that's how they eventually got together.

And the person that struck the bargain? He was dragged screaming through the center of town by his ribcage late one night as the ancient departed. The people living in town heard his shrieks and some of them looked and they saw a huge figure, indistinguishable in the darkness, dragging one long arm behind it with a single claw hooked through the chest of a writhing man. He left behind a long, thin trail of blood that ended abruptly at the first field at the edge of town.

There is often collateral damage with these creatures. Never forget that. The purity of your intentions or your love will not save you or those around you. The only thing that can is your strength and your will to fight.

Or you know, just *not making bargains with ancient creatures to begin with.*

I'm a campground manager. I've told you before that the town is hardly innocent. That man heard the knocking at the door of the nursing home and went and answered, knowing that *nothing human* knocks so late and asks to be let inside. But he saw an opportunity to stave off death and took it, even though it meant others would die. This is hardly the only story I have. The problem with everyone here being more aware of these creatures due to my campground is that they also think they can *handle* these other powers, that they can master them, and it never turns out well.

They like to pretend they're blameless. Sometimes I wonder if the reason they turned on me so quickly is because I am not afraid and I am not ashamed of what I've done and *they are*. They're in denial. 'The teacher's father would never make a bargain with an ancient power, he was such a nice old man, not like that family that runs the campground and thinks they can tell us what to do just because they're the driving force behind our local economy. And if I get everyone else to believe that Kate and her old land is the real reason these creatures that prey on us exist and it's not because life is cruel and unfair and we're helpless to change that… then with enough people believing the same as me… that must mean *I'm right.*'

Or perhaps I'm reading too much into it and they're really just a bunch of willfully ignorant assholes. Unfortunately, I do live here, and I have to get along with them. It's not like I can just let them suffer the consequences like I do on my campground because there will always be new campers to replace the ones that die.

THE TOWN SHOULD FEAR ME

Posted Mar 22 2020 00:01:47 GMT-0400

I think the town is back to normal. Last time I went to the grocery store everyone scurried out of my way and no one made eye contact. They're afraid of me. As they should be. You see, with the town not daring to oppose me and the sheriff gone... I can do whatever I want. And recently that was a bit of kidnapping.

I reached out to Turtle to see how she's doing. A lot of you are concerned about her while she's been away for the winter so I figured I'd better just confirm for certain if she's coming back. She's fine and she is not coming back. She got in touch with someone local whose land just became an old land and they desperately need help. I think it was a bookstore? Or maybe a bakery? I wasn't paying that close attention, I'm afraid. Some sort of family-owned business that's been passed down, much like mine has. Anyway, she's going to work for them and maybe help them figure out the rules of their new status. I swear it was a bookstore but she also said something about "the fires" and that's why I keep thinking it's a bakery...

Maybe it's both? I don't know. Whatever. I got my own problems here.

Anyway.

I went to the police station on Monday. The old sheriff stopped by my house to pick me up. This is unusual. I don't typically interact with the police outside of when they're called to my campground and even then it's mere formality. I hand off paperwork and sometimes a body. They don't ask questions. The handful of times I've been inside the station were for surprisingly mundane things - like picking up a camper that had gotten a bit too rowdy and had to sleep it off in a cell.

Yes, I pick them up. After the hitchhiking incidents I don't want to leave them to their own devices on how to get back to the campground.

The old sheriff told me on the drive over that they'd been interviewing everyone that was in the town hall, he said. The local police force was helping. Without an acting sheriff they've fallen naturally back into following his lead. I asked him if he was considering running for office once this was all over. He'd get it. Easy. He looked pensive at the question, his eyes softening as he stared at the road ahead of us.

"No," he finally said. "There's a lot of power with being sheriff but it's also a broad area of responsibility. I think I'd prefer to keep my focus local."

My campground, in other words.

"Who do you think is going to run?"

"Someone from out of town. Everyone around here will be too spooked. The last two sheriffs had something bad happen to them, after all."

That's fair, I suppose. It's a reasonable concern. The unofficial tradition around here is that my family deals with everyone on the campground, the sheriff deals with everything off the campground, and the police deal with speed traps and drunks and everything normal.

The police station is small. There's a cramped reception and then a hallway leading to where the police have their offices and a single conference room. The jail cells are in the basement. The old sheriff led me to the conference room where a couple officers I recognized were gathered. They nodded at me politely as I entered.

They wanted to review their findings from the interviews. There were a few things of interest to me in particular, they felt. The town had initially been divided over what to do about my campground. The police had even broken up some fights in the bar over it. But at the town hall meeting, they'd all been convinced. The not-brother hadn't said much, just introduced himself and said he was here to destroy my campground and they'd all agreed that yes, this was the right thing to do.

The people who were convinced prior reported nothing unusual about this.

The people who were on my side recalled that it felt *wrong* at the time. It grated against the back of their mind, like the same sense of unease that led them to double-check that all the doors were locked late at night. One of them called it an 'intrusive thought.' Something that was being forced upon them.

Everyone felt that way when they were willed to stop me. Some of the interviewees said it was like they were trapped inside their own mind, screaming, trying to break through to the surface, but something held them down. Like drowning, like straining to break the surface tension but the water would just not yield and allow them up for air.

If you think none of this matters because the not-brother is dead - I disagree. It matters very much. There is a difference between the not-brother's control and the man with no shadow's control. From what I've learned of the two, it was the not-brother that had the *entire* town under his control and he was the one that gave the order for them to try to stop me en masse.

It means that the man with no shadow does not have control of the entire town. He had to rely on the not-brother for that and now the not-brother is dead.

I cannot tell you how relieved I am by this.

The interviewees had another tidbit of information. In the moment of the not-brother's death they felt something. Snippets of the not-brother's thoughts, its emotions. Fragments. Not everyone had the same memories. The police were able to piece together a semblance of a coherent narrative. The not-brother died angry, but not at me. At the man with no shadow. In the moment of his death he realized he'd been betrayed - that the man with no shadow valued his life not at all and was willing to gamble with it and the bet had gone against him. He hated us both as he died.

I am less relieved by this information. Perhaps it is satisfying to know the not-brother died this way, but it means that the man with no shadow was willing to risk losing his pawn by exposing him so publicly. It means that the not-brother's usefulness was dwindling. The man with no shadow doesn't *need* the entire town turned against me.

I didn't reveal these thoughts to the police. I just quietly listened, thanked them for their work, and left. The old sheriff told me when we got into his car that he'd brought me out to the police station for another purpose. He wanted a plausible reason to get me out of the house. There was somewhere else he wanted to visit but he didn't want to draw attention to it. He didn't trust anyone in town.

The arrest of the pharmacist that tried to poison me had sent ripples through the local medical community. These ripples had unearthed someone that wanted to speak to us. He was frightened, though, and so we were going to meet him someplace discreet. Someplace where neither us nor him would be easily recognized by the locals.

Outside a bowling alley in another town, to be specific. The sheriff pulled up next to a young man wearing a bright red t-shirt and he got in the backseat and then the sheriff drove off. I glanced back at him. He looked frightened and avoided making eye contact with me. I introduced myself, just to relieve the tension, and he said that he knew who I was. Or at least, he knew me by reputation.

"I work in the hospital," he said. "I don't want to tell you my name. But I need to tell you about something that's been going on for a long time now."

It started years ago. I pressed the young man for an exact date and he couldn't give me one, as he'd only pieced the timeline together from records. But roughly speaking it was after the man with no shadow's second release from the campground. The man worked in the ER as a nurse. Or at least, he did for a while. Not anymore, he transferred after he noticed what was happening. He suspected it was still going on. But every now and then they'd get someone in the ER from my campground that was desperately sick. There would be no physical injuries, but the person's heart rate would be erratic, their oxygen count was low, and they'd soon go into cardiac arrest and succumb. It was a pattern. Not many, perhaps two a year. He'd only noticed because after one incident he'd started looking through the records and then tracking them going forwards.

The hospital recorded their deaths as from underlying health issues. He'd accessed the health history of one such patient and didn't find anything to indicate this was the case.

I knew the people he was talking about. I'd made the decision to call 911 on some of them. At the time, I'd also assumed it was some underlying health condition and the hospital had confirmed with me it was natural causes when I followed up.

He hesitated a moment in his story, staring out the window and fidgeting. I gently reminded him that I see a *lot* of weird shit and nothing he said would be unbelievable to me.

There was one patient, he said. A young man. Looked healthy, not the kind you'd expect to find gasping for air on a gurney. They'd given him epinephrine, thinking it was an allergic reaction. Then, right before his heart stopped, the young man sat straight up in the bed and grabbed the nurse.

"I'm scared," he gasped, clutching at the nurse's arm. "There's something - in the woods."

The campground. The monsters it harbored. And the nurse noticed - just before he collapsed again and before the heart monitor sounded its alarm - that the young man's shadow wasn't right.

It was almost gone. What little remained was tattered, like it'd been torn to shreds.

After that he began to look at the shadows of all the people that died of natural causes in the ER. Most were normal. Very few were not. And of those few, he noticed another pattern.

The final cause of death was always written by the same doctor. It didn't matter who had *actually* been present. The electronic record was always entered or amended by the same person.

The old sheriff thanked him for his courage in telling us what was happening inside the hospital. It was hard enough to recognize the patterns, he said, and even harder to jeopardize his position by coming forwards. He gently suggested the nurse look for a position elsewhere. In another county, perhaps. Just to be safe. Or at the very least, take a vacation until this was all over. Then he dropped him off back at the bowling alley and we sat in silence for a little bit as he drove back towards the campground.

"The man with no shadow has a doctor under his control," I said. "So what? I think we knew he had people in the medical profession when that pharmacist tried to poison me."

"Look at the big picture," the old sheriff replied gently. "Think of the timeline. This doctor started covering for the man with no shadow's victims after his second release. I think the important takeaway from this is he didn't *just* visit the sheriff or the woman your uncle was having an affair with."

I was quiet for a moment. His words conjured a terrible reality, one that I did not feel ready to confront.

"I can't trust anyone," I whispered. "He could have gone to all the key people around town in the time allowed him."

I glanced sideways at the old sheriff suspiciously. He didn't take his gaze off the road, but I think he noticed nonetheless.

"He can't control me, Kate," he said gently.

"Are you like Bryan, then? Some distant ancestor that wasn't human?"

"No. But let's just say there's someone that protects me and leave it at that."

Sometimes I wonder if my campground draws in humans as well. People that don't quite fit in with the rest of the world because there's a spark of something unnatural in them.

And I know there's been some speculation about this so let me reiterate: my family line is 100% human. Believe me, we checked. And we didn't trust that everyone was telling the truth, infidelity is obviously a thing after all, we got an actual source that could tell. I'm ordinary. Just a girl with a gun and a list of rules.

"Let's go visit the doctor," the old sheriff suggested.

"And... kill him?"

"No." He paused. "Well, maybe. But let's keep that as the last resort."

I called the police station and a few minutes later we had an address and thirty minutes later we were pulling into the driveway of the doctor's house. It was a long drive, winding through a grassy yard to a three-car drive. We have clusters of these sorts of houses in scenic areas. You know how groups of animals have their own names? A murder of crows. A conspiracy of ravens. What do you call a group of rich people with big houses sporting too many gables?

Around here, they're called 'easy targets', especially when the police have told you they'll ignore any alerts from the security system company.

We went in through a window when he didn't answer the door. The old sheriff took a rifle from the back of the truck and bashed in the glass with the stock. That set off the alarm, as we expected, and the old sheriff ignored it and tossed his jacket over the ledge to cover the broken glass and we climbed in.

The interior was dark. None of the lights were on. And the furniture... it looked ransacked. Everything was pushed away from the windows, to the far end of the room. Piled against the wall, sofa upended to make room for chairs, possessions stacked on top of seat cushions and littering the floor underneath the end table to leave the rest of the floor barren.

"This is... weird," I whispered uneasily.

We cleared the first floor. Every room was the same - all the contents stacked as far from the windows as possible. Then we went upstairs. The stairway ascended into darkness. It was an unnatural gloom, deeper than merely having the lights off. The old sheriff switched on a flashlight and peered into the first room. The windows were covered with layers of black plastic. The edges were sealed over and over with duct tape. No sunlight was able to get through. He cleared that room while I stood watch at the doorway. There was no furniture. The rooms were completely barren.

We found the doctor in the second to last room. The old sheriff had hesitated before entering, only because he was looking into the master bedroom. That was where all the furniture from the second floor was. It was stacked up to the ceiling. It cast long, jagged shadows on the far wall as the old sheriff's flashlight beam played over the interior. I admit that I was being careless - I was looking too, wondering what drove the doctor to do such a thing. I wasn't watching the room we were about to enter.

The doctor emerged from the darkness at a run. He bodily hit the sheriff, who staggered back a pace with a grunt. The doctor's hands were wrapped around some kind of weapon. His eyes were wide and unfocused. He ripped it free and waved it wildly in front of him, panting desperately with fear.

"Get out!" he shrieked. "GET OUT!"

The old sheriff backed away, telling him easy, easy, just calm down. We weren't here to hurt him. The doctor lunged again with his knife, screaming that we had to get out, that we were going to get him killed. And all the while the old sheriff was trying to talk him down.

I didn't feel we were getting anywhere with that.

I took careful aim and kicked, driving my heel into his knee. He shrieked and went down and then the old sheriff smashed his flashlight on the back of the man's head. A box knife fell from his hands and onto the carpet.

The sheriff handcuffed him while he recovered his senses and I took the opportunity to tear the plastic off the windows. Sunlight poured in. And the doctor began to shriek, screaming that the shadows were going to devour him. The sheriff stared dubiously at the wall where his shadow stood. I peeled back the old sheriff's shirt to look at the wound in his arm. It wasn't too deep. Might need a stitch or two though.

"Do you think we should be concerned about the shadows?" he asked nervously.

"We'd be *fucked* if the man with no shadow could control shadows outside the campground," I said scornfully. "Boundaries are special, though, and my campground has borders. He can't get out."

We hauled the doctor downstairs and to the yard. Then I waited while the old sheriff got the first aid kit out to bandage his wound. If it weren't for Perchta, I might have slit the doctor's throat and dumped his body within eyeshot of the man with no shadow's grove. I had to be content with merely kicking him a few times while he was down, just to hear him yell. I was wearing my work boots, too. Probably cracked at least one rib before the old sheriff gruffly told me to knock it off.

"He made a lot of trouble for me," I complained as we wrestled him into the car.

"If I beat the shit out of everyone that ever caused me trouble I would *not* have this cordial of a relationship with your family."

I didn't really have a way to reply to that.

We took him to the old sheriff's property and dumped him in an empty shed in the backyard. The old sheriff went to the ER to get his arm stitched up and I waited with his wife. She's a pleasant lady. She's his second wife. The first died and a year and a day after her death, he married again, to a stranger no one in town had met before. I hadn't really sat down and talked to her before and we had coffee and I can't remember much of the conversation for some weird reason.

When the old sheriff returned, he said we'd go talk to the doctor now. See if we could get anything useful out of him.

"Am I bad cop? What do I do?" I asked as we crossed the yard.

"Just stand there and look like yourself. You don't need to say anything. In fact… please don't."

I felt a little offended.

The doctor was huddled in the darkest corner of the shed. All the fight was gone from him. He was willing to talk. Unfortunately, It was a lot of hysterical babbling. Something about how the shadows were watching him and how he saw their faces. I can only assume that the faces are of the people who died and whose records he falsified and his guilt has finally broken him. After a lot of prodding, the old sheriff got a few things of use from him. A man had come to his office at the hospital. He'd been startled by the intrusion at first and stood, meaning to tell the stranger to leave, but then the stranger had greeted him and sat down and said he just wanted to have a conversation. He just had a few questions. The doctor decided to indulge him and the man asked about his work a bit and then the doctor belonged to the man with no shadow.

After that, the man with no shadow introduced himself as *something* from the campground. He'd gloated, briefly, that everything was in motion and he'd had a *very* successful day of getting all his pawns in order. And the doctor would be one of his pawns, wouldn't he? There was an important job for him.

"That family doesn't trust me," he hissed. "Understandable, but let's keep it at that, shall we? Make sure they never find out what else I can do."

Then I inherited the campground and things changed for the man with no shadow.

"He's angry," the doctor wept. "I feel it. So angry. Ever since you wrote the rules."

Because I included him in them. My breath caught in my chest. He'd been hoping to remain largely ignored all this time, understood to be malicious, but perhaps not as great a threat as some of the other campground denizens. But what he did with my friends had left quite the impression and instead of merely avoiding him myself, I'd written him down and told *everyone* to avoid him.

I'd robbed him of his prey and his power.

No wonder he wanted me gone.

After that, the doctor settled on one thought and that consumed what was left of his mind.

"He eats them," he wept, over and over. "He's going to eat me too."

That's it. That's all we could get from him. As we were leaving, the doctor begged us to seal off all the cracks and leave the lights off. No light could get in, he babbled. He's powerless in the darkness. The old sheriff obligingly stuffed a bunch of ragged towels under the crack of the door to block out the light, which was far more courteous than anything I would have done.

"Is it safe to leave him here?" I asked, as he did this. "What if he gets out and you're not around? What about your wife?"

He smiled faintly.

"She's safer than I am," he said.

And I knew exactly the nature of his protection with that small statement. I will not tell you what it is, for while I believe I am enough removed from the agreement that it wouldn't matter, I do not wish to take chances. If you figure it out, please keep it to yourself. I don't think you'll do any harm, but let's be polite.

For your own safety.

I'm a campground manager. I'm angry at myself for missing the signs. The man with no shadow *has* been preying on my campers all along and I never realized it. I thought we were losing people to normal reasons: severe allergies, dehydration, heart problems. And perhaps we were, but there were also some that were being devoured. I think about what it was like when he ripped my shadow's arm off. I remember how much it hurt.

I can't imagine how they suffered before they died.

It's time to put an end to the man with no shadow. Finally, I think I've got the leverage with the town to do it. The police are on my side, after the incident at the town hall. The general public won't interfere. The doctor said the man with no shadow is powerless in the darkness, but frankly there's not a lot I can do with that. So I'm going to contact the fire

175

department to get them out here with their trucks and then with them standing by to contain it - I'm going to burn his grove to ash.

I'VE LOST MY CAMPGROUND

Posted Mar 29 2020 21:11:48 GMT-0400

I run a private campground. My position has been under attack, however, and I don't understand why. I swore that I was going to win, that I'd keep fighting, and I even had a few victories.

Turns out it was never a fair fight to begin with. I never stood a chance.

A little time has passed since I last posted. I've been waiting for the right opportunity. In the meantime, the buyer has been asking around about my land. I got a call from some locals that were back on my side after the town hall incident, telling me he was down at the general store making small talk and then at the bakery doing the same thing. Looking for answers. And he sure got them. Now that he's seen that my land - and our town - is a little *unusual* I guess the locals feel he's one of us now and just opened right up and told him everything.

A few hours after the locals let me know the situation, I got a call from the buyer himself on our camp line. He clearly was not keeping it together very well. After a bit of rambling about the expected (I can't believe what happened, I thought that *thing* was my *friend*, etc, etc) he finally managed to make his way around to the reason for his call. The locals had told him about how my land is special because it's been passed down through the family. He had a brilliant solution: sell the campground to him and reset the timer. He could keep it for a year, long enough for it to lose the 'old land' status (please note that we don't actually know how long it has to be out of our possession, but a year is a decent guess), and then he'd sell it back. He could even put it in the contract. He'd thought about just bailing on the whole thing and going home and looking for some other land to purchase in a different area, but then he realized that was the coward's way out and he couldn't just abandon the town when he had an opportunity to *help*. He sounded so naively excited that I almost felt sorry to tell him that wouldn't work.

I wasn't honest with him. I didn't tell him he was my cousin.

I gave him the same reasons I've given all of you. My land provides a home and without it, the denizens will be forced to wander in search of a new one. Perhaps some will fade out of existence. The majority, however, will roam and be weakened and perhaps even feed more often as the land saps their strength away. And then there are the ones that are trapped on my land. I left it up to his imagination what releasing them could lead to.

Did he ever notice, I continued, how the old stories faded out of popularity? How we don't tell our children about the monsters in the woods anymore? It's not that they're not relevant anymore. He just had the good fortune to grow up somewhere *safe*. The world is safe because of old land. Because we concentrate and keep those creatures away from the rest of humanity.

I'm not entirely sure if that's true. It's a theory I've had for a while but haven't any way to prove it. However, it made for a convincing lie, seeing as I had no desire to tell him that he was my cousin and the pawn of the man with no shadow from before his birth.

Also, If he is under the man with no shadow's sway, I don't want to let his master know that I've figured this out. If he isn't... well, the buyer has had enough upsetting revelations already. He'll find out when this is over, I guess.

And speaking of that...

You all gave me a lot of advice. I couldn't take all of it because the logistics of obtaining some supplies in a timely manner just wasn't feasible, but there were a couple things I could do. I checked the family records to make sure the grove wasn't sacred in any way. The only entry I found was when the land was marked as "uncampable" by my grandfather.

'New inhabitant at grove in block D14. 4 campers affected, 3 dead.'

Literally that's the only thing in the journal. Grandpa kept records grudgingly. Then he redid the map to carve out the grove as uncampable land and broke block D14 up into two pieces and left his ancestors to deal with any further problems. And let me tell you, have I gotten my share of complaints about that grove. 'Oh, so a perfectly fine grove with shaded and level ground is considered uncampable but the 65 degree slope that we can't put anything on because it turns into mud every time it rains is perfectly campable?' For the record, it is NOT 65 degrees and it only turns into mud because the camp uphill can't dig a proper fucking trench for their cooking runoff, but whatever, I'm the campground manager, I get to deal with land allocation squabbles along with the inhuman creatures that kill trespassers.

Rule # 5: If you're camping on an incline, dig a 1" wide and 3" deep trench that will direct water around your tents and common area. This will minimize flooding.

I also went around to some of the other more benevolent inhabitants to see if I could scrounge up backup. Everyone's OTP, the man with the skull cup, doesn't have a spot where he can be found that I'm aware of and he didn't deign to appear either, so he wasn't going to be of help. I went to the thing in the dark and while I'm pretty sure it's come out of hibernation and is awake, it didn't answer. I'm going to assume its silence meant that it doesn't care how this turns out. I, uh, did run into the dancers.

They were raking out the bonfire ashes to prepare the pit for a new camping season. I was surprised to see this, as I'd always assumed one of my staff did it. I suppose I was wrong. The sheriff wasn't there and the lead dancer said he was off gathering more firewood, when I asked. I told her about the situation with the man with no shadow and asked if they would help. She shrugged dismissively and looked instead at the progress being made on the pile of ashes and charred bits of wood.

"I don't have a particular preference as to who owns this land," she replied. "So no, I'm not going to help. The man with no shadow will leave us alone. You, however, would drive us out if you knew how."

I hesitated. Maybe I would have in the past, but now I wasn't so certain. I was trying to think of how to put this into words when one of the dancers dredged another layer of ash out of the bonfire and with it came a human ribcage and I decided that perhaps it was time to be going.

So the inhabitants of the campground weren't going to be of any help. I can't blame them. We don't have a friendly relationship with most of them.

As for materials… well, I had to settle for a lot of gasoline, some old rags, and empty bottles. Then I had to wait for it to not rain for a few days. I needed the ground dry enough to burn. Enough to drive him out of his grove and then we'd deal with him ourselves, the same as we dealt with the not-brother.

Guns and dogs.

I had both Bryan and the old sheriff willing to help. We'd go in daylight. The doctor's warning was alarming, but we didn't see a way to completely deprive him of his ability to access shadows. Not without broadcasting our intentions to do so and giving him an opportunity to escape. Going at night might limit his abilities somewhat, but it would also hinder ours. The old sheriff feared that between the darkness around us and the fire in front of us, our visibility would be too hindered to get a good shot in on the man with no shadow. It's a compromise, made only because we don't have to kill him in this attempt. Destroying his grove will be enough and then, once he is cast out into the woods, we can hunt him down.

For the curious, the doctor is doing… okay. The old sheriff thinks he'll recover once we kill the man with no shadow. At least, recover enough to be functional. He'll have to learn to live with his guilt.

It's been raining a lot this past week. Earlier today I went down to the treeline to check how dry it was and was, yet again, sorely disappointed. However, I noticed something else, when I turned back to the house. There were cars out near the barn. The one I renovated into a store. This was odd, as the gates were closed. Certainly, someone could have jumped the fence and cut the lock, but it didn't seem like something anyone would do. I warily made my way towards the barn. There were a LOT of cars. The handful of parking spaces were filled and they'd parked in the wide street (more of a courtyard, honestly) that ran around the barn and overflowed onto the side roads that ran through the campground.

I recognized a handful of the vehicles and my heart sank. They were from town. There were cars with out of state license tags too.

It was painfully apparent what was happening.

My childhood all over again. My friends, called out to the woods and held as hostage for the man with no shadow's demands. Who else could have brought this many people here?

This was an eventuality I'd considered. Except... I'd expected perhaps a handful of people. Those ringleaders who he'd roped into leading the campaign against me within the town. People that... wouldn't be missed as much as others.

Not this many. Not the campers.

What could I do? What the hell could I have done about this? I couldn't abandon them to their fate. That would be monstrous.

I called Bryan and then I called the old sheriff. I told them we needed to delay another day. It was still too damp. I did not tell them what was happening. They didn't deserve to be dragged into this and there was little they could do to help me.

I went to the grove.

I think I understand a little more of my mother, how she must have felt walking alone to the grove so many years ago, knowing she would have to give *something* to save my friends. I felt light. Like I was floating. The sun was too bright in my eyes. The forest around me didn't feel entirely real, like I was separate from myself.

We don't get to kill the monsters that hunt us. We can only delay. In the end, they are still the predators, and we are only the prey. I've known this my whole life and it was folly to think a few minor victories would change that.

I finally found myself at the grove. There must have been at least fifty people, all kneeling, each paired up with someone else. They knelt, knee to knee, facing one another. One was passive, hands resting on their legs, staring straight ahead without movement or emotion. The other... held a gun to the forehead of their victim. They were of all ages. Some looked like teenagers, trembling and crying but unable to move the gun away from its intended target. Others were older, white-haired and resigned, eyes empty with despair. At the fore of them all, between two trees that bowed over to each other, forming a gateway of sorts, was the man with no shadow.

"Kate!" he cried, as if we were happy to see me. Perhaps he was. He threw his arms out in welcome and I stopped short of the grove's border, refusing to let him touch me, much less *hug* me in a pantomime of friendship. "So glad you came. I didn't have a way to send you a message so I just had to hope you'd figure it out. Perhaps you *are* a bit clever after all."

"This is a bit crueler than the last time you took hostages."

I glanced at the pair nearest to the border. Two men, one as immobile as a statue, the other knelt there, terrified, hopeless, his shoulders rising and falling with his panicked breathing.

"Well, you *are* older now," the man with no shadow said cheerfully. "I didn't want to traumatize a child. But I'm not entirely cruel. You see, only *half* of them die if you refuse me."

He snapped, to illustrate his point, and the man closest to the border pulled the trigger. I flinched at the gunshot and then kept my gaze averted as he began to cry out in wordless anguish, horrified at what he'd just done. Some of the other people around the grove began to cry more audibly, whimpering in terror. And in a clear, calm voice the man with no shadow told the man who had held the gun to get up, leave the campground, and go home.

"That was… unnecessary," I said stiffly, as the man did as he'd been ordered.

Reluctantly, I glanced at the body. At the bits of bone and brain matter spewed onto the grass.

"Just making sure you understand the consequences," he murmured. "You are clever and perhaps you think you can still find a way to fight this. That's your nature. I realize that now, after you killed the not-brother. That was well-played, although I confess I hadn't been paying him the attention he needed. His usefulness was coming to an end."

"What did you promise him?"

"Prey." He shrugged indifferently. "He tried to slip back into the campground, you know, after you ran him out. I intercepted him. Told him he was going about it all wrong, that he couldn't control *you,* but he could control the town. And I could claim for us the campground if he did that for me."

"So you could bring them here," I spat. "Use the whole town as hostages."

"Oh Kate," he sighed. "I could have done this at any time. I could have done this years ago. I could have called to all those unwitting campers that didn't pay attention to my lack of a shadow and they would have come. I didn't need the town as hostages. Certainly, it makes it a little more difficult for… what comes next… but I'll improvise. After you're deposed."

After I'm deposed. The phrase rattled around in my head and then I grasped his meaning - he wasn't done. This was only one step in some larger plan.

Like a web I was caught in and I couldn't see the whole.

"What *are* you trying to do?" I whispered.

He smiled and held out his hand to me.

"Step inside my grove," he murmured, "and perhaps I'll tell you. And then I'll let everyone go."

Let me tell you something, as someone that has gone through some shit. We, as a species, will sacrifice for others. This is our nature. When we are the ones who sacrifice ourselves, it feels like the *right* thing to do and the burden we carry is made lighter. It is easy to be the one that suffers for the sake of others.

Helplessness, however, will destroy you.

It is a poison. We ingest it unknowingly and it eats at us inside, it clouds our souls, it breaks our hearts bit by bit, the cracks so tiny we don't understand why we hurt. Perhaps we see the signs - we cry when we shouldn't, we cannot focus on the things we love - but we shrug them off and keep going, because our wounds are invisible. We're dying in silence.

I was helpless there at the entrance to the grove.

I have been helpless for a long time. My courage is merely the flight of the hunted deer that knows all it can do is run until a misstep spells its doom. I wonder how deep the poison has sunk, if perhaps it is now the marrow of my bones.

And part of me just wants the hurting to stop.

I gave my hand to the man with no shadow. His fingers closed over mine and he pulled and I followed and he led me into the grove.

I next remember being back in my own house. Hours had passed. When I ran to the barn, it was empty. All the cars were gone and I was alone on the campground.

I am not the man with no shadow's pawn, I know this much. The tea from the lady with extra eyes held. The old sheriff said it was like a voice in his ear and I hear no voice and I feel no compulsion.

However, I *am* bound to my agreement. I don't remember the details. They float in my mind like mist and fade away when I come close, no matter how hard I try to force them into clarity. I can tell a few things. Tonight, at midnight, I will be at my house, and the man with no shadow will come and he will bring a contract and then I will sign it. I tested this agreement. I tried to leave and was overcome with sickness, a weakness that nearly took my ability to walk and my keys fell from hands that lacked the strength to hold them.

The hours until midnight were my own, however.

I drafted up a contract transferring the campground. I took the language from my will, hoping that would be enough to be legal once it was signed and notarized. I hesitated at filling out the recipient, however. I don't know who to trust. I don't know if I can trust myself. The obvious choice was my brother - that's what's in my will - but... the man with no shadow has been preparing this for a long time. I have no idea who isn't in his sway.

There was at least one person on this campground who was solidly opposed to him. I printed the document with a blank spot for the name. Then I folded it, stuffed it in an envelope, and started out into the woods.

I walked for hours. I traversed the entirety of my campground, walking through the woods, off the roads. Straying from the road for too long is an invitation for trouble, but I was desperate. I needed to find the one person on the campground who has never given me any doubt as to their intentions towards me. Surely they'd know what to do. They've helped me so much already, after all.

Instead, I found the man with the skull cup.

He stood blocking my way, a handful of feet in front of me, and I wondered how I hadn't seen him sooner. Like he'd stepped out from between the slender trees and thin air, or perhaps I simply hadn't been paying attention in my distress. His expression was severe, harsher than his usual blank disinterest. The corners of his mouth were creased with his frown and his eyes were narrow slits.

"Should you be wandering the woods like this?" he asked.

"They're *my* woods," I replied testily.

"I was not questioning that. I was questioning if this was the most productive use of what time is left for you."

He knew. Somehow, he knew.

"I'm looking for the lady with extra eyes!" I snapped. "I don't know who else to trust."

His gaze dropped to the letter that I clutched in one hand. I warily took a step back.

"Do you know what this is?" I asked.

He nodded faintly.

"Then tell me what name I should put on it!"

I waited, breathless. I don't know if I intended to take his suggestion. I truly didn't know who was on my side anymore. He'd helped me, but perhaps that, too, was a ruse. Perhaps he only protected me to lead me to this point. I just wanted to hear him say it, if perhaps that would confirm or deny some wild theory that bubbled half-formed in my head, the product of my self-doubt and fears.

Instead, he snatched at the letter. I jerked my hand back in surprise and his fingers closed on my arm instead and then he squeezed, pressing the bones together until it felt like they would snap, and my fingers went weak and the letter fell from my hand. He grabbed it out of the air and stepped back. I hesitated, my hand halfway to the gun at my waist, but reason caught me. It wasn't worth it. I could always print another if he didn't give it back.

"I need a name," I continued. "If I'm going to lose this campground I should at least lose it to someone who isn't one of *his* pawns. Tell me who you want to manage this land."

He tore the letter in half, then half again, and let the pieces fall to the ground.

"*I chose you,*" he hissed, staring me in the eyes. "Don't disappoint me."

He turned abruptly and began to walk away.

"But... help me!" I cried.

"Save yourself this time, Kate," he called back to me. "Did you not kill the master of the vanishing house?"

"That was different! It was already dying!"

"Then perish. Old land is no place for the weak."

I'm a campground manager. I don't know what to do next.

I've called the old sheriff and told him that if there's a new owner in the morning or in the next few days... kill them. Even if it's my brother. He sounded bewildered and asked if I was going to do something dumb, so I told him no, that I was just... afraid. And he tried to reassure me. He did. Said that our plan would work, that without his grove the man with no shadow would be vulnerable and we could hunt him down at our leisure. That it would all be okay and I just had to see this through.

I half-listened and then hung up.

I know some of you will criticize me for not telling him everything and asking his help, but I can't drag him down with me. He's lost enough already because of me with all those years spent in the vanishing house.

I'm going to shut the computer down and go into my study now. I don't want to answer comments this time. I don't want to hear what I should or should not have done. We all have our limits and the man with no shadow found the line that I could not cross. I just want to be alone with my books and my family's journals until the man with no shadow comes to enforce our agreement and it all ends for me.

RULE #10 – THE THING IN THE DARK

Posted Mar 30 2020 21:14:07 GMT-0400

The man with no shadow came at midnight. I'd given myself one last sunset, before going inside for the evening. It was muted by clouds, a have of mauve, darkening to puce along the ridge of the ebony trees. I watched from my front porch, wondering if it would be the last sunset I would see, here in my family's house where I was raised and where my parents died and where all my prior generations have sheltered from the terrors of the night.

Then I waited inside by the window, watching.

Two figures approached from the road. The man with no shadow's hair shone, catching the moonlight. Beside him was a shorter figure, unrecognizable in the gloom, his shadow stretching long beside him. The little girl waited for them at the fence and the man with no shadow spoke to her and she turned and left, her steps dragging reluctantly in the damp grass. Then he came and knocked on my front door.

"Invite us in, Kate," the man with no shadow said gently.

I did. I suppose that was part of our agreement from the grove.

His companion was the buyer. My cousin. He glanced around him in delight, taking in the aged wooden crossbeams of the ceiling, the dated wallpaper, and the photographs of my family from when I was a child that I didn't have the heart to replace.

"This is quaint," he finally said. "It's very charming. I can see why you've been so reluctant to part with it, Kate. But I think it'll be for the best. That incident with the town hall was horrible and now everyone can put all this behind them."

For a moment I was stunned. The buyer had no idea what was really happening here. He didn't seem like he was under the man with no shadow's control because *he wasn't*. He was just being duped.

Behind him, out of eyeshot of the buyer, the man with no shadow gave me a thin, warning smile. He set a stack of paper and a seal on the table.

"Let's get this all signed," the man with no shadow said. "I normally don't work this late."

"Of course, of course."

The buyer hastily sat down at the dining room table and waited patiently. I joined them more slowly, my back to the wall. The man with no shadow flipped over the first page and shoved it towards me. I took it, mechanically, and there was something tight in my chest and my fingers were numb.

"It's all pretty standard sale of a property," the man with no shadow said tonelessly. "Give it a read and then initial at the bottom."

He pushed a pen in my direction. I took it. I initialed. I couldn't *not* initial. Like a hand was over my own, guiding my motions. I wanted to scream, I wanted to weep, but I only stared stupidly at the papers that the man with no shadow was handing me, one by one, dryly explaining what each one was before asking for an initial and then collecting them to form a second stack of completed paperwork. Across from me, the buyer waited anxiously, excited in his ignorance as to what was happening here.

"So how do you two know each other?" I asked.

The words came with difficulty. It was like my mouth was full of sap and my tongue stuck to the roof of my mouth. The man with no shadow's eyes narrowed with annoyance.

"Oh, we don't really know each other," the buyer said. "I just got a recommendation for a notary in town and called her and then she said she couldn't do it for several weeks but then she called me back an hour ago, apologizing for interrupting so late, saying that she'd just heard from a friend and he could finalize the sale but he'd only be in town until tomorrow. So I needed to get down to the campsite as soon as I could if I wanted everything signed in a reasonable timeframe. And sure, it's midnight, but she said she'd checked with everyone and you were both fine with it."

The notary was under the man with no shadow's control. That knowledge was useless to me now.

"It is late, isn't it," I sighed. "Do you want some tea?"

The buyer happily agreed. I got up and went into the kitchen. Behind me, the man with no shadow excused himself to help. I forced myself to focus on filling the kettle, even when he came up behind me and stood at my back, mere inches apart. I felt his breath on the back of my head.

"You're *stalling*," he hissed.

"Damn right I am," I replied. "What happens if I stall long enough to get past the midnight hour?"

A special time of night. When the day ends and a new one begins. The significance was not lost on me.

"That won't happen. You agreed to finish before then."

I stepped back, forcing him to move lest I step on his toes. He hovered close by, looming over me as I turned on the stove and began pulling out cups while the water heated.

"Did our agreement stipulate that I had to get this done as quickly as possible?" I asked tersely.

"No," he admitted. "I wish I had."

"What happens after the campground belongs to the buyer?"

I turned and found myself face-to-face with him. He stared down at me with a hatred that I suppose I'd earned by now.

"I drag you back to my grove and devour your shadow, bit by bit. I'll rip your shadow's legs off first, so you can't escape, and then take my time with the rest of you. Perhaps if you hadn't been so *difficult* I would have given you a quick death but… I'm not inclined to do so anymore. It could be days, Kate," he whispered. "Weeks, even."

He half-raised his hand and I felt something brush along the back of my arm, like the touch of a moth's wings. I glanced aside and saw his hand poised so that his shadow - if it existed - would be touching my own.

The kettle began to scream on the stove. I turned to take it off and pour and briefly thought I could just fling the boiling water right in his face.

"None of that, now," he admonished. "We have an agreement."

He returned to the dining room. I was a little slower to follow, carrying a tray of tea. I confess that I used the lady with extra eye's tea for the man with no shadow's cup and he took one sip, coughed violently, and stared daggers at me while I finished initializing the rest of the pages.

The last page. I stared at it, startled to see my own demise in such an innocuous thing. A single piece of paper. An empty line where my signature was going to go. My fingers rested on the pen.

"I know it's overwhelming," the buyer chirped. "But like you said yourself - this will be a *good* change. You can even go back to school and finish your degree like you wanted to, right?"

I really wish I'd remembered what our conversation on the phone had been. No doubt I'd made the call from the grove under the man with no shadow's guidance. The buyer was still chattering about how I could always come back and visit, of course, and how he could even keep me on as assistant manager or something since he'll probably need help in the transition period. I wasn't paying attention, my focus entirely on the single piece of paper that would put an end to all of this.

I only snapped out of my daze because he'd stopped talking.

"Do you hear someone… crying?" he asked.

"That's the little girl," I replied dully. "The one you saw at the fence. She killed my mother. Don't worry about her, she can't get inside."

The buyer stared in consternation at the window behind me. The little girl's weeping came from the other side of the glass. The man with no shadow was silently digging his nails into the surface of the table and staring at me in outright hatred.

I picked up the pen.

And as the little girl wept behind me, I had a moment of clarity.

I stood. I turned, ostensibly to untie the drapes and let them cover the blinds with another layer to block the noise, but instead I grabbed the cord and yanked the blinds up. Then, as the man with no shadow began to call my name and demand I stop, I opened the window.

And the little girl started to climb in, her shoulders heaving with her sobs as she stretched out her hands to clutch at either side of the wall.

"No!" the man with no shadow shouted, standing and lunging for me. His fingers closed around my wrist and he began dragging me away from the window. "I haven't worked *this hard* to let you win!"

He wasn't speaking to me. I realized this, distantly, as he pulled me through the house and towards the front door while the crying of the little girl drifted after us. He was speaking to *her*.

"*Move* Kate," he swore. "Damn you!"

Behind us, the buyer began to scream. A long, uninterrupted shriek. I know it well. It is the scream of someone that is in the process of dying and cannot do anything to save themselves, but nor can they hasten their demise.

The man with no shadow dragged me through the house and to the front door. Ripped it open and switched his grip to the front of my shirt before dragging me behind him across the yard. Getting me over the property line. Only once we were past the road and in the field that led to the forest did he pause and spin to face me, his hand still tight in the fabric of my shirt.

"New plan," he snarled. "I rip you apart right here. You get a fast - albeit agonizing - death after all. Then I start this *all over* with your fucking brother."

I laughed, hearing the touch of hysteria in my own voice.

"Your buyer is dead," I said mockingly. "She's probably spreading his intestines across the walls. What are you going to do about *that*?"

Pain shot through my abdomen. I doubled over but did not fall, some terrible pressure held me up. I doubled up around it, like a spike in my gut, the pain lancing all the way through to my back. I coughed and tasted blood.

"I'll figure it out," the man with no shadow said calmly. "You might want to save your breath for screaming. It might help with the pain."

Another burst of agony, higher up, just below my ribs. I did scream. Like the buyer had.

"Or perhaps it won't," the man with no shadow said thoughtfully.

And then he pitched backwards with a cry of his own, I was dropped to the ground, and a gunshot echoed through the night sky.

The old sheriff isn't an idiot. He knew that something was wrong and while I wasn't going to ask for help, he should still keep watch with his rifle.

I struggled to stand. My fingers clutched at my abdomen as pain lanced through my body and my lungs seized up in reflex. Nothing but unbroken skin. My shadow was what he attacked, I told himself firmly. Only my shadow. I could survive it - but only if I kept moving.

I took a second while the man with no shadow was reeling to take stock of my surroundings. He'd dragged me out the front and down towards the woods. The treeline was only a few yards away.

The sensible choice would have been the road. The path to it was free of trees, hopefully giving the sheriff another shot. Following it would get me off the property and out of the man with no shadow's reach. But he was between me and the road and he was getting to his feet, panting hard with pain, but his eyes were bright and remained focused on his quarry.

I chose the woods.

Perhaps it was instinct telling me where to go. The woods are where we fight our monsters, after all, and emerge from them changed - or not at all.

Or perhaps I was blinded by pain and fear and merely got lucky.

I stumbled through the trees, catching myself on their trunks to keep my balance. The man with no shadow followed in a dash, but he was not directly chasing me - he was trying to get under cover. Another gunshot broke the silence and I used the noise to move quickly, just enough distance to break line of sight between us.

Then the hunt was on. The man with no shadow pursued, but quietly, as a hunter stalks their prey. I, too, tried to stifle my breathing and step carefully so as not to give away my position with an errant branch. I can be quiet when I need to be. We grew up in the woods, after all, and my brother and I played our games of chase and hide and seek. When I was older, I hunted through these woods. I'd learned my lessons well.

Still, despite the darkness and my silence, I could not quite shake the man with no shadow. His pursuit was not entirely by human means and I could do nothing for his preternatural senses.

Then, as my strength waned and the pain of my injuries threatened to drag me to my knees, I put my hand out for support and while my fingers touched the cool bark before me, I could no longer see them. I could no longer see anything at all.

All light had gone out.

Instinctively, I squeezed my eyes shut. Somewhere behind me and to the right, I heard the man with no shadow stop as well. His hiss of indrawn breath was stunningly loud in the forest and I knew exactly what his direction was.

The thing in the dark. I could wait for it to pass. And then what? Resume the chase, one that I was losing by inches as the minutes slid by? I'd broken his line of sight but I couldn't simply hide and wait for him to pass by, as he seemed to be following through senses other than sight and hearing. And while injured, he was not weakening as quickly as I was. It was only a matter of time until he found me.

Or…

I turned. The man with no shadow's ragged breathing was faint, but there was no other sound in the woods at this moment. I honed in on it, breaking into as fast of a run as I dared, my hands stretched out before me and I ran tree to tree, pulling myself forwards by touch alone. All around me the forest began to shake. It was like a strong wind, rattling the leaves and snapping the branches. I heard the man with no shadow cry out - just enough sound to push me forwards those last few feet - and then my hand closed on his shirt.

"Here!" I cried. "We're here!"

And I opened my eyes.

The wind intensified. I saw the dirt and leaves of the forest floor rise up around me in the gale, but there was still no light, it was like they were outlined on top of the darkness and somehow I could see regardless, and there was *something* alive in that wind. Small pieces of debris struck my exposed skin like the sting of a wasp. The man with no shadow grabbed my wrists, trying to pry himself free of me, but I did not relent. We would die together.

Then we were falling. All time seemed to stop and I froze, waiting for that final impact, and I *did* land hard on dry leaves and brittle branches. But I was alive. The wind was gone. The air around us was cool and tasted damp. There was no light. My eyes widened, instinctively trying to find *some* spark of luminescence, but there was none.

"What have you *done?*" the man with no shadow hissed. I heard him stand.

"I kind of expected us to die," I said, also standing. It left me breathless and I clutched at my abdomen and waited for the pain to pass.

"No. This is *much* worse."

I raised a hand and walked forwards until my fingers touched something. I traced its contour gently, feeling the seam of wood stripped clean of bark, felt it curve upwards and downwards like the rib of a ship. Then I felt it move away from my hand and I froze and then after a few minutes it drifted back and my fingers were once again touching its cool surface.

Like it was breathing.

I knew where we were.

We were inside the thing in the dark.

A PLACE WITHOUT SHADOWS

Posted Mar 31 2020 21:22:24 GMT-0400

For a moment, I was at a loss on what to do. I hadn't thought this through because, well, I didn't think I'd *need* to, on account of being dead and all. The man with no shadow had no intention of dying just yet, however.

"How about a truce for today?" he said from behind me. "We'll both get out of here and then tomorrow we can go back to trying to kill each other. I stabbed you, your friend shot me, I think we're even."

"You're helpless here, aren't you? There are no shadows."

A long pause and then he admitted that yes, he was. But neither could I hurt him. In fact, he said reluctantly, without shadows he couldn't interact with the corporal world at all. He existed - and he touched my hand to illustrate his point - but he couldn't influence it. No matter how he tried, he couldn't, say, force me to budge with a shove. His tone was flat as he told me this but I felt this was humiliating for him, to be forced to admit his weaknesses. I asked why he was telling me this.

"Because I need you to realize I'm harmless," he replied in frustration, "so that you don't waste time trying to get rid of me. I might need someone that can interact with the physical world to get out of here."

"And why would I need you?"

"Do you think you can find the way out?"

I was about to answer that yes, I could, but then I hesitated. My initial thought had been to simply follow the right-hand rule until I found the exit, but this was not a maze. This was the body of the thing in the darkness. I could hardly hope to navigate the veins of my own body and find a way out, after all. The man with no shadow told me, with a calm I certainly did not share, that while he couldn't guarantee we'd escape, he could at least lead us to the creature's mouth. He sensed it. The head and the heart - the domains of thought and life. They were things that creatures like him knew on instinct, honing in on them much like a cat hones in on the scent of a mouse.

So I agreed. We had an uneasy truce. I might have been willing to die in the woods but now I wasn't so convinced that I wanted to spend what time was left to me wandering the corridors of some unspeakable creature with my worst enemy until I perished of thirst.

I wouldn't make a good martyr.

We walked along in relative quiet. I kept one hand against the side of the corridor, my fingers sliding from rib to rib. The flesh was woven branches and dry leaves. Small bits of debris cracked under my feet as I walked. Not all of it was wood. Small bones, mostly, from rabbits or squirrels. Sometimes my feet slipped on something larger, perhaps a deer, and there were a handful that felt like they could be human.

"I don't suppose you'd tell me what you're trying to do," I said, "seeing as I still have a shot at killing you. But will you tell me if you've harmed the lady with extra eyes, like you said you would?"

"Not yet. I intend to kill her though, once you're dead. I don't understand your affection for her."

"That's because to you, everyone is a tool to be used and discarded," I muttered.

He made a soft noise of disgust.

"And the black sheep?" I asked. "Are you willing to tell me who that is? I'm sure you're aware that I accused my own brother already. *Is* it him? Or was the buyer not as naive as I thought?"

He laughed.

"I love how paranoid you are!" he crowed. "Delightful. No, it's not family. It's the print shop owner. The idiot was dropping off your order of campground rule pamphlets a few years back and I was there waiting for him."

Well that's fucking ironic.

"The buyer *was* under my control," the man with no shadow sighed. "I wouldn't leave such an important piece up to chance. I just didn't exert overt influence. It was subtle. Suggestions, here and there, so that he didn't realize it and so that it wasn't apparent to others. Trickier to manage, but I had to keep you fooled."

I didn't want to admit that he'd succeeded, so I said nothing at all. We walked a bit further. I had to pause and catch my breath, pressing a hand to the spot just below my ribs where the man with no shadow had stabbed through my shadow. He remarked that perhaps I wasn't as resilient as he'd thought and he'd have to take care not to kill me prematurely, when he had me in his grove. Not until he was satisfied that I'd suffered enough.

"Shut up," I hissed.

He started to speak, some other petty, cutting comment, and then he obligingly did as I asked.

He heard the noise too. The crack of branches from ahead of us. I shrank into the recess between ribs, my back against the matted debris. I felt the man with no shadow crouch at my back, his hands resting lightly on my shoulders, and he quietly whispered in my ear that it was a human approaching, but that perhaps it'd be best to let it continue on past us.

I held still, scarcely daring to breathe. Their footsteps drew closer and then they stopped entirely and for a moment all I could hear was labored, halting breathing. Then bony fingers latched onto my wrist.

I shrieked and jerked away, thrashing and twisting in an attempt to throw them off. Their grip was unrelenting and they drew closer, I could smell the stink of them - stale sweat and rot - and then their fingertips caressed my face, feeling the flesh of my cheek and the line of my jaw.

"Please," a female voice croaked, raspy with disuse. "Help me. I've been here for so long."

One of my lost campers.

"She's not begging you to save her," the man with no shadow said coldly from a safe distance away. The asshole had abandoned me the moment she grabbed my wrist. "She wants to die."

"How do you know?"

"I know her thoughts. I know everyone's thoughts. I know you want to kill me."

"You can read minds?" I asked suspiciously, still trying to pry her fingers off my wrist. She continued to beg for help, an endless litany of 'please'.

"I can if the thoughts are broadcast loud enough. You *really* want me dead and she *really* wants to die."

I reached up and seized her by the shoulders. She finally let go of my wrist and fell silent, reduced to a trembling, shaking wretch before me in the darkness. Her skin was stretched tight across her bones, like even her very muscles had wasted away.

"How long have you been here?" I asked.

"I know you," she finally replied, her voice soft with wonder. "You tried to save me."

"You followed the lights."

I... don't even want to do the math on how many years she's been here. Too many. This was what I faced, I realized with horror. This is what would happen if we didn't escape. Condemned to wander the body of the thing in the dark for eternity as my body shriveled for want of water and food and light.

"Okay," I exhaled. "Come with us. We're going to get out of here."

"This is a mistake," the man with no shadow muttered from behind us as we started walking again. "Sentiment only gets you hurt. Haven't you realized that by now?"

I coaxed more information from the young woman as we walked. There were others, she said, wandering in the dark. Some had given up and lay down and stopped moving and in time the wood and the leaves covered them up. They weren't dead, she said. She'd found one, cocooned into the wall, and she put her hand through the branches and felt their breathing and the beat of their heart. This wasn't what she wanted to become, so she kept moving. Constantly. Always moving, always searching for a way *out*. And her breathing grew quicker and I went silent for a little while so that her panic could subside enough for her to remain coherent. The man with no shadow gave us directions when we came to forks in the corridors and sometimes he hesitated or even told us to turn around and take the other passage.

One of them had tried to kill her, she said. He hadn't been here long and was mindless in his terror. He wasn't himself and he'd lunged at her and she sidestepped, knowing how to navigate this darkness better than he. And then she'd shoved him, into the wall, and wrenched a sharp length of wood from the ribs and stabbed him through the stomach with it. He'd remained there, pinned to the interlaced branches, and then they grew to cover him up and muffled his screams. Sometimes she found herself in that corridor again, by accident. She knew it because she could still hear him screaming from his tomb.

Sometimes, she said in a small voice, she would sit and listen to his cries just to hear another human voice for a little while.

She wanted to die so this would end. But just as he couldn't die, neither could she. She was already trapped in a body that should have died a thousand times over from deprivation and some horrific power kept her bound inside her bones.

I dropped back a few paces so that I could talk to the man with no shadow.

"Do you think she'll die as soon as we escape this thing?" I whispered.

"Probably. But that's what she wants."

I was quiet. I wanted to disagree. I wanted to save her, like I'd failed to do so many years ago. Yet after so long in the darkness… perhaps there is no way to come back from this. Perhaps if I were trapped for so long I would feel the same.

"You're afraid," the man with no shadow said.

"Reading my thoughts again?" I snapped.

"I don't need to in order to realize that. I *will* find the head of our captor, Kate. And then you get us out."

He told us to turn again and then stopped. He asked me to put my hands against the wall and tell him what I felt. I swept my palms along it, to the left and right, then up and down, and when I reached up - I felt a ledge. My heart sank. This maze was in three dimensions. But the man with no shadow sounded more confident now, saying that this was why he kept getting turned around, and maybe we could make some *real* progress now. I boosted the young woman up first and then she turned and helped pull me up into the tunnel. Then I reached down for the man with no shadow. He was as light as a feather and it took almost no effort at all to pull him up after us.

Then we kept going. Onwards and up along the slope until it opened into a new passageway. Our progress was better now that the man with no shadow understood more of what we were looking for. I hate to say it, but I do think we wouldn't have found our way out without him. We had a few more passageways leading up, one so steep we had to half-climb, pulling ourselves from rib to rib. Then the man with no shadow warned us that we were going to pass by the heart of the creature.

"What's in the heart?" the young woman asked.

"I have no idea and no desire to find out," he replied tersely. "Those places aren't meant for... lessor... creatures like myself and certainly not for mortals."

It was tense going after that. I was on edge, every part of me straining to hear some sort of sound other than the snap of branches and bones beneath our feet, and fearing that I would. Then my hand slipped off the rib and found only empty air beyond. The man with no shadow said to keep going and I stepped out into the open space, expecting to find another rib just a few paces beyond. Nothing. This passageway was wider than the others. I opened my mouth to warn the others and tell them to move to the other side of the tunnel when a whispering raced up out of that gulf and I froze. Like the rustle of leaves.

The ground beneath me shifted. I let out a cry of surprise and then everything was sliding, the leaves and the bones and the branches rolling and tumbling under my feet and I went down and slid with them, the carpet beneath me turning into a river of debris. It pulled me down into the hallway and then everything stopped. I tumbled a few more feet and hastily picked myself up, listening intently, hearing only the startled cries of the young woman and the swearing of the man with no shadow as they came after me. For a moment, everything was still.

Then the floor began to slide again. I lunged this time and my hands closed on a rib. I put one arm over it, locking my body in place as the floor rushed past me, drawn inexorably further down the tunnel towards what I now realized was a vast, empty chamber.

The heart was beating. Drawing everything in towards it.

And then I realized that I could *see*. There was light coming from the heart. Pale gray, diffuse, but light nonetheless and more than enough for my sun-starved eyes.

I turned to look inside once the floor settled in the lull between heartbeats.

The beast waited for me.

The one that will someday kill me.

I saw the glow of its white eyes in the darkness. I felt its presence, felt its patient desire.

Whenever someone goes missing I know that the thing in the dark swallowed them up because I dream of the beast. I dream of my death. And that was what waited for me inside its heart.

The lost camper reached me first. She slammed into the wall, having kept her feet despite the shifting terrain. Her fingers clawed at the rib, she couldn't find purchase, and then she slid back towards the heart and I reached out and her hand closed on mine. My arm trembled to hold onto the rib, keeping us both anchored there, then the floor's flow slowed and stopped.

I saw her face. White like bone, impossibly hollow with hunger, lips cracked and peeling, her eyes narrowed against the light. Her hair was almost gone, just a few tattered patches clinging to her scalp.

"Grab hold of the wall," I urged her, panting with exertion. "That heart is going to beat again."

She looked back at the archway and the chamber beyond. The beast waited for me, its double set of eyes opening and closing as it blinked patiently, knowing it was only a matter of time before I died under its claws. My heart pounded painfully in my chest.

"There's nothing in there," she said.

She resisted my hold, stepping towards the heart. I tightened my grip around her hand, crushing it between my fingers in desperation. The heart would beat again soon and she'd fall away and I'd lose her like I lost her years ago. I yelled at her to please, grab hold, don't do this to me again. Not again. I was so tired of losing people. I couldn't watch her die.

And she looked up at me and I saw that this was what she was yearning for, it was exactly as the man with no shadow said, and she saw nothing inside the heart because there was no death that she feared.

A heartbeat.

And I let her go.

She half-fell, half-ran into the heart, and it swallowed her up and there was a burst of light, like the birth of a star, and I shut my eyes tight against the brilliance.

A hand closed on my arm. The man with no shadow, given form by the presence of light, and he pulled at me, yelling that I had to move, that we had to get away from it before it pulled us in as well. So we did. We fought our way up. There was a cadence now. I flattened my body to the wall against a rib and waited for the river of debris to pass and for the floor to grow calm and then I ran forwards until I heard that whispering approaching from the chamber behind me, telling me to seek an anchor once more. And the entire time the man with no shadow didn't let go of me, refusing to lose me to the beast that waited inside the heart, just as he refused to lose me to the little girl.

We emerged into the t-intersection and threw ourselves to the side, huddling against the wall in a recess between spars. The heart whispered and the debris beneath us shifted, but faintly, and only a few pieces rattled their way into the passageway. I watched them dance and roll in the light cast by the heart. I was too numb to even weep for her death.

"*Twice*," the man with no shadow snarled. "This makes *twice* I saved you. The pleasure of killing you with my own hands had better make up for this."

I had no indication of what he was going to do, not until there was a wrenching sensation in my side and then blinding pain. I remember screaming and then I remember nothing and then I was flat on my back, waking to pain, disoriented and feeling like I would slip away back into the darkness at the slightest movement. It hurt to breathe. Like one of my lungs was filled with fire. I took shallow, halting breaths, and my eyes filled with tears.

"You should still be able to walk," the man with no shadow said calmly, standing over me. "I can be precise when I want to."

"Why…?" I moaned.

"I only need you alive to get out of here," he replied grimly. "I don't need you *whole* and you are far less of a threat with a maimed shadow. Now get up. I've dragged you as far as I can. The light is gone again."

I didn't. Not right away. The man with no shadow sighed and crouched nearby. I heard the rustle of his clothing. He told me that certainly, I could lie there and wish for death, but we'd both seen that death wouldn't come here, hadn't we? Besides, that wasn't in my nature. He'd made some mistakes in all of this; no plan went flawlessly. But his biggest mistake had been underestimating my capacity to keep fighting even when I should have given up long ago.

As he spoke, my fingers curled on a piece of bone. It'd broken in two, leaving behind a jagged end. I slipped this into my belt as I got up, letting the noise of my struggles to stand mask the sound of me concealing it.

Yes. I was still willing to fight.

I struggled onward, guided by the man with no shadow's directions. I needed light in order to kill him, after all, and for that I needed to escape. That was the mantra that kept me going. I needed light to kill him. I called myself prey in a prior post, but prey can still fight back, even to its last breath. Weakened by pain and injury, I drove myself forwards, fighting that urge to sink back to the ground because I knew that if I rested even for a moment I might not get back up again. The bone stake I carried with me was what kept me going. It and the promise it represented. One last chance to fight back.

The passageway sloped upwards. A long, gradual climb, but one that left me drained nonetheless. I stumbled the last few steps through the widening mouth and into an open space that echoed with my ragged breathing. The head of the thing in the dark, the man with no shadow whispered to me. Just as he'd promised.

"Now," he murmured and made no effort to disguise his malice, "it's your turn. Beg it to let us go."

"That's your plan?" I gasped, shaking with exhaustion.

"It's all I have. You're the campground manager. It might actually listen to you."

I didn't ask what we'd do if this failed. I knew the answer. We'd wander the corridors, desperately seeking a way out, until our will broke and we sought the heart and the death that waited for us within. I wondered what was waiting for the man with no shadow. What kind of death he feared.

"Hello?" I called into that vast emptiness. "It's Kate. I'm here. You swallowed me up."

I held my breath and waited. Silence.

"I've tried to do what you told me," I continued, my voice trembling in desperation. "I've tried to get others to do the same. But we make mistakes and all I can offer is a plea for you to release me, so that I can keep trying."

The ground beneath us lurched. I stumbled and fell and then a body landed across my legs; the man with no shadow, cursing under his breath.

The thing in the dark was waking up.

Its voice came from all around us.

"You gave me a home," it rumbled. "You gave the land near me to people who are kind. They leave me offerings in the summer, of food and drink, of which I cannot partake but it is an offering nonetheless."

The senior camp. They had an excellent cook who also brewed her own beer. Of course.

"I forgive this transgression," it continued. "Just this once."

The blackness in front of me split open and light poured in - sunlight, and after the hours of darkness it brought tears of pain and relief to my eyes. An opening yawned in front of me like the mouth of a cave, jagged with branches and roots like teeth. I saw the blurry outlines of trees beyond, shining in the light. We were inside the thing in the dark's mouth, I realized. I stumbled forwards and a hand seized my arm. The man with no shadow was by my side, his fingers digging into my flesh, and his face tight with fear. He stayed close to my side and I realized this was why he wanted me alive, so that he could slip out unnoticed with me. But the thing in the dark was not naive and it had its own designs.

"You I do not forgive," the thing rumbled and I felt liquid trickle out of my right ear as I lost all hearing in it.

Behind us, the branches and leaves whispered and converged, rolling into a ridge and then they engulfed the man with no shadow's feet. He jerked, like a fish on a line, and toppled as the thing in the dark began to drag him back into its maw. He screamed in incandescent rage and threw out his hands and even though I tried to step away, I was weak and slow, and his grip closed on my leg. I began to slide, being pulled back into the darkness, and the opening before us began to close. The thing in the dark was not a patient creature and it would only afford me one chance to claim my freedom.

The weak perish. There is no mercy here in the forest.

I twisted. I seized the bone from where it rested in my belt. And the man with no shadow's eyes widened with horror as he realized my intention, but it was too late, he was already holding on with both hands while the carpet of branches and leaves continued to engulf him, already covering his body up to his knees.

I drove the sharp end of the bone through where the shadow of his wrists would land.

He screamed and I jerked hard on my leg and was free. Then I was half-running, half-crawling towards the narrowing gap, and I grabbed hold of the broken half of a tree and pulled myself through, squeezing between its teeth, and then I rolled down the mound and came to a rest on the damp soil of the forest.

Beside me sat the mound that housed the thing in the dark. It was silent and still but for a moment, I thought I could hear the man with no shadow. Screaming.

I think it was only my imagination.

I believe I fainted after that.

I next remember being carried. There were arms under my shoulders and under my knees and when I looked down at them, there were plain metal rings around the fingers. I slipped away again and next awoke in my own bed. The old sheriff was there. He said he'd been keeping watch over the house in case I came back, while Bryan searched the forest with the dogs. He told me it was almost sundown. I'd been missing for most of the day.

I told him the man with no shadow was gone. Then I had him bring me my laptop and I began to type all this up, before the details began to fade.

Today I saw the doctor. I have a few scrapes from my falls, but otherwise my only serious injury is my shadow and they can't do anything about that. If I stand in front of a wall I can see clearly how much the man with no shadow tore away. An entire lung would be gone, had he attacked my corporal body. I don't like looking at it. I'm weak and I'm winded easily, but I'll recover in time. I still can't hear out my right ear, either. My eardrum ruptured from the thing in the dark's voice, but it will heal. It's actually ruptured before from infection, when I was a child, so the scar tissue was what split open again.

Otherwise, I've been spending my time today resting and recovering. I made some calls to the people in town who were in that grove. They remember what happened. They heard the man with no shadow call them and tell them to come to the campground, so they did. Some were told to come with a gun, and they did. I told them the man with no shadow was gone, to assure them they were safe, and they said that they knew. Somehow, they knew. Not dead. Just... gone. Like a weight was off their shoulders.

I keep thinking about how the thing in the dark refused to let him go. It's been bothering me as to why. I've never had any indication that the thing in the dark was anything other than indifferent towards the other creatures it shared the campground with. Then, after I got done calling the people in town... I realized why it had been angry.

I'd recognized one of the campers that was in that grove with a gun held to their head. I don't know a lot of campers. They all tend to blur together over time. But this one, I know this one because they're one of the special ones that I see more than others and have a reason to stand out in my mind. They're part of the senior camp, the one that I put next to the thing in the dark because I know they'll be careful not to disturb it.

They're one of the people that leave offerings. And the man with no shadow would have killed them. He knew what he'd done. That's why he needed me alive.

On one hand, I am intensely grateful there was one of the senior camp among those the man with no shadow was going to kill. I'm not sure if the thing in the dark would have dragged him back into the darkness otherwise. On the other hand... out of everyone that camps here, they should *really* have known better than to talk to him.

We all make mistakes, I guess.

I called a family meeting today to update everyone on the situation. My brother was there. He rarely attends. I apologized for keeping everyone ignorant as to the full scope of the situation, but explained that we were dealing with something that could manipulate minds and it was hard to tell who to trust. My brother looked put-out at that, but I suppose that's understandable. I think him being at the meeting at all was his way of saying I was forgiven.

Then one of my cousins spoke up with something that would have been really nice to know *years* ago. (okay they're actually a second cousin but I have a lot of those and a lot of cousins and you're not here to listen to genealogy so I'm just going to call them all cousins and leave it at that)

She did 23andMe a while back and found a relative we didn't know about. Yes. The buyer. She thought it would be wonderful to connect with this side of the family and arranged for him to come out to the campsite. My cousin admitted that she was remiss in not telling him the rules before he came. She thought it would be safe if he was only here for a few hours, but she didn't think about how my entire family, no matter how distantly related, are targets. But he never showed. And he never answered any of her messages and she assumed he'd chickened out and was now ghosting her.

I think we can fill in the blanks from there. He reached the campsite and the man with no shadow greeted him. They had a conversation.

I wonder if my cousin was *also* under the man with no shadow's influence or if this was just a happy coincidence for him. Regardless, there's a new rule for the family. No more 23andMe. No more ancestry ANYTHING. We don't need to be bringing more surprise relatives here that don't know what they're getting into.

I'm a campground manager. I've still got a lot of work to do. I'm not convinced that getting rid of the man with no shadow is going to keep this from being a bad year. I'm going to be wary. I'm going to keep watching and doing whatever I can to keep my town and my campers safe. I'm going to keep telling you about my land and my rules and why they exist. It's spring, after all, and it's time to open my campground.

You should come visit.

And this year, when I send out my "how to survive camping" pamphlets with the list of rules, they will be shorter by two. The not-brother is dead. And the man with no shadow will never escape.

201

–

ABOUT THE AUTHOR

Bonnie Quinn is a hobbyist author with delusions of fame, fortune, and competence. She spends her free time painting (badly), programming (passably), or playing computer games. She writes when she should be sleeping. Bonnie lives with her three cats and hopes to someday be the neighborhood's crazy cat lady.

Printed in Great Britain
by Amazon

62487209R00128